Praise for

What people are saying about *See Me* and *Hear Me,* the first two books in the Breaking the Rules Series:

"It is not only a great book for young adults, but for all people who at some stage of their life did not want to be seen."

*Kim Anisi, 5- Star Review for Reader's Favourite*

"As I write this there's another national case of school bullying in the news. This issue is not going away, but books like *See Me* can help youth who suffer understand that they are not alone, and that speaking up, though difficult, is often the first step toward a solution."

*Shelley Leedahl, Sask Book Reviewer*

"A moving look into the lives of two young teens who try to find their way through the struggles in their lives."

*Carol Marit, Grade 4 Teacher*

"*See Me* is a sensitive and authentic portrayal of middle school that will leave you yearning for the next installment."

*Karen Henderson, Elementary School Librarian*

"Such a wonderful story of perseverance and doing what is just in order to create a better world for victims of bullying."

*Sue Twemlow, Teacher*

"Follow Hannah as she finds her voice, learns about true friendship, loyalty and the power of truth. H.R. Hobbs brings a realism to her storytelling that everyone is going to want to experience."

*Carla Hildebrandt, Educational Psychologist*

"I am sure readers will sympathize with and feel the pain and injustice the characters are experiencing. I hope they will also discover their own humanity when they lift their visors and see all the uniquely beautiful butterflies we all are."

*Karen Kloibhofer*

# Contents

| | |
|---|---|
| Also by H.R. Hobbs | v |
| Chapter 1 | 1 |
| Chapter 2 | 10 |
| Chapter 3 | 19 |
| Chapter 4 | 27 |
| Chapter 5 | 37 |
| Chapter 6 | 41 |
| Chapter 7 | 47 |
| Chapter 8 | 51 |
| Chapter 9 | 59 |
| Chapter 10 | 63 |
| Chapter 11 | 69 |
| Chapter 12 | 73 |
| Chapter 13 | 78 |
| Chapter 14 | 82 |
| Chapter 15 | 85 |
| Chapter 16 | 89 |
| Chapter 17 | 95 |
| Chapter 18 | 98 |
| Chapter 19 | 104 |
| Chapter 20 | 109 |
| Chapter 21 | 112 |
| Chapter 22 | 119 |
| Chapter 23 | 129 |
| Chapter 24 | 133 |
| Chapter 25 | 140 |
| Chapter 26 | 147 |
| Chapter 27 | 150 |
| Chapter 28 | 159 |
| Chapter 29 | 165 |
| Chapter 30 | 171 |

| | |
|---|---|
| Chapter 31 | 180 |
| Chapter 32 | 184 |
| Chapter 33 | 190 |
| Chapter 34 | 200 |
| Chapter 35 | 208 |
| Chapter 36 | 212 |
| Chapter 37 | 217 |
| Chapter 38 | 222 |
| Chapter 39 | 230 |
| | |
| Mailing List | 235 |
| Acknowledgments | 237 |
| About the Author | 239 |

# Also by H.R. Hobbs

Want to know what rules Hannah and Chip broke first? Check out the first two books in the series: *See Me* and *Hear Me*!

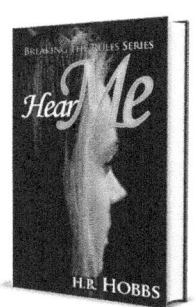

Copyright 2019 H. R. Hobbs

All rights reserved. No part of this publication may be reproduced, distributed, or transmitted in any form or by any means, including photocopying, recording, or electronic or mechanical methods, without the prior written permission of the published, except in the case of brief quotations embodied in reviews and certain other non-commercial uses permitted by copyright law.

ISBN: 978-0-9953448-3-9

ISBN: 978-0-9953448-4-6 (ebook)

*To Brody, Jude and Brooklyn:*
*For bringing a sparkle to my eye with your crazy dance moves, love of dinosaurs and trolls, infectious giggles and curiosity.*
*May you always be this way!*

# WATCH ME

Book 3 in the Breaking the Rules Series

H.R. HOBBS

## Chapter 1

I am going to kill Chip for this—if I live through it.

My hair flew back, and the skin on my face pulled tight as my cheeks moved toward my ears. All I could see were blue sky and clouds, close enough to touch. Suspended there, I would have admired the breathtaking view, if I had any breath left. I slammed my eyes shut so I wouldn't see the ground racing toward me. Clutching the bar in front of me, I prayed for it to be over.

It had been Alex's great idea to come to the fair. I'd hoped my birthday money would last me through the summer, but I hadn't seen my friends since school let out, so I said "Yes." Now I was regretting that decision.

After what seemed like an eternity, we slowed to a stop, and I took a deep breath.

"That was awesome!" came from my right. That would be Trudy.

"Awesome? It was freakin' fantastic!" I heard from my left. That would be Chip. The bar that kept me from plunging to my death released, taking my arms with it.

Trudy's voice chimed in, "Let's do it again!"

"Hannah!" Chip's voice came from in front of me. "Open your eyes. It's over. You survived."

I cautiously removed my fingers from the padding on the bar and cracked my eyes open.

"I'm alive?"

"Yes, but we're going again." Hands in his pockets, Alex bounced on his toes in front of me.

"I'm sitting the next one out." I pushed off the armrest and attempted to stand on rubbery legs. I immediately tilted to the left. The only thing keeping me from face planting on the platform was Trudy's grip on my arm.

Chip grabbed my other arm. "Yeah, maybe you should sit this one out."

With the two of them supporting me, I hobbled like an old woman down the ramp.

"You guys go ahead. I'll wait here for you." I leaned against the rails surrounding the loading area.

"You're sure?" Trudy asked, battling between concern for me and wanting to get on the ride again.

"I'll be fine. Go."

Trudy and Chip exchanged a worried glance. "GO!" I waved them toward the entrance.

"All right, we're going," Chip answered, and the three of them *finally* got in line. Chip looked back at me again. I ignored my churning stomach and plastered a smile on my face while giving him a thumbs up. He held my stare before turning back to Alex and Trudy. I relaxed against the railing. As I watched them laugh and joke with each other in the line, I smiled to myself, a real one this time. If you'd told me a year ago that I'd be at the fair with three friends, I would've thought you were crazy. Back then, I protected myself by never letting anyone get close to me, but these three had managed to break down the walls I'd surrounded myself with.

I watched them get on the rollercoaster. They were near the back this time, not front and center as we'd been only moments before. The car started its slow ascent, arms reaching to the sky as they climbed the first hill. Screams filled the air as they descended into a sharp turn. *And that's why they call it The Screamer.* My stomach rolled just watching them. The car moved to the far side of the structure, and soon I could only tell where they were by the screams that erupted as they flew up and down the hills.

---

I PLANNED to keep my word and wait for them, but my rolling stomach and the smell of fried dough drew me to the stalls that lined both sides of the asphalt walkway. My attention bounced between the games, food, flashing lights, and music. I smiled as I passed a dad holding up his son who smashed gophers with a rubber mallet before the time ran out. People crowded around the games where they popped balloons with darts, tossed rings on milk bottles, or shot basketballs. No chance I'd win a prize on those games! I chuckled. The games couldn't distract me though; I followed my nose down the center of the midway.

It led me to a food stand selling everything deep-fried. I glanced at the menu. *Deep-fried butter? Ew. No way. Deep-fried pickles? Another No. Deep-fried Mars bars. Now we're talking!* I hustled over to the order window.

"What can I get ya?" An apron with grease-stains and dried dough appeared at eye level.

I placed my order and the apron disappeared with a grunt. Leaning against the counter, my mouth watered as I waited for my piece of heaven.

Angry voices jarred me out of my dreams of battered-covered deliciousness, tossing me from my dream into a nightmare.

"This game is rigged. I hit that last target. Now give me my prize!" A chill ran down my spine as I recognized the voice.

Cautiously, I walked to the end of the food stall and peeked around the corner. There they were, the cause of many sleepless nights. Logan, Cody, and Mason stood in front of a shooting game, arguing with the vendor. They were our classmates, and to be honest, the school bullies. It seemed strange to see them without Brady, but he'd disappeared in November after breaking his probation for beating Chip. Rumour had it that after he completed his sentence, he was living with an aunt and uncle in a nearby town.

Even without Brady, seeing the three of them made my stomach roll.

"Look, the rules clearly state that the bell has to ring, and the target has to fall over to be counted. The target is still upright and you and I both know it didn't ding." This came from the young man running the booth. He was older than me by a few years. His blonde hair was long on top and he wore jeans and a t-shirt. He didn't look like your typical fair vendor. His body language said "don't mess with me" as he stood with his arms folded on his chest.

"It did so. You guys saw it go down, didn't you?" Logan's hand slapped Cody's chest for confirmation.

"I did."

"Me too," Mason added.

"Yeah, well, I didn't, and I give out the prizes. Do you want to try again?" He waited with his hands on his hips.

"What's the point? You're just going to rip me off anyway."

Logan threw the gun on the counter, and the three of them stalked away. The man shrugged and rearranged the guns on the counter for the next customer.

"Mars Bar!" came from inside the food stand.

I left my hiding spot and picked up my order.

Not waiting a second longer, I bit into the crunchy coating and closed my eyes in delight as the gooey, chocolatey goodness hit my taste buds. *Yep, heaven on a stick.*

"There you are!" Chip, Trudy, and Alex walked toward me just as my tongue came out to catch any icing sugar on my lips.

"I thought you were going to wait for us, but it looks like the enticing smell of a deep-fried heart attack got to you first," Trudy joked, bumping my elbow.

"Careful." I moved out of her reach. "I don't want to lose one piece of this."

I waited for Alex to weigh in on my disappearing act, but he was studying the menu.

"Deep-fried pickle," he nodded at the board and went to the order window.

"I don't know how you guys can put that stuff in your body."

I narrowed my eyes at Trudy. "This?" I waved the stick at her. "This is the very reason you come to the fair."

"Not me. It gives me the heebie-jeebies just thinking about eating it," she shuddered.

"I'm with Hannah," Alex returned. "I think it should be its own food group. Preferably at the bottom of the pyramid."

I smiled and took another bite.

"What's next? The Ferris wheel?" Chip looked at the various rides we hadn't ridden yet. "Or will it be the teacups, Hannah?"

"Very funny." I took another bite. As I chewed, I remembered the scene I'd just witnessed. "You just missed some of our favourite people." At their confused looks, I added, "Logan, Cody, and Mason were just here."

Chip went from confused to concerned. "What happened?"

"Nothing," I reassured him. "They were trying to weasel a prize out of the guy running the shooting booth." I pointed to where he was lining up the guns for the next customer. "But he wasn't having any of it. So, they threw a little fit and left. They didn't even know I was here."

Chip didn't say anything, just scanned the crowd to see if they were still around.

"At least someone in this town doesn't let them get away with everything," Trudy said.

"Pickle's up!" came from the food booth, and Alex jogged over to get his order.

As Alex wolfed down his pickle, we browsed the various stalls. Trudy opted for a shish kebob of fresh fruit; Chip tried the ring toss game with no luck.

"So—" Chip clapped his hands. "Which ride is next?"

"The Ferris wheel doesn't look too bad." Trudy motioned in its direction. "Let's give it a try. It can't be as awful as the rollercoaster."

The wheel was stopped, and I could see people in the top basket waving to the crowd below. I felt the Mars Bar roll around in my stomach, and my face heated up at the thought of being so high in the air.

"If you look straight ahead and don't look down, it's not so bad."

Trudy gave me a reassuring pat on the back. "That's what they told us to do when we were learning how to do pyramids for cheerleading."

Trudy's words of encouragement didn't help. I shivered at the image her comment brought to mind. Both because it involved being high in the air and that the advice probably came from Stephanie. And that thought right there made me determined to get on the Ferris wheel. I wasn't going to let my dislike for Stephanie keep me from having fun. *It's going to be fun, right?* I stuffed down my fear and nausea. *I can do this!*

"Let's go!" Trudy's face lit up at my words, and we started for the Ferris wheel. It was getting harder to maneuver through the crowds as we wandered around the fairgrounds. We finally came to a standstill when people began cutting in front of us on their way to the grandstand.

"What's going on over there?" Trudy stood on her tiptoes to look over the crowd. The sounds of clapping and cheering reached us.

"Let's go check it out. Maybe it's a concert."

Chip ducked between the people walking past and headed to the stage. Seeing the black curtains, I knew that Chip was wrong. A podium stood in the center of the stage with a sign on the front of it that read "Get the job done, vote Jacob Robinson." A man in a suit with hair slicked back stood at the podium waiting for the crowd to settle. We came to a stop near the front of the stage.

"It's time for change," the man's voice blasted from the speakers. "For too long, this town has been run by a mayor satisfied by the status quo." Random cheers came from the crowd.

Chip looked at me and mouthed, "Status quo?" I shrugged.

"We've watched our town crumble despite rising taxes. It's time to put a stop to the lack luster developments that have plagued our town for so long. And I know just the man to turn things around. Ladies and gentlemen—" He pointed to the left. "I give you the next mayor of Acadia, Jacob Robinson!"

Part of the crowd cheered and waved signs like the one that hung on the stage. Others stood silently. Jacob Robinson appeared, waving his arms above his head and smiling at the crowd. He came to a stop behind the podium, basking in the adoration of his fans. He hadn't changed since the last time I'd seen him, the day Brady had been expelled from school for framing Trudy with a water bottle full of alcohol. He wore a black suit with a white shirt, which must have been sweltering in the summer sun. His white teeth stood out from his tanned skin as he smiled toward the crowd.

Mrs. Robinson stood behind him to the right in a flowered dress. Her ever-present pearls hung around her neck, and her blond curls were styled in a halo around her head. The heat didn't seem to affect her either as she stood with her hands clasped in front of her. Seeing the two of them standing so perfectly on stage, the memories flooded my thoughts and that familiar sick feeling was back, worse than before. Suddenly, we were back in the courtroom and Jacob Robinson was sitting behind Brady, wearing the same confident smile he wore now as their lawyer tore holes in my memories of the night Chip was beaten. That confident smile was replaced with disgust the day he beat Brady for getting expelled from school and breaking his probation. Jacob Robinson wore numerous masks, and I didn't trust any of them.

"No sign of Brady," I whispered to Chip. *Was he still banished from Acadia?*

"He'd never bring him out here," Chip spoke out the side of his mouth. "That's the first thing he cleaned up—his son's scandal."

Two gigantic men flanked Jacob Robinson on the stage. Both wore suits, dark sunglasses, and expressions that said, "Don't mess with me." *What did he need bodyguards for? Did he think he was a celebrity?* Robinson continued to smile as he looked out over the crowd and gripped both sides of the podium. *What a snake.* The crowd quieted, and Mr. Robinson paused before speaking.

"First, I'd like to thank everyone for taking the time to hear what I have to say. These are important events for families to attend together. For those of you who know me, you know that I've always been a civic-minded member of the community. I've sat on the Chamber of Commerce board and Town Council for the past five years. I've been a member of our district's school board…"

I rolled my eyes. The only reason he had anything to do with the school was to protect Brady.

"And I have been President of the committee that is looking at the feasibility of a new sports complex." Cheers went up from the crowd. "I believe that we need to get Acadia back on track, and that means cleaning up the town. We need to be able to entice people to open businesses, buy homes, put down roots, and raise a family."

More cheering. People were really eating up his garbage.

"I believe that a leader needs to walk the walk, not just talk the talk, so I'm going to take the first step as a concerned citizen. We all know the old mill on the east side of town has been an eye sore for some time now."

The crowd booed. Chip snorted at his words.

"This guy is too much." He muttered to himself.

"We've heard a lot of talk about cleaning it up or selling it to someone who will start it up again. Well, I don't know about you, but I'm tired of empty promises, and I'm going to do something about it." He paused as cheers went up. "As of this morning, I am now the owner of Birchfield Mill." The crowd cheered loudly at his words, and he stood and smiled, waiting for them to quiet again. "I promise to clean up or re-purpose the mill so that it will no longer be known as the eyesore on the east side." The crowd cheered again. "And from there, I promise to clean up the whole town." The crowd erupted, and Robinson drank it in.

Finally, he motioned for quiet. "If you agree with me and want Acadia to move forward, be progressive—vote me in as mayor." As the crowd chanted "Jacob! Jacob!" he and his wife stepped off the front of the stage and began shaking hands with people in the crowd. His bodyguards, one in front and one behind, moved people out of the way. Suddenly, a bright flash blinded me. I looked for the source and realized it was the sun reflecting off a pin from one of the bodyguard's suits. It had the initials "JR" on it with a check mark beside the initials.

As Jacob Robinson started to make his way toward us, Chip turned. "Let's get out of here."

The three of us trailed behind as Chip cut a swath through the remaining supporters.

"They're scraping the bottom of the barrel if they think that Jacob

Robinson is going to make a good mayor," Alex said, once we reached the Ferris wheel.

"If he wants to clean something up he should look at his own family," Trudy added as we got in line.

"Maybe that's why Brady hasn't come back," Alex said. "He probably doesn't want to remind people that he's raised a juvenile delinquent."

Alex was probably right. I'd seen first-hand what happened when Brady embarrassed his father. He was safer out of his dad's reach.

## Chapter 2

We moved to the front of the line for the Ferris wheel. Trudy and I got in a basket as Chip and Alex got into the one behind us. Once the baskets were full, the wheel began to move. As I shifted to look below, the basket teetered back and forth; I screamed, terrified we were going to spill out.

"Relax, Hannah," Trudy tried to assure me. "We aren't going to tip over."

"I guess I haven't recovered from The Screamer." We began to move, and I clutched the bar that lay across my lap.

"Keep your eyes open this time. The view from up here is unbelievable."

Remembering Trudy's advice, I scanned the horizon. Golden fields of wheat mixed with seas of flowering canola stretched in every direction from the edge of town as far as the eye could see. From the basket, I watched a truck travel down the gravel road to the east, a cloud of dust hanging in the air behind it. I was on top of the world. Trudy was right—it was unbelievable.

Movement on the ground drew my eyes from the landscape to the fairgrounds below. From this height, we were able to see what goes on behind the scenes at the fair. Trailers for both animals and people were scattered behind vendor stalls. Two people in particular caught my attention—the young man from the shooting booth and a large man who was talking to him. From their gestures, it appeared they were having a heated discussion. The larger man shook his head and pointed at the exit. The young man said something, but the larger man stalked off. The young man stood for a moment before he bent over and picked up a duffel bag off the ground. The basket started moving, obscuring my view for a moment. When the spot came back into sight, no one was there.

"What are you looking at?" The basket rocked again when I jumped at the sound of Trudy's voice. I grabbed the frame of the basket in an attempt to steady it (and my thumping heart).

"I think that guy just got fired." I pointed to the young man who was now walking down the fair's main street.

"How do you know that?" She leaned ahead, and the basket tipped forward.

My fingers clutched the bar tighter. "Will you quit moving!"

She slowly leaned back. "Sorry. Why do you think he got fired?" she asked without moving, her voice quiet.

"He was arguing with a guy. I think it was his boss."

"That's strange. I can't imagine what you'd have to do to get fired from a fair. It's not a job that you could screw up too badly, is it?" I had no idea, but some of the people who worked the booths were . . . let's just say, I'd be scared to fire them.

Knowing the way the "Brady Bunch" (our nickname for Brady and his gang) worked, I wouldn't be surprised if they'd complained to the young man's boss. They had hurting others to protect themselves down to an art. Get someone else to take the blame (Dylan), deny that you had anything to do with it (Brady), use your connections to keep you out of trouble (all of them, but mostly Brady). Going to the boss was a move that had their names written all over it.

"If Logan complained that he didn't get the prize he thought he'd won, that might be enough to get someone fired."

"Those guys cause trouble everywhere they go." Trudy glared at the ground below us. I wasn't about to disagree. She knew better than anyone what they were capable of.

The Ferris wheel came to a stop on the platform. As soon as we were released from our basket, I shot off the platform and straight down the ramp to wait for Chip and Alex.

"How'd you survive this one Hannah? Did you open your eyes for even part of it?" Alex teased as he and Chip joined us off to the side of the loading area.

"Ha ha, very funny."

"I know. But you didn't answer my question."

"I'll have you know, I kept my eyes open for the whole ride. Ask Trudy."

Alex turned to Trudy for confirmation. "Yeah, her eyes were open the whole time."

I gave Alex a satisfied smile.

Surprised that Chip wasn't giving me a hard time, I saw he was checking messages on his phone.

"Something wrong?" I asked.

He slipped his phone into his pocket.

"No." He threw his arm around my shoulders. "Well, I guess we don't need to go on the teacup ride then."

I elbowed him in the ribs, and he bent over pretending I'd hurt him.

"Hannah, that's a wicked elbow you got there. You know I was just kidding."

"It just slipped. Sorry."

Chip rubbed his side. "You're not sorry at all."

We continued to banter back and forth until we came to another food stand. This time Chip stepped up to the order window.

"Anyone want anything?" he asked.

I reached into the back pocket of my jeans for my money.

"Can you get me a pop, please?" I asked sweetly.

"Well, since you asked so nicely, I guess I can." Chip took the five-dollar bill I handed him and went to order.

"Excuse me," said a man behind me. I turned and froze. Standing there, holding a ten-dollar bill was the guy from the shooting booth. "I think you dropped this."

I reached into my pocket and found it empty. That was the last of my money.

When I didn't answer or take the money, he frowned.

"It fell out of your pocket a second ago." He gestured for me to take the money. And when I stood there not answering, he asked, "Are you okay?" The young man was even taller up close, which would have intimidated me except for the confused look on his face.

*He must think I'm an idiot!* An embarrassing heat crawled up my face. *Take the money, Hannah!*

I stuck my hand out and nearly knocked the bill out of his.

"Uh, thanks," I replied and took the money.

"No problem." He smiled and walked away.

Chip handed me my cola. "What did he want?"

My eyes followed the young man. "He noticed I'd dropped some money and gave it back to me."

"Huh, most people would just put it in their pocket," Chip observed before inhaling half of his hot dog.

"I know." As I watched him disappear into the crowd, I noticed he walked with a slight limp. If he just got fired, he probably needed the money more than I did.

"Let's try the games." Alex led us to one of the stalls.

The encounter with the young man was quickly forgotten, as we tried our luck at the games of chance down the fairway. Alex was determined to win a prize at the ring toss. It only took him half an hour and ten dollars to get a small bear, which he promptly gave to Trudy.

"You didn't take all that time and money to win this for me, did you?" Her tone and face reflected her shock. "Because you didn't have to."

"I know," Alex told her, "I just wanted to see if I could do it." He shrugged his shoulders. "Now that I know I can, I don't need the bear anymore." He stuffed his hands in his pockets and headed for the exit.

Chip shook his head at Alex's reply, "Only you could take a kind gesture and turn it into a personal mission."

"Well, thanks," Trudy said to his retreating back.

My feet slowed as we passed a mysterious looking tent, and I stopped out of curiosity. Beaded curtains in ocean blue were pulled back to reveal a table covered in a matching tablecloth. Tacked to the top of the curtains were three tarot cards and a sign advertising palm readings. A pair of hands tipped with claw-like nails lay clasped on the table. A ring with a large red gem hung loosely on the boney finger of one hand. I peered closely, trying to make out who the hands belonged to, but the darkness prevented me from seeing the lone occupant.

"Madame Asteroid?" Alex read the name on the sign. "Bet she's out of this world," he chuckled at his joke.

"It's Astraea," I said absently, trying to see into the tent.

"Hannah," Chip's voice jarred me out of my study, "are you coming or not?"

I looked back at the opening to the tent. My curiosity got the better of me. "Not," I answered and entered the booth. At the back of the tent, candles burned in groups of three, throwing the figure seated at the table into shadow. Scattered among the candles, gems of different colours winked in the dim light. Tinny music played softly in the background. I slowly lowered myself into the chair across from the shadowed occupant.

"Ten dollars," The low voice demanded, as bracelets tinkled and one of the claws turned palm up. Now that my eyes had adjusted to the darkness, I could see she looked just as I had imagined. She had to be close to my grandma's age with long blond hair that fell around her shoulders, covering most of the dark purple blouse that she wore. Beads from the handkerchief on her head lay in rows across her forehead. Furrows of skin radiated from the corners of her eyes.

I dropped the last of my money on the table. She raised her piercing gaze and smiled as she tucked the money into the front of her blouse.

"Give me your hand," she gestured with her fingers, "and I will tell you many important things."

"Hannah, what are you doing?" Chip's voice came from outside the tent. "You don't actually believe in this stuff, do you?"

"Silence!" the palm reader demanded lifting her hand.

Surprisingly, there was no reply.

The palm reader turned my hand over where it lay on the tablecloth. A jolt of electricity ran up my arm at her touch. Her hands were hot as she gently pulled back my fingers and peered at my palm. Saying nothing, she ran her index finger over the lines of my hand. She lifted her head and closed her eyes.

Suddenly, her eyes sprang open. She stared at me.

"This is your lifeline." She traced her finger along the middle of my palm. "Your lifeline says that you are going to stand alone in a forest with predators all around you." She stopped. *That's it? I paid ten dollars for that?* I started to pull my hand back, but she gripped my fingers tighter. "You will fight many battles that will take a lot out of you, but you will triumph and become stronger with each one."

I knew the look on my face was skeptical. I didn't see myself fighting any battles now or in the future.

"You don't believe me?" Her eyebrows came down as she again pierced me with her gaze. "These lines tell me that you have fought battles already, yes?"

I squirmed in my chair under her assessing gaze. It seemed like all I had done for the last year was fight battles. I'd fought battles with myself. I'd broken my rules to bring Brady to justice for Chip's beating. Is that what she meant? I had battled to let myself be seen. Battled to let myself be heard. I stood up to Coach Sanders and Principal Struthers to clear Trudy's name when Brady targeted her for revenge. I'd even battled my own beliefs about Brady. I'd done all of those things. The freaky part was Madame Astraea knew them too.

"I can tell by the look on your face that this is true."

*She read palms, not minds. Right?*

I reluctantly nodded my head. The ghost of a smile touched her lips.

She gently traced another line—her finger going back and forth hypnotically as she spoke to my palm.

"Yes, you have been seen and heard. Now,"—I leaned forward to look at the line she traced—"the next battle you face will be the biggest you've ever encountered but know that this battle will not only be important to you, but to those you champion. This battle will be the biggest yet, against a formidable opponent." She paused and looked up. "Again, you don't believe me."

"It's not that." I stammered as her eyebrows settled into a scary frown. "I get the battles I've already fought, but I don't see how I'll do battle for someone else."

"Madame Astraea sees all." She let go of my hand. "Never doubt this." With a clatter of bangles, she placed her hands palms down on the table. "I have no more for you," she declared, regally leaning back in her chair and disappearing back into the shadows. I guess we were finished.

I stuck my head out of the tent, temporarily blinded by the sun. My eyes adjusted, and I could see Chip, Trudy, and Alex waiting near the entrance.

"So," Trudy said her eyes bright with excitement, "what did she tell you?"

"Well, she looked at my lifeline and said I would have many battles in my life," I mumbled looking at my shoes.

"Battles? What kind of battles?" Alex asked. "Like between the Rebels and the Empire?"

"Not everything comes back to Star Wars, Alex." Trudy countered.

Shock registered on Alex's face. "Ah, yes, it does. It's the age-old battle of good against evil."

Trudy scoffed, "What do you know about the battle between good and evil? Ninety-nine percent of the time you're staring at your phone."

"Where do you think I learned about good and evil?"

They bickered back and forth. Finally, when Trudy had enough, she crossed her arms and turned her back to Alex.

"Let's get back to Hannah's palm reading. Did she say what kind of battles you'd have to fight?"

"No, just that I'd fought some already and that the next one would be important to me and 'those I would champion.'" I made air quotes with my fingers. "Whatever that means," I shrugged.

"It means," Alex said, "a person who fights for a cause or for someone else." He nudged Trudy with his shoulder. "You see, sometimes those games pay off. Besides, that fortune teller stuff is fake. Give me ten dollars, and I'll read your fortune."

Trudy rolled her eyes. "Did she give you any clue as to who or what that might be?"

"No, she just said it would be important."

Chip, who hadn't said anything up to this point, asked, "She's right, you've fought some pretty big battles in the last year or so. Maybe that's what she's talking about?"

"No," I shook my head, "I asked about that too."

"Well, maybe it will reveal itself sometime in the future." Chip wiggled his fingers around my head, imitating something spooky. "Or maybe it's right around the corner. Either way, there isn't much we can do about it."

Chip was right, it was probably just a bunch of hocus pocus.

*July 7, 2018*

*Summer vacation! My favourite time of the year! Sunshine, sleeping in, and doing whatever I want. Only a week in, and I've had my first big adventure—going to the fair without my parents! Chip, Trudy, Alex, and I went to the fair today. It was AWESOME!*

*The deep-fried Mars bar was the highlight. My mouth still waters just thinking about it. Oh, and I got my palm read by Madame Astraea—weird name, I know, but it's something I've always wanted to do and never had the courage to. I wanted to know if I'd have a long, happy life and all she talked about was the battles I'd fought for Chip and Trudy against Brady and the school and the ones I had left to fight. Not what I expected at all. And honestly, I'm tired of fighting battles. In fact, I'm hoping she's wrong and I can sit the next one out.*

*The rides were terrifying—The Screamer was the worst—and I was the chicken who didn't want to go on them. Chip convinced me that I could do it, and I did it, even though I was sure at one point we were all going to die.*

*The downside to the fair—we saw Logan, Mason, and Cody. They didn't see us, thank goodness. Oh, you'll never guess who's running for mayor! Jacob Robinson! He was giving a speech at the grandstand about how he'll clean up Acadia. There isn't a worse candidate out there! Do the people of Acadia want a mayor who beats his son and gives money to the school to keep his son out of trouble? He's the last person that should be mayor! If I was old enough to vote, at least then I'd feel like I was doing something! Can he convince enough people to vote for him? I know my parents wouldn't, but there might be lots of people out there who might think he's right. They may think it's time for a change, but Jacob Robinson is not the change this town needs. Why are the most corrupt people the ones who want all the power?*

## Chapter 3

The next day, I was burrowed under a blanket on the couch watching videos on my phone when it dinged.
*Feel like some ice cream?*
I quickly texted back.
*Of course, when have I ever turned down ice cream?*
*Never ☺ I'll be over in 10.*

Chip and I really needed to have a talk about giving me ten minutes to get ready. I was still in my pajamas for goodness sake! They were my Princess Leia ones. The ones mom bought last year after the Halloween dance at school. I'd never hear the end of it if Chip saw me in these! It was 1:00 p.m., but it was summer holiday, and I planned to spend as much time as possible lounging around.

That didn't mean I had nothing to do. To earn some pocket money, my mom left me a list of chores. Dad usually checked to see if I'd done them on the nights he was home, which wasn't often. He was still picking up as many extra shifts as he could. I had no problem doing dishes and vacuuming in my pajamas, which is what I'd done this morning. But I needed to change my clothes if we were going down to the Milky Way for ice cream. George, the owner, didn't say much about a lot of things, but I don't think he'd appreciate me wearing pajamas in his shop.

I'd had time to find some loose change on my parents' dresser and was lacing up my sneakers when the doorbell rang.

"Come in," I yelled from where I sat on the step.

Chip stuck his head in the door.

"You ready to go?"

I tightened the bow on my shoelaces, grabbed my keys, and felt my pocket for my money. "All set," I answered, joining him on the front step. A wave of hot air hit me the moment I stepped out the door. I squinted against the sunlight.

"I guess summer is finally here," I noted as we made our way down the street.

"I know. Our air conditioner is broken. That's why I thought we should go for ice cream; the house is like a sauna."

"How's your mom making out in this heat?" Chip's mom hadn't been feeling well for the last couple of weeks. Being sick in this heat would make me miserable.

"I left her in her room with the blinds drawn and our only fan on. My grandparents are coming over to take her to the hospital, and she refused to let me go. She pretty much ordered me to get out of the house for a while."

"Still no idea what's going on with her?"

"None. She's really tired and doesn't have much of an appetite. It's been dragging on for so long, I'm starting to worry. She's so stubborn. She won't listen to me or my grandparents."

"Well, I guess we know where you get your stubbornness from, don't we?"

Chip snorted at my comment.

"If there's anything I can do, let me know. I'm sure it's nothing but a bug of some kind."

He nodded but didn't answer.

We took the long way to the ice cream parlor, avoiding the shorter route that took us past the alley where Brady and gang jumped Chip. We'd never talked about it, but since Chip's beating, we hadn't walked past that alley. I know if it was me, I wouldn't want to walk by the place where I nearly died.

Chip held the door for me as we entered the shop. Designed like a fifties diner, there was a long counter with stools in front. A black and white checkered floor gave the place a vintage feel. George was wiping down the counter when we entered and gave us a nod of recognition. We took the table by the window.

Chip grabbed the plastic-coated menu stuck between the napkin dispenser and the sugar. He studied it as George ambled over—his bald head nearly level with the pendulum light that hung above our table.

He planted his hands on his hips and asked, "What can I get you kids today?"

Chip handed the menu to me and said, "I'll have the root beer float, please."

George nodded and looked expectantly at me.

"What about you little lady? No, wait. Let me guess." He held up a finger. "A double scoop Tiger Tiger cone." He smiled, proud of himself.

"Please," I replied.

I heard him mumble as he walked away, "Kids these days, no sense of adventure."

"I think I insulted George," I whispered to Chip, who was gazing out the window.

"Huh?" He looked at me and then to George. "I'm sure he'll get over it. You can't be the first person who always orders the same thing."

I knew Chip was teasing, or trying to anyway, but the usual sparkle was gone from his eyes and he dropped his gaze to the table.

"You're worried," I stated the obvious.

And I was worried that Chip was worried. Even with his broken arm two years ago, Chip managed to be upbeat. He was the most relaxed, carefree person I knew, and to see that liveliness gone meant that this was probably not a simple case of the flu.

Chip drummed his fingers on the table not meeting my eyes. "I've just never seen my mom like this before. I can't remember the last time she was this sick. She'd catch a cold and have a cough and a runny nose for a couple of days, but this has been going on since before school ended. She'd still cook meals, go to work, and clean the house when she got home. But this isn't the same. She puts on a good front, but now she's not even doing that. She drags herself out of bed every morning with barely enough time to get to work, and she has a nap every night when she gets home. I'm helping out by cooking supper and cleaning up, but by the time I'm done, she's back in bed for the night. And she hasn't argued with me once about helping her."

"Has she been to the doctor? What does he say?"

"She's been to Dr. Tompkins twice. Each time he tells her there's a virus going around, antibiotics aren't going to work, and she'll have to wait it out. But it's not getting any better. My grandparents are starting to worry too. They want to take her to the city and at least get a second opinion."

"That sounds like a good idea if she's not getting any better."

"Yeah, but she refuses to go. She says she trusts Dr. Tompkins, and if he says she's going to get better, she will."

Dr. Tompkins has been the town doctor since before I was born. He reminded me of Humpty Dumpty. A short, squat little man with a strong French accent despite having lived in Acadia for more than twenty years. I made Mom come with me to my appointments because I couldn't understand him. He's respected by everyone, but he's getting along in years.

George returned to our table with our order, and Chip swirled the straw around the glass to mix the ice cream and root beer.

"Something just isn't right," he stopped swirling and took a slurp of his float.

"With your float?" George stopped and scowled back at our table.

"No, no," Chip stammered. "The float's great, George. I was talking about something else."

George returned to wiping down the counter.

We ate our ice cream in silence.

"Maybe my mom can talk to her," I offered. "She's a nurse after all. Maybe your mom will open up to her. Tell her if there's something else going on."

Chip raised his eyes from his float.

"Do you think she would?"

I was sure of it. Like Chip and I, our moms had become friends over the last year. Chip's beating and Brady's court trial brought them together, and they had remained friends since.

"I'll ask her. She's not at work tomorrow; maybe she can stop by and see your mom."

Chip gave me an absent nod and went back to his stirring while I licked at my cone before it dribbled down my hand.

I pushed the door of the shop open and stepped onto the street. We walked slowly, and I looked in the shop windows as we passed by. We waited at the corner and crossed to the next block. That's when I noticed that someone was sitting alone on the steps of the drug store. As we drew near, I could see it was the guy from the shooting booth. He sat leaning against the building, his leg propped on the duffel bag beside him. He had on the same clothing from the other day, jeans and t-shirt. As we got closer, the door to the pharmacy opened and Mr. Collins, the pharmacist, came out and talked to the young man. After what seemed like a few words from Mr. Collins, the young man got up and started walking down the street in front of us. He was definitely limping today. Mr. Collins remained standing on the step, watching him go. When he was satisfied he was gone, he turned and went back into the store.

The young man stopped at the corner and glanced our way before crossing the street. For a second, I thought he might recognize me from the fair. If he did, he didn't show it. He entered the park, threw his duffel bag on the ground, and sat on a bench.

"Isn't that the guy who found your money on the ground at the fair?" Chip commented after we passed the park.

"Yeah, it is. He's also the guy Logan and Cody were trying to gyp too. And I'm pretty sure I saw him get fired while Trudy and I were on the Ferris wheel." I took a furtive glance back to where he sat on the bench. "I wonder why he's still here. The fair has moved on, you'd think he would have too."

"Mr. Collins didn't seem to like him sitting on his shop steps. Where do you think he's staying?" He stopped as if the idea had just occurred to him and turned back to where we'd come from.

"It doesn't look like he's staying anywhere? Why else would he be carrying his duffel bag around?"

"Yeah, but why wouldn't he leave? He could catch the bus or hitch a ride to the city. Do you think he's stuck here?"

"Looks like it. Maybe he's looking for a job?"

"Not a lot of those in Acadia." Chip voiced what I knew to be true. Acadia was a small town with few job opportunities. When Chip didn't suggest we talk to the young man, I knew that the situation with his mom was more serious than he was letting on. Chip never missed a chance to help someone in need. For him not to get involved told me that his mind was definitely on something else.

---

I WASN'T REALLY HUNGRY, thanks to the treat Chip and I had earlier in the afternoon, but part of my summer chores was to get supper ready each night. With my chores finished, I got comfortable on the couch.

I had ordered some books from the library, so I opened the app on my phone to see if any of them were in yet. I had a long list of books that I wanted to get through this summer. No school meant it was my time to catch up on books that I wanted to read, not the assigned ones for class. Out of the ten I'd ordered, only one had come in so far, and I had finished it yesterday.

At the top of the library home page was an announcement about a summer contest. I scrolled past it and tapped "my books" at the top of the screen and looked to see when I could expect my next book.

That's where my parents found me when they arrived home at the same time from work. I was surprised to see them both standing there when I peered over the top of the couch. They rarely got home at the same time.

"How was your day, Hannah?" Mom called as she hung up her sweater. "Did you put the potatoes and carrots in with roast?"

"Good. Yeah, they've been in there for about an hour." I went back to my phone.

"Are your chores done or did you spend all day on your phone?"

Dad asked, entering the kitchen and getting a glass and the bottle of liquor from the cupboard above the refrigerator.

"Yes, they're done, and no I didn't. Chip and I went for ice cream this afternoon," I picked up the remote and turned on the television knowing my dad would be joining me soon.

Dad folded himself into his recliner. "Turn it to the news."

I clicked through the channels to the local news. Well, not really local, it came from the city, but they often carried news stories from Acadia.

The announcer quickly grabbed both our attention. "With the civic elections just around the corner, we are focusing on the candidates from various towns across the province. Today we're spotlighting Acadia's two mayoral candidates. We have returning Mayor Clarence Aldridge and first-time candidate Jacob Robinson."

My eyes shot toward my dad to see his reaction. When he slammed his chair into the upright position, I knew this was the first he'd heard of it.

"He's running for mayor?" Dad grabbed his glass and took a drink. "That's all we need, that blowhard running our town."

A picture of Jacob Robinson came onto the screen and the announcer continued. "Robinson is focusing his campaign on cleaning up the Birchfield mill. Abandoned fifteen years ago, the mill is an environmental hazard to the community, according to Robinson. He had this to say, "Mayor Aldridge has let this go on for far too long. I promise to clean up not only the mill, but I also vow to make Acadia a shining example of wealth and prosperity in this region."

"He could start with his own son and let the town take care of itself."

"He held a big rally at the fair," I commented, drawing my dad's gaze. "There were a lot of supporters there, a lot of people cheering for what he had to say too."

"And what did he have to say?"

"Pretty much the same thing he said on the news. He's going to clean up the town. Mayor Aldridge has let things go to pot."

"Well, he's not getting my vote. I don't care if Aldridge runs the town into the gutter."

The announcer moved on to the next story and Dad got up and refilled his glass.

I wasn't surprised by my dad's harsh reaction to the latest development. What was shocking was that my dad and I finally found something we could agree on. That never happened.

## Chapter 4

Two days later, Chip texted to see if I'd asked Mom about talking to Shelley, so I invited myself over. When the door opened, I was face to chest with Darth Vader, not the real one, the one on Chip's shirt.

"Good morning, Vader," I commented as I walked past him into the house. Chip didn't reply, closing the door behind me. Something was different. We moved into the living room. A game of Fortnite sat open on Chip's laptop. Then it struck me; it was so quiet.

"Your mom not home today?" I sat on the sofa across from Chip.

"No, she's here. She's resting. She's not feeling so great today," he said all of this while staring at his laptop.

"She's still sleeping in the afternoon?" I asked his profile. Shelley was usually bustling around the house whenever I was over. Chip said she'd been tired. Was she getting worse?

"Lately, she does. She's not sleeping at night, so she naps during the day. She started her vacation on Monday and she's had a nap every afternoon."

"They didn't find anything when your grandparents took her to the hospital?"

Chip shook his head. "They ran some tests, and she goes tomorrow to find out the results. She doesn't know it yet, but I'm going with her."

I recognized the determined set of his jaw and knew there was nothing Shelley could say that would convince him to stay at home. Chip felt it was his responsibility to look after his mom ever since they'd moved to Acadia. He would want to know what he could do for his mom and then he'd do whatever he could to make her well again.

"Chip," his mom's voice came from down the hallway.

Chip jumped up from his chair and went to her room. Minutes later, he went to the kitchen, returning with a glass of water and disappearing down the hallway. He came back, and without a word, sat down.

"Everything okay?"

"She gets thirsty, and sometimes she's just too tired to get out of bed."

"Is there anything I can do, Chip?"

"I wish there was Hannah, but right now we just need to find out what's wrong. I'm hoping your mom can help with that. Then we can do something."

I watched while Chip tried to play his game. I noticed how distracted he was because he turned his head every time he heard a sound coming from down the hallway. What could I say to make him feel better? Honestly, I didn't think there was anything that would make him feel better. Nothing that would cheer him up, anyway. Shelley appeared in the doorway, leaning against the entrance to the hallway for support. At first, I didn't recognize her. Her yoga pants and t-shirt hung on her body, her hair was dull and limp. Shelley's usually healthy-looking skin was gray, and she had black rings under her eyes. Now I understood why Chip was so worried. I thought I should go.

"Hannah, I didn't know you were here. Chip why didn't you tell me?" The soft tone of her voice took the sting out of her accusation.

"Hi, Shelley," I waved as Chip helped his mom to the couch and sat on the arm beside her, his arm wrapped protectively around her shoulder.

"How is your summer going? I hope you're having more fun than

Chip. He spends all his time hovering over me as if I'm an invalid. You'd think I'd never been sick before," she chuckled, but Chip's expression never changed.

"Summer is going okay. I've got chores to do, but other than that, it's great so far."

"Can I get you anything, Mom? Are you cold? Thirsty?"

"I'm fine, Chip. Why don't you and Hannah go do something? Get out of the house for a while. I'm just going to sit here and watch some television." She gestured toward the coffee table. "Hand me the remote, please."

"I was going to go to the library. I've got some books I need to pick up. It shouldn't take too long," I offered.

"Great idea!" Shelley patted Chip on the knee. "Get some fresh air. It'll take your mind off worrying about me. Doctor Tompkins said everything will be fine. Go with Hannah."

After some thought, Chip rose from the couch. "We'll be back in an hour. Sit right there until I get back."

"Yes, sir!" Shelley saluted Chip's order.

"Very funny, Mom. I mean it. I expect you to be in this spot when I get back."

"I will. Now go and have some fun."

Shelley aimed the remote at the television as Chip and I moved to the door. Chip gave one last look at his mom before crossing the threshold.

"Go, Chip," she called, her eyes trained on the television.

"Good to know your mom has eyes in the back of her head too," I joked, hoping to lighten the heavy mood that followed us out of the house.

It didn't help. Chip responded, "Other than my grandparents, she's all I've got."

We walked in the cooling shade of the tree-lined street. Kids on bikes and scooters zoomed by us the closer we got to the library.

Lost in thought, it took me a while to realize Chip wasn't beside me. I turned around to find him looking in the window of the sporting goods store on Main Street.

"What are you doing?" I asked, walking back to where he stood looking through the window. "Do you want to go in?" I noticed he wasn't looking at the display of golf equipment, he was looking at the 'Help Wanted' sign taped to the glass.

"You're looking for a job?"

Chip studied the sign before turning to me. "I might have to. Mom is nearly out of sick days. We're just lucky she had some vacation time saved up or she'd be off work without any pay." He looked back at the sign. "I might have to get a job to help out. Or at least enough to get the air conditioner fixed."

I didn't know what to say. Chip was carrying the weight of the world on his shoulders. He not only had his mom's health to worry about, but also how they were going to survive if she was seriously sick. I didn't think people could hire you unless you were sixteen, but I wasn't about to tell Chip that. He didn't need something else to be discouraged about.

"It's going to work out, Chip." I hoped what I was saying was true. Chip gave the poster one last look. After that, I noticed that Chip checked every store front we passed for a Help Wanted sign.

The library was quiet when we entered. Two kids, younger than us, were playing a game on the computers by the front counter. A third person was hunched over a computer by the window. The librarian, Mrs. Mackie, was signing out books for a customer. Mrs. Mackie had been the librarian for close to a hundred years, I figured. I got in line, and Chip headed towards the stacks. The woman in front of me thanked the librarian and left.

"Hi, Hannah. Here to pick up your books?"

"Hi, Mrs. Mackie. Yes, I got a notification that a couple of the books I ordered are in."

She turned to the shelves behind her.

"Here they are. Oh, this one looks good." She held up the latest book in a series of popular fantasy novels. "And how is your writing going? That piece you performed at the Slam Poetry contest was so inspiring. Have you been writing for long?" she asked while scanning my books and looked at me expectantly as she handed them over.

"Umm . . . for a while now." Hoping she'd let it go at that. No one even knew about my writing until Brady stole my notebook last year, which was how I liked it. Despite having performed my poetry twice in front of people, it wasn't something I liked to talk about.

"Really? I didn't know you were a writer, and you've been coming to the library for years. Did you see the poster for the multi-media contest we're running this summer?" She pointed to the door. It was the same one I'd seen on the library website. "There's a $200 cash prize and they may use your piece in an upcoming promotion that could air on television. You should think about it. It would be a real feather in our cap to have someone from Acadia win."

I turned to look for Chip. I needed to get out of there before Mrs. Mackie had me all signed up for the contest. School was out, and I didn't plan on doing anything even close to school work for the rest of the summer. Chip was nowhere in sight.

"I'll think about it, Mrs. Mackie. Thanks."

"Well, let me know. I can help you with the submission. The entry deadline is August seventeenth."

"Great." I took the bag of books she gave me and headed to the rows of shelves to find Chip. *Where is he? We need to get out of here!* The first two rows were empty. It wasn't until I got to the final row of shelves that I found him standing in the aisle reading a book. As I got closer and noted that we were in the health section, more specifically, the section that dealt with illness, I knew what he was looking for.

I casually asked, "Whatcha readin'?"

His head came up as he snapped the book closed and put it back on the shelf. "Nothing."

"*The Natural Way to Healing*?" I read the title. "That doesn't sound like nothing. That sounds like you're looking for information for your mom."

"I have to do something, Hannah." He ran his fingers through his hair. "I tried to search online, but I can't take the chance of going over on our data or Mom catching me, but I can't just sit around and hope that Dr. Tompkins is going to make her better. According to my grandparents, it's a sixth month waiting list to see any specialist. We need to do something." He started walking to the end of the row.

"What did the book say?" I hurried to catch up to him.

"I couldn't find any of her symptoms in there, but I didn't get far." He kept walking, not turning back to talk to me.

I grabbed his arm as we made it to the end of the aisle and he stopped.

"Let's go back and look then. I'll help. Maybe there's another book here that will give you some answers."

At first, I thought he was going to refuse my offer, but he finally turned and went back to the book on the shelf.

"How can your mom 'heal naturally' if you don't know what your mom has?" I asked, scanning the book titles in the section. Chip opened the book he'd been reading earlier, and we both continued his hunt for answers without speaking.

"Why don't we try the internet again?" I asked. My book held no answers to Shelley's illness. "There's a computer free by the windows."

With a sigh, Chip returned his book to the shelf, "Why not?"

I dropped my books on the table beside the last available computer and sat down. Chip pulled a chair up beside me. I realized that the person sitting at the computer next to me was the guy from the fair. Today, he wore a dull green military jacket over his T-shirt. I looked at his screen and saw he was messaging back and forth with someone named Louise.

At that moment, he turned in my direction, and I quickly looked back to the screen in front of me. I clicked on the web browser.

"So, what should I put? What are some of your mom's symptoms?" My fingers hovered over the keys.

"It started with a cough and fever about two months ago." I typed "cough" and "fever" into the search bar. "Then, the fever went away, but she still had the cough and no energy. That's about it."

I added "no energy for two months" and hit Enter. The screen changed, and a number of titles came up.

I clicked on the first one. Chip and I read the list to ourselves. It started with the flu and ended with a number of cancers.

"Where's your thyroid," I asked. It was the only one I didn't recognize.

"Around your neck somewhere," Chip said as he continued reading the list.

"It sounds like it could be one of"—I paused and counted the various illnesses listed—"about forty different things. Are there any other symptoms she has?"

"Not that I've seen."

"What about weight loss or lack of appetite? I've never seen your mom look this thin."

"Yeah, add those. It's just so frustrating. She won't tell me much about how she's been feeling." Chip frowned. "I'm afraid she's keeping her symptoms from me so I don't worry."

The clacking of keys beside me interrupted my train of thought. I casually peeked at the other screen again and saw messages coming and going rapidly. One caught my eye before it disappeared, "Ben I don't have the money. Sorry."

*Ben! His name is Ben!* I pressed my lips together and turned to Chip, ready to blurt out my discovery, but he sat with his head down, fingers buried in his hair, his elbows resting on his knees. Chip's head came up with a jerk when the young man beside us pushed back his chair and grabbed his duffel bag off the floor. He pushed past an elderly man waiting at the counter and was out of the library in seconds.

"Did you find what you were looking for?" Mrs. Mackie called after him, but he didn't answer.

"What was that about?" Chip's eyes followed Ben's departure from the library.

I looked at the computer screen, but the conversation was gone, the screen saver taking its place.

My cheeks heated. "He was trying to get someone to send him money, but they couldn't. I think he's upset."

"You read his conversation?"

"Just one message, then it disappeared. I wasn't reading it on purpose. I just happened to glance in that general direction and saw the message." My face was on fire at this point.

"You're quite the detective." Chip gave me a lopsided grin. "I never thought that shy, unassuming Hannah would snoop into someone's private conversations. Especially after the whole school heard what was in your journal incident."

"I didn't read the whole thing. Just one message."

"I'm not accusing you of anything. I was just kidding, Hannah."

"Ha ha. Let's get back to finding out what's wrong with your mom." The laughter left Chip's eyes, and I felt bad for reminding him why we were there. I avoided looking at Chip while I jiggled the mouse to wake up the screen.

An hour later, and twenty websites behind us, we still didn't have any answers.

"I've had enough, Hannah. We're no closer to figuring out what's wrong with my mom than we were when we sat down."

"There's one more site here that looks promising." I scrolled to the next link on the page.

"The only thing we know is that we don't have enough information to narrow down what it could be. I'm going home and asking my mom if she's got any other symptoms, then we can try again."

"You're sure?"

"Yep, come on. Let's get out of here." I exited the search page and picked up my books.

Chip noted the titles. "You're still reading fantasy books? Hannah, I need to introduce you to some better literature."

"Yeah? *Captain Underpants*? Or no, wait . . . like a Marvel comic? That's the only thing I ever see you read. Don't knock my taste in books."

"I'll have you know Stan Lee is considered a writing genius in some circles."

"No doubt,"—I pushed open the door to the library—"just not in my circle."

We stepped out on to the street. The sun continued to beat down and waves of heat rose off the pavement.

On our way to his house, we passed the park where I wrote the poem about Chip. It was the day after Brady read my journal to the class. Too scared to show my face at school, I wrote a poem about how brave Chip was and how he didn't care what people thought of him. If

Brady hadn't handed it in as an assignment, I'd probably have given it to Chip at some point.

A mom was waiting for her toddler to come down the slide while trying to rock her baby in a stroller. The swings were empty, and on impulse, I dropped my books on the grass and ran over to sit on one. Chip stood on the sidewalk looking at me and then reluctantly joined me as I pumped my legs and gained momentum.

"Bet I get higher than you," I taunted, pulling back on the chains.

"Never!" Chip replied, driving to catch up with me. We kept at it, and soon all I saw were clouds as I flew upward. It reminded me of the rollercoaster, but instead of closing my eyes, I revelled in the freedom of the swing moving back and forth. I laughed as hair covered my face and I swung backward. Not long ago, I was alone, but today I had my best friend beside me. Despite the worry over Shelley, I was shocked at how dramatically my life had changed and how I had changed since Chip barged into my life and demanded to be my friend.

Chip and I were soon swinging in sync, and I realized he was going to push ahead of me if I didn't keep up my momentum.

"I'm close, Hannah."

"Close doesn't count."

"Two more should do it," his voice called from beside me.

I pulled harder on the chains, but the next swing showed Chip's feet higher than mine.

"I win!"

"No, you don't. Your legs are longer than mine!" I argued, the chains biting into my hands as I pulled on them.

"Okay, next swing, whoever's butt is higher, is the winner."

"You're on!"

Pulling with all my strength, my swing flew back and then forward. As I reached the top of my swing, I looked to my left and saw Chip even higher than I was.

"YES!" Chip pumped his arms in the air and then quickly grabbed the chains. As the swings slowed, I dragged my foot in the dirt and came to a stop.

"Winner, winner, chicken dinner," Chip laughed, flying into the air while his swing was still moving back and forth.

"Yeah, yeah. You won. Don't be a sore winner."

"Me? Chip the Champion; it has a nice ring to it. Feel free to call me that from now on."

Chip wore a smile from ear to ear—a smile I hadn't seen all day. In fact, I hadn't seen it since the fair.

I smiled despite my loss. If Chip was smiling, it was a win in my book.

## Chapter 5

I placed the pan of pork chops on the counter and flipped the oven mitts down beside them. It was 5:45 p.m., and I expected mom and dad to walk through the door any minute. I mashed the potatoes until they were fluffy clouds and then popped the lid back on the pot. Plates and cutlery were on the table along with a salad. The frosty pitcher of iced tea was all that was missing.

Now that supper was ready, and I had nothing to occupy my brain with, I thought about the trip Chip and I took to the library. I could only imagine how it would feel to know that your one remaining parent, or the only one you had any contact with, was sick, and you were helpless to do anything about it. Shelley and his grandparents were the only family Chip had, and he protected them fiercely. Asking my mom to talk to Shelley was the least I could do to help him. I was hoping that since supper was ready, Mom and I could have a chat before Dad got home.

At five minutes to six, Mom came through the front door carrying the mail and her lunch bag. She dropped everything on the floor, sat down to take off her sneakers, leaned back against the wall, and let out a sigh.

Her head rolled to the side and she opened her eyes, "Supper smells delicious, Hannah. Is your dad home yet?" She sat up straight, put both hands on her knees, and stood up.

"Not yet." I went to the sink as she plodded upstairs. While Mom changed, I reached into the soapy water and fished around for the utensils I'd used to make supper.

"Anything I need to do?" Mom asked, taking the pitcher of iced tea from the fridge and filling a glass off the table.

"No, I think I have everything ready for supper, but there is something I'd like to ask you about." I took the dishtowel off the stove and started drying the utensils in the sink.

"Sure, what is it?" She leaned on the counter and took a long drink out of her glass.

I didn't answer right away. Now that the moment was here, I struggled to find the words to ask her, so I pretended to concentrate on polishing a stainless-steel flipper to a brilliant shine.

"Hannah, you're going to wear the finish off that thing. What is it? You know you can talk to me about anything."

I knew that. But I didn't trust myself to say the words without breaking down.

I took a deep breath. "It's about Shelley." I put the flipper in the utensil drawer.

Mom frowned and put down her glass. "Shelley Cavanagh? What about her? Is it Chip's dad? Is he around?"

"What? No! This has nothing to do with Chip's dad." I stepped back from the fierce scowl on her face. *Wow! That went south fast!*

The scowl disappeared from her face. "Sorry, I worry about him showing up unexpectedly."

*Really? Why would she worry about that? Chip hadn't seen his dad for nearly two years.*

"Chip wanted me to ask you to talk to her."

"What about?"

My voice quavered, and I tried to swallow around the lump in my throat. "Chip's really worried about her. She can't seem to shake this 'flu' as Dr. Tompkins calls it, and he's afraid that she's keeping something from him or that the doctor isn't taking this as seriously as he should."

Leaving her glass, Mom rounded the counter and pulled me into her arms, trapping a spoon and spatula between our bodies. After a moment, she pulled back and searched my face.

"I just talked to Shelley last week. She didn't mention anything. What's got Chip worried?" She brushed my bangs from my face. I turned and put the utensils in the container by the stove, folded the dishtowel, and put it on the counter, giving me time to get my emotions under control.

I recounted my visit to Chip's and our fact-finding mission to the library. As I explained Shelley's symptoms, her face softened, and I saw the concern in her eyes. She took my hands in hers.

"What do you want me to do?" I'd lowered my head, and she peered at me through my bangs.

"Would you talk to Shelley? See if there's something she's not telling Chip? I think he just needs some reassurance." She smiled and pulled me in for another hug.

"Of course, I will."

"Thanks Mom," I wheezed out through the crush of her hug.

"No problem." She let me go and headed for the table. "Now, let's eat. I'm starving."

Mom told me about her day as we ate our supper. The usual hospital stuff, but I asked questions in the right spots, and I could tell from her stories that she really loved her job. Dad texted to say he was on a call and wouldn't be home for a couple of hours. As I put the leftovers on a plate for Dad to warm up when he got home, Mom finished up the dishes. We worked in silence, but it wasn't awkward. Instead, it was comfortable, and I realized that my relationship with my mom had changed in the last year too. For the better. We talked more, and I was able to tell her things that I never would have before. My dad? Well, that was a different story. Not much had changed there, and I saw even less of him now that he was working more. It seemed the only thing we could agree on was our dislike for Jacob Robinson.

*July 10, 2018*

*Today Chip told me his mom was sick. He's really worried that she's keeping something from him. I hope he's wrong. Mom's going to talk to Shelley, and I hope she tells her the truth. Maybe mom can convince her to see another doctor to get a second opinion. I understand how Chip feels. If my mom was sick, I'd want to know what was going on. I couldn't imagine watching her get weaker and weaker and not being able to do something about it. I'll call Chip later and see if he wants to do something tomorrow. Maybe some time with friends will take his mind off things.*

## Chapter 6

I laid my towel on the grass and sat down. All around me, kids laughed and splashed in the water. As they ran by, they sprayed me with water like a dog shaking out his coat—I yelped as the drops of water hit me—paying no attention as they hustled to the end of the waterslide line. The stairway was full of kids clutching their arms trying to stay warm.

A bag landed on the grass beside me, followed by a towel, and then Trudy.

"Hey. How long have you been here?" she asked, digging in her bag and coming up with a bottle of sunscreen.

"Not long. Nice bathing suit."

"You think so? My mom bought it for me." Trudy proceeded to slather sunscreen on her legs and arms. "I'm not sure orange is my colour."

"Yeah, I think green is your colour." Alex sat on the grass in front of us dressed in jeans and a t-shirt.

"Where's your swimming trunks? You do know that when we agreed to meet at the pool, the idea was to swim, right?" Trudy asked, snapping the lid on her lotion and throwing it in her bag.

"I got it right here." Alex held up his swim bag. "I'll get changed in a sec. Chip in the pool already?"

I plucked at the grass. I'd called Chip last night to see if he wanted to go swimming today. It was the last time the four of us could get together before Trudy left for camp. She was going to spend the next five weeks as a junior counsellor at Twin Pines Camp. Chip refused at first. The only way I could get him to agree to come was to tell him that I'd talked to my mom.

"He'll be here. He must be running late." I hoped I was right and Chip hadn't decided to stay home.

While Alex went to change, Trudy and I watched the kids coming off the waterslides into the pool. Two toddlers stood in the shallow end dueling with water noodles as their mothers looked on.

When Alex came back, Chip was with him, and I let out a sigh of relief. They loped across the deck, towels thrown over their shoulders. Smaller kids scurried around them, and when a ball landed right in front of them, Chip picked it up and threw it back into the pool.

"You're late, Mr. Punctuality," I teased as Chip flipped his towel out and sat down.

"Yeah, I had to help my mom with a couple of things before I left," he said, straightening the corners of his towel. He wouldn't meet my eyes, so I knew that "helping" really meant he was doing something to make her feel better. "I tried to get our air conditioner working, but I didn't have much luck. No thanks to Google."

We laid on the grass and watched the kids. Trudy and Alex got up to go down the waterslide.

"You guys coming?" Alex stood on his towel waiting.

"Of course, we are," Chip answered and jumped to his feet. He held a hand out to help me up. Standing close to him, I leaned over and whispered, "I was afraid you wouldn't come."

"Mom overheard our phone call last night and demanded I come today. She seems to be feeling better, or she's trying to convince me she is. So here I am." He spread his hands and shrugged.

"I'm glad you're here. Don't worry, Mom promised to talk to her soon."

Chip's shouldered sagged. "Thanks, Hannah. I just need to know Mom is going to be okay."

"She will be. Now come on, let's do some water sliding." I grabbed his hand, and we joined Trudy and Alex where they stood at the end of the line.

The afternoon flew by. We must have gone down the waterslides at least twenty times, and it wasn't until Trudy said that her legs were going to give out if she had to climb the stairs again that we moved to the pool. Well, three of us moved to the pool. Alex sat in the shallow end with the toddlers, showing them the *correct* way to duel with water noodles. We teased him after, but he felt he'd performed an important community service. I'd thought swinging with Chip yesterday had been fun, but swimming with my friends was even better.

I flopped down on my towel and used it to wipe my face. My eyes burned from the chlorine and my hair was a scraggly mess around my shoulders.

Alex grabbed his towel and dried off.

"I have to go." He rubbed the towel over his hair, and it stood on end when he finished. "I promised my mom I'd cut the grass before my dad got home. Later." Before we could say good-bye, he was heading to the change rooms.

"See ya around, Alex," Chip called after him. He waved in response.

Trudy packed her bag. "I better get home too. I've still got things to get ready before I leave. I'll talk to you tomorrow, Hannah. Bye, Chip."

We sat and watched the kids play for a while. It always surprised me when Chip and I had moments like this. He was the only person I could share silence with and not feel uncomfortable. When my hair and suit were nearly dry, I knew I needed to get home to make supper.

"I need to get going," I told Chip.

"Yeah, I should get home too," he answered, but didn't move until I pulled my towel from underneath him.

We picked our stuff up off the grass and walked around the splashing children. The playground beside the pool was busy. The moms who had been at the pool were now sitting on the grass as their kids crawled around the play structure. One kid, a little boy in blue shorts and sun hat, ran away from his mother laughing. She let him get away before getting up to chase after him. He ran toward one of the many benches in the park, and it was then that I noticed Ben sitting on the bench in the shade of the tree. *This is crazy!* I elbowed Chip.

"Eric! Come back here," his mother called trying to catch up to him, fear replacing the laughter in her voice. It was obvious she'd seen Ben and was trying to prevent her son from going near him. Curious, I stopped.

Eric ignored his mother and instead crawled onto the bench. He grinned at Ben, and I saw his lips move. Ben said something to the boy and ruffled his hair. Eric's mom quickly scooped the toddler into her arms.

"Eric! Mommy told you not to talk to strangers," she scolded. At the tone of her voice, the boy began to cry. She forced a smile in Ben's direction while bouncing the boy and patting his back. "No offense, but he's so friendly he'll go up to anyone, and I'm deathly afraid one day it will be the wrong person. You hear about babies being snatched up all the time."

Where only seconds ago, Ben was smiling, his face was now blank.

Putting her son in the stroller, she ignored his cries and joined her friend who was waiting for her on the path. In front of us now, their conversation carried back to us.

"Who was that?" the friend asked.

"I have no idea. I've never seen him here before."

"What do you think he has in that duffel bag? Do you think he's homeless?"

"I hope not. You hear how those homeless people are nothing but addicts who wander from town to town mooching off people until the community kicks them out or they move on. Who knows, he could have some mental health issues too. I'm going to ask around and see if anyone else has seen him lurking around the parks. I should mention it to Claudia. Her husband works on the police force." They reached the opening in the chain link fence that was the entrance to the park. One behind the other, they went through and walked down the sidewalk in the shade of the trees that lined the street.

I stopped at the entrance and looked back to the bench in the park. It was empty.

Chip stood looking in the same direction. "I think you were right—he's stuck here."

I thought about the mom's reaction. She didn't seem the least bit concerned about how her words may have made Ben feel. In fact, it was like she didn't see him at all. Like he was invisible to her. I shook my head as that thought stuck and reminded me of how I used to like to be invisible—I even had rules for it, rules I never broke—until I met Chip. And for the most part, I don't think about my rules very often any more.

"Why are you shaking your head?" Chip asked as we stepped up on the curb of the second block.

"I feel bad for him."

Chip turned with a frown on his face. "The little kid? I'm sure he'll be all right."

"No. The guy at the park. Ben. That mom was so rude to him," my voice shook with frustration. "He didn't do anything except ruffle the boy's hair, and the mom treated him like he had a contagious disease."

"I'm sure she was just trying to look out for her son. You have to admit, we don't get many people around here like him. I'm sure she was just scared."

"Like him?" I asked, my voice rising. "And just who is he like? We don't know what his story is. He might be homeless, he might not. Just because we don't have many homeless people here doesn't mean that we treat people who come into our town as outsiders looking to attack our children, push them off the steps of our store, or worse, treat them like they don't exist altogether. Different isn't bad. Why can't people understand that?"

"Well, coming from someone who was once a stranger and considered an outsider, I agree with you. Even after a year of living here, I still feel like I'll never be accepted as one of Acadia's own, even if my grandparents have lived here their whole lives."

I felt bad for snapping at Chip. I knew Acadia hadn't been very welcoming when he moved here. I knew he still felt like he didn't belong.

Maybe Chip was right. Ben wasn't asking for help and maybe we had no right to butt into his business. Lost in thought, I was nearly clotheslined by an evergreen branch. Chip quickly grabbed me and I started and then smiled in thanks before picking our conversation up where we'd left off. I thought back to the person he was texting with. He must have someone who could help him.

"The bus would be the obvious choice to get out of town. Maybe he's just waiting for someone to send him some money."

"Yeah, maybe."

"Do you think we should ask him?" Ben looked harmless and he did give me back the money I'd dropped, so he was probably honest, but I wasn't sure about talking to him.

"Sure, why not? *If* we see him again, we could ask." Chip shrugged.

I still wasn't sure. There was no point worrying about it. The chances of us seeing him again were slim. He probably had family or friends who could help him. Right?

## Chapter 7

I shifted from one foot to the other beside a display of oil filters while Chip talked to Charlie, the owner of Proctor's Garage. This was the third business we'd visited today, and from the looks of things, it wasn't going to be our last. Charlie stood behind the counter and shook his head at Chip. The dejected slope of Chip's shoulders told me what Charlie's answer had been.

"I take it that's a 'No?'"

Chip nodded and pulled the door open.

"Same reason as the last place?" I asked.

"Yeah." he kicked a rock. "It sucks being fourteen."

I wasn't surprised Chip wasn't having any luck, but I wasn't about to tell him that.

It had been two weeks, and Chip was more determined than ever to get their air conditioner fixed. Shelley had already told him she was against it, but changing Chip's mind was like trying to get the earth to spin in the opposite direction. After spending an hour trying to convince him it wasn't necessary and no one would probably hire him, she threw up her hands with a frustrated "fine" and told him to go ahead, but added, it was only a summer job. Once school started,

Chip would have to quit. Chip agreed, and we'd spent most of the afternoon trying to find him a job.

"If the government says you can't work until you're sixteen, business owners don't have much choice Chip."

"The government—always sticking its nose in other people's business—there has to be a way to get around this." Head down, hands in his pockets, Chip scuffed his feet along the cement of the sidewalk. And he was right, it sucked being fourteen, worrying about your sick mom and taking on adult responsibilities. I knew Chip wouldn't give up until he found a way. Lost in thought, it wasn't until the last minute that I noticed a woman chasing a large brown and black dog coming toward us. I pushed Chip into the grass to avoid a collision.

"Geez, Hannah. What was that for?"

At that moment, the dog stopped and lowered its black nose and sniffed Chip's feet.

"Hey, boy. Where did you come from?" Chip asked as he ruffled the fur around the dog's neck. The dog barked.

"Scout, come here!" The young woman carrying a leash ran up to us. She looked to be in her early thirties with short brown hair. She clipped the leash to the dog's collar. "Thank you. I've been chasing her for two blocks. If you hadn't stopped her, I'd still be running." She paused to catch her breath. "She isn't usually this friendly to strangers."

"I like dogs," Chip said and knelt down to continue scratching Scout's neck. With her tongue hanging out, Scout panted and turned her head so that Chip could hit the right spots.

"She likes you too." The owner stuck out her hand. "I'm Christy."

Chip stood and shook hands. "I'm Chip and this is Hannah." He gestured to me.

"Hi, Hannah."

"How long have you had her?" Chip asked, now giving Scout a full-body rub, which if the movement of her tail was any indication, she was enjoying immensely.

"I rescued her about six months ago." Christy ran her hand down Scout's back.

"She's beautiful," I said. And as if she understood me, Scout turned and licked my hand.

"She is. She's great company. And, honestly, she gives me a little security, but I work shift work and I just don't have the time it takes to give her the exercise she needs."

As soon as the words left her mouth, Chip's head came up from where it was buried in Scout's coat. I recognized the look in his eye immediately. It was the same one he had when he was convincing me to get on the rollercoaster.

Chip stood.

"I'll do it for you." Scout butted her head against Chip's knee, and he absentmindedly stroked the dog's coat. Excitement shone in his eyes as he waited for Christy's answer.

"You would?" She appeared to be thinking it over as she stared down the road behind us. "I don't know. You have a dog of your own?"

"No. My dad wouldn't let me have pets and now that it's just my mom and I, we can't really afford it."

Christy didn't look sold on the idea.

"But I've always wanted one, and I'm very reliable. Right, Hannah?"

Shocked that I'd suddenly become part of the negotiation, I stuttered, "Right. . . . I mean, yes. He's very reliable. The most reliable person I know. He is *so* reliable."

Christy held up her hand, smiling.

"I think I get the picture." She thought for a second, her face serious. "What would you charge?"

I knew Chip wanted this job badly, but not wanting to appear too eager, he replied, "What are you willing to pay?"

Christy smiled, "You want to negotiate? I like that. Okay, five dollars a day."

Chip tilted his head, "Ten."

Christy countered, "Seven."

"Seven fifty and you have a deal." Chip stuck out his hand and Christy shook it.

She smiled. "We'll make it an even eight. Can you start tomorrow?"

"Sure! What time do you want me?"

"If you can come around nine that would be great." She pulled her phone from her back pocket while at the same time wrapping the leash around her other wrist, as Scout was now interested in the grass along the sidewalk. "What's your phone number, and I'll text you the address?"

They exchanged phone numbers, and Chip promised to be at Christy's by nine the following morning.

"Scout and I need to get going or I'm going to be late for work. Nice meeting you, Hannah. Thanks again for your help. See you tomorrow, Chip." Christy pulled on Scout's leash, and they continued down the street.

"It looks like your job search is over."

"I know! Isn't it great? Now I just need to find some more people who need a dog walker." Chip walked faster, and I jogged to catch up.

"More people? What do you mean?" I slowed to a stop. Chip took four more steps before he noticed I wasn't beside him.

He turned and waved his arm at me. "Hannah, come on. I've got posters to make."

I blinked and remained where I was. "Posters?" I shook my head. "Okay Chip, I'm lost. What are you talking about?"

"I'm not going to walk one dog, Hannah. I'm going to walk as many as I can. Think about it." He held up his index finger. "Every dog represents forty dollars a week. Five dogs a week—two hundred dollars. Ten dogs—four hundred dollars. This is a gold mine, Hannah. And that's only for an hour walk. There are eight hours in a day. I could make three hundred and twenty dollars a day." He paused and finally took a breath.

"Glad you're putting those genius math skills to use."

"Come on, Hannah. We've got work to do." He stalked away, faster than before. Rather than being left behind, I ran to catch up.

## Chapter 8

"Chip, I need a break!" My feet hurt. I'd never seen Chip like this before. He was on a mission and nothing was going to stand in his way.

"Two more and I'll buy you ice cream." Chip stood beside a light pole and stuck out his hand.

"We've still got a stack of flyers to put up," I complained as I held one against the pole and he proceeded to wrap tape around the top and bottom.

"Two more. I promise." he walked toward the next pole. "By then we'll be at the Milky Way," he added to entice me to keep moving.

We'd been at this since ten o'clock this morning, right after he took Scout for his first walk, which, considering how Scout pulled him all over town, Chip should've been exhausted, even if it didn't play Scout out. It was now three o'clock and I was pretty sure there wasn't a street light in Acadia that didn't have one of Chip's dog walking flyers plastered to it.

I grunted and forced myself to walk behind him. He stood at the next pole and waited. I slapped the flyer onto the pole and looked longingly at the ice cream shop, imagining the taste of licorice and orange on my tongue.

"Last one, come on." Chip jolted me out of my ice cream daydream. I tried to lift my hand off the flyer—it wouldn't move. My fingertips and wrist were taped to the pole on top of the flyer. Chip, tape gun in hand, bent over laughing.

"I can't believe you didn't feel me taping you to the pole," he laughed again.

"Very funny." I yanked, but the tape didn't give. "I was daydreaming about ice cream. Chip get me out of here now," I demanded, as a couple came out of the bakery we were standing in front of. At first, they smiled, thinking I was leaning against the pole, but when they saw my hand, they frowned in confusion. "This is embarrassing," I hissed.

Chip hiccupped with laughter. "I don't know, Hannah. I think it's great advertising. Do you think you could stay here all day? You're drawing attention to the sign. Or maybe curl your fingers in so you're pointing at my phone number."

Chip's laughter erupted again, until he realized that he was the only one laughing. I stood with my hand on my hip, steam coming out of my ears. Careful not to get too close to my free hand, Chip released me from the poster. I rubbed my wrist while shooting him an irritated look.

"You have to admit, it was kind of funny."

He looked sheepish when I didn't reply.

"Okay, okay. How about some ice cream?" He took the leftover posters from me and steered me in the direction of the Milky Way.

"I was dreaming about a double scoop, but now it's going to cost you a triple scoop, and we're eating it in the shop." There was no way I wasn't going to enjoy the air conditioning while I had the chance.

Chip held the door to the shop open. "You got it."

The cool air hit me as I crossed the threshold. I closed my eyes and drank it in, lifting my hair off the back of my neck, letting the cool air soothe me.

"Are we going to order, Hannah? Or just stand here and enjoy George's air conditioning?"

"It feels so good, I'm not sure."

"Well, let's at least get a booth, so we're not holding up traffic by the door." I opened my eyes to see the shop was packed, and I was blocking the entrance.

I let my hair drop, and I walked to the first available booth along the wall and slid in. Chip got in line for ice cream, but there were five people in front of him. He was going to be a minute, so I rested my head on the back of the booth and closed my eyes.

"Hannah, quick, before I lose all your ice cream."

I blinked my eyes open to the biggest cone I'd ever seen. I'd asked for three scoops, but they were huge.

"Take it," Chip gestured with the cone, while at the same time licking a vanilla cone that was starting to lean like Pisa. I wrapped my hands around the tiny cone afraid the mountain of ice cream would crumble from the weight.

"Heaven," I whispered reverently starting at the bottom and taking a long lick to the very top of my cone.

"Here. You might want to wipe your nose." Chip handed me a paper napkin from the dispenser on the table.

I pulled the metal dispenser over, looked at my reflection, and quickly rubbed the ice cream off my nose.

"Thanks."

"You'd tell me if I had ice cream on my face, wouldn't you?"

"Um . . . yes?" I replied with a small smile, but after taping my hand to the pole, I wasn't sure.

The door to the shop opened. Logan, Cody, and Mason entered the shop dressed in basketball shorts, t-shirts, and sneakers. Mason had a basketball tucked under his arm.

"Nab that booth," Logan waved at the last remaining booth in the shop, which happened to be the one directly in front of us.

"I want a chocolate sundae." Cody placed a couple of bills in Logan's hand. The booth shook as Cody sat down, his back to Chip. Not wanting to draw attention to ourselves, we ate our cones silently.

Logan and Mason got in line behind two ladies. Mason bounced the basketball on the floor as he waited.

"Enough!" came from behind the counter. George peered over the top of the freezer, a cone in one hand and a pail of ice cream in the other. "—or you're going to be eating outside." The shop was instantly quiet. All eyes were on Logan and Mason. George continued to stare at Mason, and his face flushed red.

"Yeah, Mason. George is going to throw you out if you bounce that again," Logan scolded, imitating George.

After a long look at Mason, he reached into the freezer and finished the cones for customers at the head of the line.

Logan and Mason continued to joke around as George finished their order. "Take your order outside," George said as he handed them their ice cream.

Chip and I both shifted uncomfortably. We knew that George wasn't afraid to take on teenage boys. He'd done it before when Brady, Logan, Mason, and the rest of their group had tried to steal a young boy's ice cream.

We knew that Logan and Mason weren't going to challenge George without Brady. They weren't that confident.

The boys grumbled, but moved to the door. Cody got up from the booth and joined them as they were leaving. Mason bounced the ball one last time on the way out. Everyone froze waiting for George's reaction, which was to give them another long look as the door closed behind them.

I let out a sigh of relief.

Murmurs started up around us.

"I always thought they only acted like that to impress Brady, but now I think they're all jerks in their own right." Chip licked his cone.

"They've been at it long enough. I don't think they know any different. But George doesn't take any crap from them. I think they were so shocked when he told them to get out that they did it without thinking."

Chip chuckled, "Yeah, I don't think I'd say 'No' to George. I think he may have wrestled in the WWE once upon a time."

I laughed, but Chip was right. George was no shrimp. His biceps were the size of tree trunks. I'm sure if he had to, he could throw Logan and the boys out the door without breaking a sweat.

Ten minutes later, we were back taping flyers to the poles on Main Street when the thud of a ball bouncing came from behind us.

"Going into the dog business, Toby?" Chip stiffened beside me at the use of his real name.

Neither of us turned around. We both knew who it was: Logan, Mason, and Cody. They hadn't gone far after being kicked out of the Milky Way, and because they obviously had time on their hands, they were still hanging around.

Finished with the sign, and ignoring the group of boys, we moved down the street to the next pole.

"You're going to be a dog walker?" Mason laughed as he peered at the sign we'd just put up.

"I don't know, Toby. Dogs can judge character pretty well, and they're going to know you're a snitch right away."

"Rather be a snitch than a jerk," Chip faced them. From my vantage point behind Chip, I clutched the flyers we had left. The scowls on their faces told me his comment had not gone over well.

Logan clenched his fist at his side and took a step forward. "You never learn, do you? We nearly beat you to death once, maybe this time we'll succeed."

As Logan stepped closer, I moved beside Chip. I didn't care if the flyers blew away, if he took one more step towards Chip, this was going to get ugly.

I was about to drop the flyers when Cody's arm landed across Logan's chest. "I think what Logan meant to say"—and he gave Logan a pointed look before returning his gaze to Chip—"was that you'd think you would've learned to keep your mouth shut when you're out numbered."

This time Chip clenched his fists and took a step forward. "Are you telling me it was my fault that you beat me up?" His face flushed and the cords in his neck became more pronounced. I gripped the back of Chip's t-shirt, ready to restrain him if necessary.

"If you hadn't stuck your nose into something that wasn't your business—you would have been fine, but you couldn't do that, so you had to be taught a lesson." Logan spit out. Fire in his eyes, he lunged forward, only to again meet the resistance of Cody's arm.

"I wasn't going to let you bully Hannah or anyone else. And—cowards that you were—you had to attack me in the dark, dressed in black. At least today, you have the guts to face me. And believe me, this has been a long-time coming. Come on. You gonna break my arm again?" The tape hit the ground, and Chip brought his fists up, twisting his shirt out of my hand.

At Chip's words, Cody's arm dropped from Logan's chest as he squared off with Logan and Mason. Chip was outnumbered three to one. I let go of the flyers. I had no idea what I was going to do. In fact, I was secretly hoping that someone or something would come along before I had to hit someone. My phone sat like a useless weight in my back pocket. Reaching for it meant I had only one hand to defend myself. Out of the blue a thought came to me. Is this the battle the palm reader was talking about? I didn't think she meant a real battle! As Chip and I stood back-to-back while the others circled around us, I thought that was about to change. Logan pulled his arm back, Chip brought his fists up, and I closed my eyes. When the sound of knuckles hitting flesh didn't happen, I slowly opened my eyes to see Ben holding Logan and Cody by the scruff of the neck. Both of them wiggled against the grip, but it didn't lessen.

"I think you three better get home before you find yourselves in a whole mess of trouble."

Logan and Cody fought to get free, and Mason even attempted to help them out, but Ben held on.

"You again? You're the guy that gypped us out of our prize at the shooting booth." Logan growled, twisting to get free of Ben's grasp.

"I'd like to say it's great to see you boys again, but it's not." Ben smiled.

"Who are you anyway?" Cody squirmed to get a look at Ben.

"Yeah, and what are you still doing in our town? The fair left days ago." Mason dodged his friends' arms and legs as they tried to get free.

"Funny thing. After my run-in with you three, my boss fired me. You boys wouldn't know anything about that would you?"

Cody grinned. "As a matter of fact—"

"We didn't do anything." Logan sent a warning look to Cody.

"Hmmm, well, I'm sure you're lying." Ben loosened his grip, but it was only so he could turn them around to face him. "I suggest that the three of you listen carefully." He included Mason on the right as he looked each of them in the eye. "I catch you threatening anyone, and I'll be reporting it to the police. Now scram, before I forget what a nice guy I am."

He pointed them down the street and with a small shove let them go. Mason had already started running, and once they were free, Logan and Cody were right behind him.

"Thanks for the help. I'm Chip." He held his hand out. "This is my friend, Hannah."

"Ben. No problem." he shook Chip's hand and smiled. "Glad to help out. The odds weren't in your favour."

"I appreciate it. I wasn't sure how it was going to go."

Ben laughed. "Well, I think you would have held your ground, but I just thought I'd even up the sides. Luckily, they reconsidered and took off. I think you should be okay for now." He reached down, picked up his duffel bag, and threw it over his shoulder.

"See you around," Chip called. Ben didn't turn around, he just threw his hand up to wave and started down the street.

I picked up the flyers that hadn't blown away and handed them to Chip.

"These are ruined." Chip crumpled the remaining flyers and threw them in the trash. "I'll make some more posters tonight, and we can put them up tomorrow."

I cheered silently to myself. This had been the longest, hottest, scariest day in a long time, and I was more than happy to go home and forget all about it.

*July 13, 2018*

*I'm tired. I'm hot. I'm burnt. Today Chip and I wallpapered Acadia with flyers for his new dog walking business. He's bound and determined that walking dogs is going to make him rich this summer. Me, I'm not so sure. Chip gave me all the figures and projections for how much money he could make—over a thousand dollars a week, IF he can convince forty dog owners to pay him to walk their dogs every day. Are there forty dogs in this town? Are there forty dog owners willing to pay him forty dollars a week? I guess we'll see. Either his phone will be blowing up with requests or quiet as a tomb. But I have to remember, this is Chip, so this is only plan A. He'll have plan B and C ready if this doesn't work out. The best part of the day? Running into our favourite people: Logan, Cody, and Mason! George kicked them out of the Milky Way and they thought it would be a great idea to hang around to harass Chip and me. We ignored them right up until they threatened Chip again. That was the last straw and right when I thought there was going to be another fight, Ben showed up. I couldn't believe how he stood up to those jerks, and by the time he was done, they were hightailing it out of there. Thank goodness for Ben.*

## Chapter 9

Who was I kidding? Chip didn't need a backup plan. His flyer campaign was a huge success. So huge, in fact, that I was walking two dogs while Chip was in front of me walking four. I had Bullet, a mini Pinscher, whose name described his personality to a T. He investigated every bush, every crack in the sidewalk, every pole, and my arm felt like it was coming out of the socket from being yanked in every direction. His only redeeming characteristic was that he didn't bark at other dogs. Dog number two, Jerry, the slowest, cutest dachshund ever, hadn't stopped barking at Bullet as he ran, jumped, and hopped in circles around us.

Chip currently had four of the large dogs as we walked down Coast Street. I'd be ready to kill Chip for getting me into this mess if it wasn't for the comedy act going on in front of me.

In fact, I had been chuckling to myself since I found Chip on my doorstep just after nine in the morning. He was standing in the middle of a dog tornado, but there was no calm in the center of this storm.

"Morning," I said, trying to hold back my laughter.

"At least you didn't say 'good morning' because it's definitely not that," he grumbled. "Get back here!" He tilted sideways as two of the dogs went to investigate something on the lawn.

"You just stop by for a visit?" I asked innocently. Jerking himself upright, the dogs milled around his feet, some wanting in the house and others trying to get back to the street. In all the confusion, Scout sat next to Chip's feet looking at him adoringly.

Chip scowled at my question. I guess I hadn't done a very good job keeping my delight at his predicament out of my voice. I was dying to tell him "I told you so." He ignored my question.

"Let me guess. It's not going so well?"

"Get out of there!" He used his foot to move one of the dogs out of Mom's flowerbed. "No, it's not going well. I thought the park would be a great place for the dogs to get some exercise. But you know what's in the park?"

Confused by his question, I answered, "Benches? Swings?" When he continued to scowl, I kept going, "Grass? Slides?"

He rolled his eyes. "No, Hannah. There are squirrels. Did you know that dogs like to chase squirrels?" I shook my head. "Neither did I. But they do. It took me fifteen minutes to get them out of there."

Unable to contain my laughter any longer, it burst out of me. The look on Chip's face had me quickly wiping the smile off mine. He looked like he was at the end of his rope, or was it leash? *Oops, no more laughing.* I coughed to cover it up.

"Hannah, you know I wouldn't ask you if I didn't need your help —" Chip tilted his head and stuck out his bottom lip. He'd learned how to give puppy dog eyes already?

I stood in the doorway, studying the chaos around him. The dogs were getting more impatient, and if I didn't help him soon, they were going to drag him off the steps and down the street. But still, I didn't answer right away.

"Hannah . . ." This time I couldn't resist the pleading note in his voice or the desperation in his eyes.

"Oh, all right. Give me a second. But you owe me."

Less than five minutes later, I found myself walking Bullet and Jerry.

Now, after pleading with Jerry to pick up his pace and yanking Bullet back from everything he needed to smell or pee on, my amusement faded. Up ahead, Chip stood at the corner waiting for the walk light or for me to catch up, I wasn't sure which. Dogs were tangled around his legs and each other, and I was afraid if he moved, he'd fall over. The light turned green, and Chip and the dogs remained where they were until my duo and I arrived.

"How are you doing? Bullet or Jerry giving you any problems?"

"These two? Nah, I mean one's like a rocket and the other is like a rock. No problems here."

"Sorry, Hannah. It's just that they are the smallest, and I didn't want them trampled by the bigger dogs." I could see what he meant. Besides Scout there was a black Labrador, Dotty; Brute the boxer; and a collie named Lucy. Scout obediently stood beside Chip while the rest of them sniffed every inch of the street corner.

"New plan," Chip wheezed out, sweat soaking the collar of his shirt. "Give me Bullet and you take"—he paused and looked at each dog—"Dotty. Hers is the pink leash. Can you untangle them and take her?"

I swiped at Dotty's leash as she went by, her head down, tracking an unknown scent. After a lot of twisting and uncrossing of leashes, I had her free.

"Okay, now give me Bullet." Chip waved his hand for the leash.

"I've got him. I'll keep these three, and you wrangle those three. Which way do you want to go?"

Chip managed to pull his phone out of his back pocket and looked at the time.

"It's just about ten. Why don't we head down Baxter Street and by then it will be time to start dropping them off."

Bullet and Jerry seemed to move faster now that Dotty joined our group, or it might be that Dotty walked slower. Whatever the reason, Jerry and Bullet were out in front and Dotty walked along side me for the rest of our trip.

We slouched on my front steps, dogs all delivered, and no catastrophes to report. It felt like we'd survived a tornado. We were both covered in dog drool and hair. Chip had leaves in his hair and scratches up his arms from when he had to rescue one of the dogs from a bush. I had burns on my wrist from Bullet pulling on his leash, and I wasn't sure I had the energy to get in the house.

"I'm sure there is some iced tea in the fridge. Do you want to come in for a drink?" I offered a parched-looking Chip.

"Nah, I need a shower. I just want to go home," he spoke to his feet, head hanging down, shoulders slumped. He looked as exhausted as I felt.

"Okay. Call me tomorrow if you need a hand." I pushed off the step and stood slowly, my muscles protesting each movement.

"I will." Chip got up gingerly. "Thanks again, Hannah. You were a life saver today."

I patted him on the back, and he winced. "Please don't touch me. I hurt everywhere."

"Sorry." I felt bad for Chip, not just for patting him on the shoulder, but because I don't think he really knew how difficult dog walking was going to be. I didn't either, but Chip wouldn't let one bad day keep him down.

He waved and started down the street. I planned to spend the rest of the day on the couch.

As I recuperated, I texted Trudy even though I knew she probably wouldn't be able to get back to me. I imagined her days were spent wrangling kids, but I thought she'd enjoy hearing about Chip's latest idea. I was right. An hour later, she replied with a string of laughing emojis.

## Chapter 10

The rest of the week followed a familiar pattern. I would offer to help Chip the next day, he'd decline and say he had it under control, and then usually around 9:05 a.m. I'd get a text: *Help!* After the second day, I planned for it and was up and ready by the time the text came.

My dogs and I had come to an understanding: I wasn't the boss, Bullet was. We went where he wanted to go, and he expected us to follow along obediently. Jerry didn't care where we went or who was the leader, as long as we went at his pace, which was slow. He wanted to check every tree, post, and blade of grass. Most of my time was spent trying to get Bullet to slow down and Jerry to speed up. Dotty was right in the middle when it came to how fast she walked, but if you stopped for even a second, she'd lay down for a rest and was very reluctant to get back up. Chip, however, had not come to an understanding with his pack. Scout was the most well-behaved. If Chip said "sit," she sat. Brute and Lucy were the complete opposite. They both took any opportunity to irritate each other. Most days, that meant Chip's three dogs were trying to go in three different directions with Chip tossed around like a boat in a storm. Meeting people on the sidewalk had also become a bit of a juggling act. Chip had to snug up

Brute's leash and maneuver him away to keep him from snapping at oncoming people. He should have been named Oscar, he was that grouchy.

Today Chip was out in front, while my trio and I trailed behind. It was another hot day, in the low thirties, and the dogs and I were all panting. For some unknown reason, Chip thought we should go down Main Street to the park. On the first block, we'd nearly taken out three pedestrians and a guy making deliveries to the grocery store.

"Can we take a break?" I called to Chip, eyeing the bench in front of the Blue Moon Café on the next block.

"Sure."

By the time we got there, the other dogs were slurping water from bowls Chip kept in his backpack.

I handed the dogs off to Chip and dug for the bowls and bottles of water I carried in mine.

After their drink, the dogs laid in the shade of the tree beside the bench while Chip and I had a drink of water and cooled off.

I closed my eyes, letting the hint of a breeze dry the sweat from my face and arms. Our peace and quiet was broken by a tug on the leashes, which signaled something had caught the dog's attention.

I peered down the street in the direction they were looking and saw Ben walking toward us. His duffel bag on his back, his t-shirt drenched in sweat.

I nudged Chip. "Huh?"

I jerked my chin to where Ben was coming down the street.

"Hey guys," he greeted when he got closer. "Looks like the posters worked! You've got a whole bunch of energy tied up there." Scout stood and sniffed Ben's feet. "Aren't you a friendly girl?" he said and ruffled her fur. "You two look beat."

"We are," Chip agreed. I nodded unable to form words.

"You haven't picked the easiest job, but a little hard work never hurts anybody." He slowly squatted, and Scout licked his face in thanks for all the rubs. "Maybe I should look into dog walking. There doesn't seem to be anyone hiring in town."

I looked at Chip in confusion. A handful of days ago, we'd seen the sign at the sporting goods store and talked to a couple of places that were looking for extra help. They just wouldn't hire Chip because of his age.

I was just about to ask Ben if he'd been to Proctor's Garage when a car pulled up beside us on the street. Ben stood, a wary look coming over his face. At the slamming of the car door, I turned to see Constable Irving coming around the front of his car.

"Chip. Hannah." Constable Irving greeted. Neither of us responded as he stood beside the bench. It was Constable Irving who let Brady off the hook when he broke his probation by being near Chip and attacking Trudy and me.

Constable Irving looked at Ben. "And you would be?"

Ben stood and put out his hand.

"Ben."

Ignoring his hand, Constable Irving studied Ben. "You're not from around here." He rested one hand on his holster.

"No, sir. I'm not."

"What's your business in town?"

Ben shifted uncomfortably. "I worked for the fair but got fired over a misunderstanding with some customers. I'm trying to scrape together enough money to get home, but there doesn't seem to be a lot of jobs available at the moment."

"Let me give you some advice. Jobs around these parts are scarce, especially for people just passing through. You are just passing through, right?" He paused, but before Ben could answer, he continued, "I suggest you move along sooner rather than later." Letting his words sink in, he turned to us. "Hannah. Chip. Those dogs aren't going to walk themselves." With that piece of advice, he turned and got in his car.

It wasn't until he'd pulled away that we all let out a collective sigh of relief. I think even the dogs had been holding their breath.

Ben hitched his duffel bag higher on his shoulders.

"On that note, I'll see you around." I watched him start down the street without looking back.

"Sometimes," Chip's voice came from beside me, "I really hate this town."

"That's not right," I said as Ben turned down one of the side streets. "I know Irving is a jerk, but why would he do that? And what's up with the big stare down?"

"I don't know, Hannah," Chip said at the same time his arm jerked out in front of him. The dogs were impatient to get moving again. With one last look in Ben's direction, I followed Chip.

"Why would he treat Ben like that? He was so rude. No, he was beyond rude. Ben hadn't done anything to deserve that kind of treatment."

"I can't tell you why he did it, Hannah. Who knows what goes on in Irving's head." Chip navigated the dogs through the entrance to the park.

"We should do something about it."

Chip stopped and let out a sigh of frustration. "What are we going to do, Hannah? Huh? We know how this town works." He let the dogs off their leashes.

Chip was right. Again. Which was irritating. Just because that was the way Acadia was didn't mean someone couldn't help Ben. And Ben needed help. I just didn't know what kind.

———

IT WAS NEARLY suppertime before I got home. I spent all day with Chip. Ben's run-in with Constable Irving was just the beginning of a horrible day. Bullet managed to get off his leash, and we chased him around the park until we cornered him by a fence. We thought Jerry had heat stroke, so we carried him for most of the hour. By the time we got the last dog home, Chip and I were hot, tired, and cranky. Today was payday and Chip offered to give me half, but I refused. I knew how important it was for him to get their air conditioner fixed. But helping my friend today meant I was late getting home and getting supper started.

Dad's truck was in the driveway when I got there. I knew I was late and that he wouldn't be impressed with my excuse. He was sitting in his recliner, still dressed in his EMT uniform, a half-empty glass in his hand.

"Where have you been all day?"

"Helping Chip," I replied, moving to the stairs to wash up before making supper.

"Do what?"

"Walk dogs."

That got his attention. He turned from the television with a questioning look.

"Walking dogs? Chip doesn't have a dog. Why would he be walking them?" The ice cubes in his glass clinked together as he it brought it to his lips.

I stood with my hand on the banister and turned back to my dad.

"He's started a dog walking business so they can get their air conditioner fixed. He's got more dogs than he can handle, so I'm helping him."

"Why does Chip need to pay for it?"

My chin dropped to my chest, and I sighed before looking up at him.

"Didn't mom tell you?"

He took a sip from his glass. "Tell me what?"

That would be "No" then.

"Shelley hasn't been feeling well for a while now. Chip's worried that it's something serious. She's missed a lot of work because of it. So, he decided that he'd get a summer job, except no one would hire him so he started his own business."

"I don't care if you want to spend your summer helping him, just make sure you're home in time to make supper." He never took his eyes from the screen while he said this.

"I'm going to wash up and then I'll start supper."

He didn't answer.

Mom was working a double shift today, so it was just dad and me for supper. The plan had been to have pizza, but because I was so late coming home, it was omelets. My dad grumbled, but didn't complain too loudly because he didn't have to make it. When I told him supper was ready, he poured himself another drink and sat down at the table. We ate in silence and when the meal was over, I cleaned up the dishes while my dad returned to his recliner. When I was done, I went straight to my room.

*July 15, 2018*

*I don't get the people in this town. Today we met up with Ben again while walking the dogs. Out of nowhere, Constable Irving shows up and more or less told him to get out of town. I can't understand how he could treat someone like that. I don't know Ben, I've only seen him around town a couple of times and talked to him twice, so I can't really judge, but I know that no one deserves to be treated like that. The way people avoid him or talk to him like he's dirt under their feet or worse, that he doesn't even exist. And I should know—I felt like I was invisible for a long time. I even tried to make myself invisible by not attracting attention to myself. Even though I didn't bother anyone, it didn't keep people, like Brady, from bothering me. I felt so alone and I'm sure Ben does too. I don't know his story, but there must be something we can do to help.*

## Chapter 11

"Stop. Please, stop." I begged Chip as we walked in the ditch south of Acadia. I swore if he sang that song about a red dirt road one more time, I was going to scream. It wasn't just the off-key singing, it was how the dogs howled along with him.

"I'm in a singing mood, Hannah." He smiled around the blade of grass in his mouth and tipped his straw hat at me. I rolled my eyes.

"I can see that," I returned. "But you and your backup singers are giving me a massive headache."

"Breathe that country air! How can you feel anything but terrific? And the dogs are loving it, too! Look at them. They can spread out and sniff to their heart's content."

He was right. After the fiasco downtown yesterday, we took the dogs on a field trip to the country. Well, not really the country, but out of town. We were on our way to the abandoned farm we discovered last year while doing our photography project. The old farm had a large yard. The dogs would have some new places to discover, and if they behaved themselves, we might be able to let them off their leashes for a while.

Chip led his pack down the path into the grove of trees that was the entrance to the farm. The dogs sniffed every tree and barked at the birds that scattered when they approached. When the tree-lined path opened into the farmyard, the dogs clambered to get free of their leashes.

The house looked the same with its huge porch and beautiful glass door. Machinery and tools sat forgotten in the tall grass. A rusty truck sat beside the barn. Nothing appeared to have changed since our last visit.

"Sorry, buddy, but you're sticking with me," I told Bullet. I still didn't trust him not to take off into the country side. Jerry was happy to just bark at everything he got close to and didn't seem interested in venturing off on his own, probably because he was all bark and no bite. Dotty found a grassy spot and sat down, so I let go of her leash and left her to sit. She immediately laid her head on her paws and closed her eyes.

Chip and the other dogs headed to the barn, and we followed along. Chip let Scout off her leash but kept a firm grip on the rest of the dogs. They sniffed, barked, and chased each other outside the barn, disappearing every so often in the tall grass.

Bullet tried to jump up on an old wooden wagon, determined to check out what was up there. He tried three times to scramble up but couldn't quite get the height he needed.

"Let me help you," I said, trying to corral his squirming body. Lifting him and Jerry up, they proceeded to give the bed of the wagon a thorough sniffing.

After about twenty minutes of checking out the barn, Lucy picked up a scent and followed it to the house. The other dogs followed and soon they were all on the porch checking every nook and cranny. Brute focused on the front door. He went back and forth, his nose sniffing the crack at the bottom of the door. Every time Chip would pull on his leash to bring him back, the dog would go right back to sniffing the door.

"Do you think there's something in there?" I asked Chip from the bottom of the porch steps. Jerry and Bullet were busy investigating what used to be a flowerbed in front of the porch. The odd flower still poked its head up amongst the weeds and grass, but they were few and far between. Bullet ate the flowers off a milkweed and then spit it out again.

"Maybe it's squirrels or a skunk," Chip guessed, cupping his hand on the screen door, attempting to peer through the glass of the front door. "It doesn't look like anything has changed since we were here last."

Brute stopped sniffing the door and barked.

"It's okay, boy." Chip patted the dog's head, but the dog continued to bark. Chip knelt amid the tangle of leashes and sniffing dogs and wrapped his arm around the boxer's neck. "What do you hear boy? It's just an old house, nothing to worry about."

He stood and whistled for the dogs. One thing they'd learned in the last week. They milled around Chip's legs waiting for direction, all except Brute, who now had his front paws on the door, growling.

"Brute, get off the door! Come on." Chip tugged on the leash, and Brute dropped to his feet but continued to growl. "Let's go guys. It's time to head back to town."

At Chip's command, the dogs leapt off the porch, all but Brute, who stood growling at the door. Chip couldn't decide what to do.

"Brute!" Chip's tone said he was done fooling around. Brute ignored Chip's command and flaunted his disobedience by lowering himself on his haunches.

Since Brute was not going to come willingly, Chip handed me the leashes for Scout and Lucy and picked Brute up from in front of the door. The strain of carrying the dog was written on Chip's red face as he struggled down the steps and over to the rest of us. Unhappy, Brute knocked Chip's hat off and continued to bark over his shoulder. Letting Brute down, Chip stood in front of him and blocked the path back to the porch. I handed Chip his hat and he slammed it on his head without a word.

Bullet and Jerry followed the bigger dogs and I picked Dotty's leash off the ground as the pack went past her. She reluctantly got to her feet and followed at her usual sedate pace.

The dogs didn't bother to mark or sniff the grove of trees we passed through to get back to the road. They checked and marked everything on their way in, and we were soon back on the road, heading for town.

"I thought for a minute you were going to have to carry Brute back to town. He sure didn't want to leave the house. What do you think he smelled or heard?" Chip and I walked along the ditch, the dogs out in front of us.

"It was probably nothing, but once he gets something in his head, it's impossible to get him to focus on anything else."

"Still, it was weird that the other dogs didn't pick up on it or get too excited."

"I don't know too much about dogs, but I'm learning that they all have their own quirks. Maybe that's just Brute; he sees and hears things when there's nothing there."

Chip could be right, but this was the first time I'd seen Brute so curious about something that he was willing to ignore what the rest of the pack was doing. Was there something in the old house? Or someone? I shivered thinking back to when Chip and I had discovered it and had gone through the house looking for things to take pictures of. We thought the house was empty, but maybe it hadn't been.

A chorus of barks brought me out of my musings. The dogs had spotted a gopher poking its head out of a hole. Seeing the unruly pack, the gopher quickly ducked back into its hole that the dogs had now surrounded. I think they thought if they barked loud enough and long enough, the gopher would stick its head out again.

Chip and I pulled and pushed the dogs away from the hole, and it took us five minutes of cajoling and offering treats before we were on our way again.

We were both panting. Between wrestling the dogs and Brute's behaviour at the farmhouse, I was ready for a break.

"Remind me again why we thought this would be a good idea?" I asked Chip.

"We thought the dogs would get into less trouble in the country."

"We got that wrong," I observed. Chip snorted his agreement.

## Chapter 12

Chip held the door open for me and we entered the Milky Way for an after-movie treat. The place was full of teenagers sitting at booths or straddling the stools at the front counter. There were three empty stools in the middle, and we quickly sat down and waited to order. George was busy scooping ice cream out of the cooler, and his wife Erma was delivering them to various tables as fast as he could make them. As she moved through the tables, I thought about how Erma was the opposite of George. She was about my height, skinny with long, brunette hair that lay in a braid down the middle of her back. The one thing they had in common was their attitude.

Chip and I chatted while we waited for Erma to take our order. I turned when someone slid onto the stool beside me. I was shocked and surprised to see Ben. He rested his hands on the counter and waited for Erma. The young couple sitting to his left looked at him too. The woman wrinkled her nose and then nudged her husband who also looked at Ben with disdain. The couple promptly got up and left.

"What can I get you?" Erma stood in front of us, her hands on the counter.

"Hannah's going to have a double scoop Tiger, Tiger," Chip told her and then looked at the multitude of items on the menu. "And I'll have a large Galaxy milkshake in honour of Star Wars."

Erma didn't bat an eye at Chip's order. She probably knew that most of the people in here had been to see *Solo* at the theatre.

"Coming right up." She looked at Ben. "What about you, son?"

"I'll have a coffee and small chocolate sundae."

Erma nodded her head and shouted to George, "Double Tiger Tiger, large Galaxy shake, and a small chocolate sundae," as she poured a coffee and placed it in front of Ben. She wiped down the counter where the couple had been sitting.

"Where you from? I haven't seen you around here before," she asked Ben, leaning on the dishrag and propping one hand on her hip.

At her question, Ben stiffened. Probably because it was the same question Constable Irving had asked. And in the same tone of voice. Ben focused on his coffee and stirred in cream and sugar. He told her the name of the town, somewhere I'd never heard of and neither had Erma. He went on to explain that it was two provinces over and that he hadn't been there for more than two years.

Chip and I must have had the same thought because neither of us said a word as Erma interrogated Ben. His answers to her questions became vague when she asked what he was doing in Acadia.

"I was working for the fair when it came to town, but my boss and I had a disagreement, and he fired me. My plan was to work my way west with the fair to get home or close to home, but now I'm going to have to find another way."

"That's too bad." Erma started wiping the counter again. "You don't have any family or friends that could help?"

"No, unfortunately—not at the moment."

Erma nodded, thoughtfully.

"Let us know if there's anything we can do to help you out."

"I appreciate it, ma'am. You wouldn't happen to be hiring, would you?" Ben asked, setting his cup on the counter. I couldn't help but notice his hopeful tone.

Erma's mouth formed a sad smile. "Sorry. George and I, we run a mom and pop place. Only enough work for the two of us despite the crowd you see here tonight. This is about the busiest we get and that's only on the weekends when the kids are out. But if I hear of anything, I'll let you know. Where are you staying?"

"Um, I'm staying with a friend," he told her. "But I don't know how long I'll be there."

"Well, stop and check in over the next couple of days. See if we've heard anything."

Ben thanked her and continued to eat his ice cream. Shouts came from the doorway, and before I turned around, I knew who it was. Logan and Cody entered the shop and looked around. Finding a group of girls from our class, they invited themselves to join them.

Chip shifted on the stool beside me. Through the mirror, on the wall across from us, I watched Erma take their order and come back to the cooler. Logan scanned the shop, and his eyes lit up when they landed on Chip and me at the counter. He got up from the booth and started to come over. I elbowed Chip and nodded to the mirror. Chip sat up straighter as Logan approached, preparing for whatever was about to happen. But Logan veered to the left and sat on the empty stool beside Ben.

"Heard you were still in town. Irving was telling us you'd had a chat? You don't seem to get the hint that people don't want you here." Ben scooped ice cream on to his spoon and ate it, ignoring Logan's remark.

When Ben didn't reply, Logan moved closer.

"I'd watch myself if I were you. You never know what can happen to a guy wandering around town alone at night." He moved back and jerked his chin at Chip and me. "Just ask Chip. He can tell you what happens. If you were smart, you'd head out of town before someone runs you out."

Ben laid his spoon on the counter and slowly turned on his stool to face Logan.

"You must be feeling pretty good about yourself. After all, you're the reason I'm in this mess. As for getting out of town, I'll leave when I'm ready."

He faced the counter again and scooped up another spoonful of ice cream.

Logan's face turned red, and this time he leaned even closer. "I wouldn't take too long if I were you."

"Logan, here's your milkshake." Erma set the cup in front of Logan. "You best join your friends"—she gestured to the booth—"before you find yourself eating it outside. Again."

Logan grabbed the cup off the counter and gave Ben another hard stare before joining his friends.

"Don't mind him," Erma said. "He's just a pip squeak with a big mouth."

"I won't," Ben replied and continued eating his ice cream. A moment later, he said, "That guy just doesn't give up, does he?" Ben pushed the sundae dish across the counter for Erma to pick up.

I realized he was talking to Chip and me. "He's like a bad cold you can't get rid of," Chip answered.

"Always threatening people?"

"Oh, yeah. Like it's his job," Chip said.

Ben finished his coffee and threw a five-dollar bill on the counter. "See you around." He picked up his duffel bag off the floor and left.

I popped the last of my cone in my mouth. "Let's go."

"Where are we going?" Chip drained the last of his milkshake and hurried to follow me out the door.

As we passed the park, I could make out Ben sitting on one of the benches, his bad leg resting on the duffel bag at his feet. He was wearing a jacket with the hood pulled over his head.

"Do you think he told Erma the truth or do you think he sleeps there?" I asked Chip.

"He spends a lot of time at the park for someone staying with friends."

"If he has no friends and no money, how is he ever going to get home?" I wondered aloud.

"I don't know, Hannah."

We continued walking, and as we passed the library, the poster for the multi-media project jumped out at me. I stopped and read it again.

"You're thinking of entering?" Chip asked, as I studied the poster.

"The prize money is $200." I looked over my shoulder to where

Ben was sitting on the bench. "Do you think that would be enough for someone to get back home?"

Chip followed my gaze. "Maybe, but you'd have to win."

"Yeah. Even if I don't, if my project is about respect for everyone, even strangers who don't have a home, maybe it would change a few people's minds about how they treat people."

Chip's eyes met mine.

"I think it's a great idea."

## Chapter 13

Mom was snuggled on the couch with her usual bowl of popcorn when I got home. *No sign of Dad. He must still be at work.* I joined her on the couch and stuck my hand in the bowl.

"Didn't you just come from the movie?" she asked as I crunched on the kernels. Mom didn't butter her popcorn, and I had to force the dry kernels down my throat.

"Yeah, why?"

"I thought you would've had your fill of popcorn, and I'll bet you stopped by the Milky Way for ice cream after." She raised her eyebrows at me.

"Yeah, we did. It just smelled so good, but it tastes terrible. You need some butter on that."

"Butter's fattening. Besides, your dad hates it with butter, so I guess I've learned to like it this way."

"Where is Dad, anyway?" I asked, dusting the popcorn off my hands.

"Out on a call," she answered absently, her attention on the television.

I had to admit, I was a little relieved he wasn't home. He'd been in a strange mood lately. I thought it was because he'd been on call more nights than usual. What else could it be?

With Mom's attention back on the home improvement show, I thought about Ben.

"Mom."

"Yes," she replied still watching the show.

"I'm going to enter a contest at the library."

"What kind of contest?" She answered, her eyes still on the television, only half-listening.

"It's a multi-media project. I'm going to do it on tolerance."

"Tolerance?" she asked, grabbing the remote off the coffee table and turning her full attention on me. "Why tolerance?"

I considered what I was going to say. I wasn't sure if my mom would approve or not. *What the heck, I'll go for it.*

"There's this guy that's been around town for the last couple of weeks. He was working for the fair and got fired. He's been here ever since. And tonight, when he came into the Milky Way, he was telling Erma that he was trying to get together the money to go home."

"What does he have to do with entering the contest?"

"I just see how people treat him. Constable Irving interrogated him the other day, Logan threatened to beat him up, and I've seen people avoid him or ignore him all together. It just isn't right mom, the attitude of the people in this town. Well, some of them anyway."

My mom considered me for a moment.

"So, you want to do this project to change that."

"Yes. The prize money is $200, and I thought if I win, I'd give the money to him to get home."

"I think it's great you want to help someone who is being treated unfairly, but you don't really know anything about him, honey. I wish we were in a position to help, but your dad and I are trying to pick up as much extra work as we can." She patted my knee when I didn't answer. "I appreciate that you feel bad for him, Hannah, but we aren't always able to help everyone we'd like to. If you'd like to make up a package of food and give it to him, I'd be okay with that." She shook my leg. "Okay?"

I nodded. I knew my mom was looking out for me, and she was

right. I didn't know much about Ben. But I had a feeling that all he needed was a hand up not a hand out. Maybe if I got to know more about Ben, I could convince her too.

"Good. Now let's see how this kitchen turns out." She stuck her hand back in the bowl, turning her attention back to the show. While she watched her show, I planned how to find out more about Ben.

---

WITH MY WRITING notebook propped on my legs, I wrote a list of questions that I wanted to ask Ben.

Where are you from?

Where were you before you came to Acadia?

Are you homeless? That's what the Mom had said in the park the other day.

How did you become homeless?

My phone dinged as I studied my list and tried to think of more questions. I didn't want them to be too personal. At the same time, I wanted people to understand that being homeless wasn't always a person's fault. But, I needed some answers to my questions.

*Do you have a plan?*

Plan? What was he talking about?

*For what?*

*How you're going to get Ben to help you with the project.*

Oh, that.

*I've got a list of questions I want to ask him. Does that count?*

*Yeah. You think he'll still be at the park?*

*I hope so. I just have to make sure I'm prepared in case we run into him again.*

*Okay, well, that's our plan then. Mom and I are going to Gramps and Grams tomorrow. See you Monday?*

*Of course.* I typed and set my phone on my bed.
Where is your family?
Why won't they help?
My list of questions got longer. I couldn't imagine being totally on my own without anyone who cared about me. What would that feel like?
What's it like to be on your own?
I couldn't imagine finding a place to sleep every night and worrying about whether or not I was safe.
How do you choose a safe place to sleep?
What do you do if you run out of money?
I tapped my pencil on my notebook trying to imagine what it would be like to live on the streets.

*July 20, 2018*

*I think the hardest part about being homeless is being alone. I don't mind being alone for an hour or two or even a day, but to have no one who cares about you or to help you, that's the worst kind of alone. To know that no one cares if something happens to you. That no one cares if you are treated badly. No one cares. I want Ben to know that someone does care. That someone wants to help him get home, not just give him a handout and hope he goes away. I want Ben to know that I see him as a human being, not someone to be ignored.*

I yawned. I hit the home button on my phone—10:30. I put my pencil and notebook on the floor beside my bed and changed into my pajamas. I sent Trudy a text telling her about Ben and the project. No answer. As I turned off the light and crawled under the covers, Ben was still on my mind.

## Chapter 14

I was the first one up on Sunday. It was the first day off my mom and dad had had together for a couple of months, so I moved quietly through the house. They hadn't seen much of each other because they'd been working so hard. Maybe a big breakfast would be a good start to everyone's day. I took eggs and bacon from the fridge, and as quietly as possible got the frying pan from under the stove. As the bacon started to sizzle and crackle, I beat some eggs in a bowl.

"Smells good," my dad commented making his way into the kitchen. He loaded up the coffee pot and turned it on. He leaned against the counter and waited for it to perk.

"I figured I could whip up some breakfast and let you and mom sleep in."

Before the coffee finished brewing, dad pulled out the pot and filled his cup. "I don't sleep in much anymore." He took a sip and went to the kitchen table.

As I took the bacon out of the frying pan and set it on a plate lined with paper towel, my mom entered the kitchen.

"Smells delicious, Hannah. What's the occasion?" She poured herself a cup of coffee.

I shrugged, "It's the first Sunday you and dad have had off together since summer holidays started. I thought you deserved a break."

"Thank you. That's sweet." She kissed the side of my head and joined dad at the breakfast table.

I poured the beaten eggs into the frying pan and popped bread into the toaster. Taking plates from the cupboard, I loaded three of them up. When everything was ready and delivered to the table, I topped off mom and dad's coffee, got myself an orange juice, and sat down.

Dad scrolled through his phone.

"Did you see this?" He gestured to a news story on his phone. Mom leaned over to have a look.

"No, but it was a big topic of discussion at work yesterday in the break room. People are wondering what he plans to do with the mill."

"Like I said before, he needs to think about cleaning up his own backyard before he starts cleaning up the town." Dad bit down on his toast.

"What does the article say?" I asked. I hadn't seen the story, I didn't follow the news like my parents did.

"More or less exactly what he said in his interview the other day." My dad skimmed the article.

"Although, this is new." He pointed to a sentence. "The rash of thefts that has been going on in our town over the last three weeks is another area of concern. I will do my best to assist the police in discovering who is terrorizing our town. The citizens of Acadia have come to expect a level of safety and pride themselves on the fact that each person is their neighbour. I pledge to find the culprit, or culprits, and bring them to justice."

I snorted at that one. Jacob Robinson might be all about justice for thieves, but he sure didn't like it for his own son. The look on his face when Brady was given probation for beating Chip wasn't a look of satisfaction at seeing justice being served, it was about getting the charges against his son dismissed.

"He wouldn't know justice if it hit him in the face," my mom added, picking up her plate and taking it to the sink. She started washing the dishes. "I'll tell you one thing, Jacob Robinson won't be getting my vote."

My dad used his toast to scrape his plate. "He's got a lot of influence in this town, Lorraine. A large number of people rely on him for their livelihood. I wouldn't be surprised if he won this election."

I picked up dad's dishes. "What about the robberies? This is the first I've heard of anyone missing things in town."

"It seems rather convenient that we suddenly have a rash of robberies right before the election." My dad continued reading, while mom and I finished the dishes.

"He's right about one thing, we do look after our neighbours," Mom added. "I can't remember the last time we had to worry about theft in Acadia."

"People are struggling." Dad refilled his coffee. "I'm not saying it's a solution, but sometimes people see it as the only solution they've got."

Mom turned her gaze to him. "Not everyone sees it as a solution." She scrubbed the frying pan.

"There's nothing saying it was someone from Acadia, Michael. We've had some strangers around town in the last couple of weeks."

She gave me a pointed look. I silently pleaded with her not to mention Ben. Besides, it wasn't fair that she would suggest he was the culprit just because he was new in town.

Dad considered what she said.

"You could be right. It just seems a little too convenient for me."

He grabbed his coffee and went out to the garage.

"Mom! Why would you say that? You have no proof it was Ben!" I nearly rubbed the pattern off the plate I was drying.

"You have no proof that it wasn't. There may be more than one coincidence going on here."

I hated that she could be right. But I was nearly a hundred percent sure that Ben was not responsible for the robberies. As I put the dishes in the cupboard, I was more determined than ever to prove her wrong.

## Chapter 15

Ugh! Monday. Usually, the day of the week doesn't matter much to me when I'm on summer holidays, but since Chip started this business, it was like being back in school. I pushed the hair out of my eyes and looked at the clock—8:30. I got a move on so I would be dressed and ready by the time he showed up.

I was sitting at the table, eating my toast when the doorbell rang. 9:10, just like clockwork. Chip stood on the step with Scout, Bullet, and Dotty. Scout and Dotty were sitting obediently, Bullet was doing his imitation of Whack a Mole.

"Sit," I said before Chip could get a word out. Bullet sat on the ground and looked up at me with a "but I'm really excited to see you" look on his face.

"I hope you're talking to Bullet and not me," Chip said with a smirk.

"Like you'd listen. Where's the rest of them?" I stepped onto the landing and took Bullet's leash. He trotted down the path to the street with his head up, ears perked, and his stubby tail moving back and forth like a windshield wiper. Chip gave Dotty a pat on the head to convince her it was time to move again.

"We have to go pick up Brute. Lucy is with her family on vacation this week."

I wasn't going to miss Brute and Lucy constantly battling to lead the pack. His owners, Mr. and Mrs. Morris, an elderly couple who lived a few blocks over, were such a cute couple. Mr. Morris used a walker to get around, which was why they weren't able to give Brute the exercise he needed. They both thought Chip walked on water. Every day, Mrs. Morris would present him with a treat, some baking she had done the day before so he had a snack while walking Brute.

Brute immediately noticed that Lucy wasn't there and as predicted, took what he felt was his rightful spot at the front of the pack. Dotty and Scout were fine with that, and even though Bullet and Jerry attempted to take the lead, Brute would swipe his head at them anytime they thought about getting out in front of him.

You wouldn't think one less dog would make much difference, but Chip and I were able to walk side by side for a change and actually talk.

"How did your planning for the contest go?" he asked me after we'd been walking for ten minutes.

"I came up with a list of questions to ask Ben." I pulled the list from my back pocket and handed it to him. "I also told my mom about my plan."

Chip stopped and unfolded the paper, which gave Dotty time to catch up to us. He scanned the questions and handed the paper back to me. "And what did she have to say?"

"She wasn't exactly thrilled with my idea. In fact, she suggested giving Ben some food instead."

"You can't blame her, Hannah. Your mom is just looking out for you." We caught up to the dogs at the corner. They really were learning to work together the longer we had them. We crossed the street.

"I know. Hey, speaking of safety, did you hear there have been a rash of robberies in town in the last three weeks. Did you know anything about it?"

"Come on, you two." Chip pulled back on the leashes as Brute and Scout stuck their heads in a lilac bush along the sidewalk. "Not until my mom mentioned it yesterday. She was telling my grandparents to be extra cautious and to make sure they kept things locked up."

"What do you think is going on? My dad thought it was really strange that this crime wave hit town right around the time that Jacob Robinson decided to run for mayor."

"I don't know if they have anything to do with each other, but it seems like pretty drastic lengths to go to for a small-town election. Besides, Mr. Aldridge seems to have history on his side." Chip nodded at the signs that dotted the front lawns along the street. We only saw one sign for Jacob Robinson. "On the other hand, it wouldn't surprise me if Robinson would do anything he could to win. Although I can't see him getting his hands dirty by doing the thefts himself."

"I can't imagine him becoming the mayor. The way he bullies the people in this town already is bad enough." Changing the subject, I asked, "How's your mom been feeling?"

By this point, we'd started down the road to the old farm. The dogs ran back and forth, and it took all of our concentration to keep their leashes from tangling up. They stopped again at the gopher hole to say "Hi," but there was no one home today. Disappointed, the dogs continued on.

"She's had a good week. She was back at work for full days and had a good day at my grandparents' yesterday. She's eating well and doesn't have to take nearly as many naps as she was before. You know, I hate to admit it, but maybe Dr. Tompkins was right, it was just a virus."

"I forgot to ask if my mom talked to her," I said as we cleared the trees and came into the yard.

"Mom didn't mention it, which she would have if she had any idea that I asked your mom to talk to her. With the good week she has had, maybe it was all in my imagination."

We let Dotty and Scout off their leashes and took the other dogs to the front porch. Brute once again dragged Chip up on the porch and sniffed at the door. Chip peered through the screen and started to motion me over with his hand.

"Hannah, come here. Look at this." Dragging Bullet and Jerry up the steps, I peered into the living area of the house.

"What? What am I looking at?"

"That chair over by the window. Last time we were here, it was against the wall. Now, it's facing into the living room."

I cupped my hands around my eyes, careful to keep the leashes wrapped around my wrist and looked again. Chip was right. The chair had been moved ninety degrees and was facing toward us. I turned to look at him.

"Do you think someone has been here?"

"The other times we've been here, everything looked the same. But this time, the chair's moved."

"Maybe the owners have been out here, and they moved it," I offered in explanation.

"Or maybe someone's using it for something else."

I stepped off the porch and looked at the windows on the second level. Everything else appeared the same as it always did. Brute was still sniffing at the door.

"Brute is pretty curious, but he's not barking today. Do you think someone was here the last time we were here?" Chip asked, his eyes round. "Or maybe the house is haunted?"

All this talk about robberies and hauntings had me on edge.

"Let's get out of here," I replied and headed for the opening in the trees with the dogs. Chip snapped leashes on Scout and Dotty, and we hurried through the trees to the road. The hairs on the back of my neck stood up like they did when I'd come up the stairs from the basement. Like someone was behind me. The shadowy opening of the barn no longer spiked my curiosity, instead, it now looked ominous. My eyes scanned the trees, and my ears strained for any sound that would indicate that we weren't alone. When we broke through the grove of trees, I glanced back at the darkened path. Seeing nothing, I hurried after Chip and the dogs.

## Chapter 16

Mom came through the door at four thirty that afternoon, carrying her lunch and the mail. I was on the couch with a sketchbook propped between my crossed legs. Music from my phone was playing as I tried planning my project.

After dropping everything on the kitchen table, my mom came and sat beside me.

"How did your day go?" she asked, peering over my shoulder at the squares I had drawn on the page.

"Good," I replied. "How was yours?"

"Long, as usual, but not too busy. What are you working on?"

"An outline for my project. I'm trying to organize some of my ideas." I pretended to look busy, hoping she'd take the hint and not ask me any questions about my day.

"I'll tell you what. I'll cook supper tonight. How's that?"

She got up and went to the kitchen. The sound of dishes and pots being moved around drowned out my music, and I realized I wasn't going to get any more work done, so I went to the kitchen.

My mom was busy browning ground beef and chopping onions.

"I forgot to ask if you talked to Chip's mom." I moved to the stove and stirred the ground beef.

"I talked to her on Friday while you and Chip were at the movie. I figured it would be a good time to chat." She came to the stove and scraped the onions into the beef with the knife. I stirred the onions into the mixture.

"What did she say?"

I reached in the cupboard for a pot big enough to cook the spaghetti and filled it with water. Giving the meat mixture another stir, I got tomato sauce and spaghetti noodles out of the pantry.

"She didn't really give me any more information than Chip gave you. I asked her about her doctor visits and gave her some pointed questions to ask Dr. Tompkins about her tests the next time she goes to see him." She scraped celery and mushrooms into the meat mixture.

"So, nothing that she might be keeping from Chip?" I asked, continuing to stir.

"Nothing she told me." She washed her hands and dried them on the dishtowel on her shoulder. "And I didn't get the impression she wasn't telling me the whole story either. She was honest about her lack of energy and flu-like symptoms. I think Chip may be overreacting. It's sweet of him, but I think he may be worrying for nothing."

"It makes sense though. He thinks he has to take care of his mom. That's what started the whole dog walking business."

"Shelley did mention that. She's worried that Chip, and you, are wasting your summer chasing dogs around when you should be enjoying yourselves." Mom opened the can of tomato sauce and poured it into the meat.

"It's funny, in the beginning I wasn't sure I'd like it, but now, after spending a couple of weeks with them every day, I'm enjoying it, and I'm getting to know each dog. Bullet is exactly as his name suggests, flying around in every direction. Brute, the leader, is like a general, marching his troops to battle. Jerry, he sniffs *everything*. I think it's because he's so low to the ground." Mom chuckled at my description. "Dotty is slow, and Scout is the protector, especially of Chip. Lucy likes to boss everyone around." I turned down the meat sauce to simmer.

My mom laughed, "I can only imagine what it would be like to get five different dogs together. At least one hasn't eaten the other."

I rolled my eyes.

"What?" she asked. "It could happen."

"They all get along really well. The only one that causes any problems is Brute. And he's just naturally cranky. The other dogs have learned what they can and can't get away with before he snaps."

"It sounds like babysitting kids."

"It is in some ways, not so much in others. At least there are no diapers to change, and they don't throw up on you."

My mom laughed, "True. Dogs may have their perks after all."

I was setting the table when my dad walked through the door. Ignoring us, he took the stairs to the next floor, and I heard the shower running. When my dad came downstairs fifteen minutes later, our plates were dished and on the table. He filled a glass with his usual after-work drink.

Mom and I were already seated when he took his place.

Without a word he picked up his fork, twirled the noodles around it, and then shoved them in his mouth.

"You really must be hungry," Mom said. "No time for lunch today?"

He took a drink from his glass, then picked his fork back up, twirling spaghetti on it again. His eyes on his plate.

"No, no time for lunch today. We had a call to the old folks home at eleven-thirty and we were there for quite awhile. By the time we got back, we were expected to sit in on a talk by one of the mental health workers for our region." *A mental health worker? Didn't they help people with depression? Is my dad depressed?* He made it sound like it happened every day, but this was the first time he'd ever mentioned someone from mental health coming to talk to them, and I could tell that my mother was surprised too as she stared at my father. He refused to meet her eyes, focusing solely on his supper.

"A mental health worker?" Mom finally found her voice. "And what did they talk to you about?"

My dad shrugged, still avoiding her gaze. "The usual issues we face on the job."

"Oh," my mom nodded, put down her fork, and clasped her hands under her chin, "like insomnia, poor appetite, and nightmares? Things like that?"

At her words, his head snapped up. She raised her eyebrows at his expression of surprise.

"Yeah, Lorraine, things like that." He looked back to his plate and took another bite of spaghetti.

"And what did this person have to say?" She stared at him, her supper forgotten.

"The same thing they say every year when they come to talk to us. I could almost give the speech myself," he grumbled and took a long drink.

"So, do they ever offer private counselling or opportunities to talk to someone about your job?" Mom picked up her fork and took a bite of her supper.

"What are you getting at Lorraine? I've done this job for seventeen years. I don't need to talk to someone about it. I talk to the guys at work—they know what it's like." Dad forced the words out through clenched teeth.

"I thought that maybe with the way you haven't been sleeping, your short temper, and how you seem to isolate yourself, that you might consider talking to one of them." They stared at each other, neither one backing down, but, instead, more intent. I thought mom could have added drinking to the list of behaviors, but I decided it would be better if I didn't get involved. In fact, I was pretty certain I shouldn't have been there for any of it. I picked up my plate and set it in the sink.

The staring contest was over when I returned to the table. Escaping the tension, I went to the living room. Dad joined me and turned on the television. As I scrolled through my phone, the sports report played in the background. *Boring.* Just before the commercial break, the announcer gave a teaser for the next section of the news: "When we come back, it was three years ago that a tragic accident occurred in Acadia. Jaime Webster revisited the small town to see how residents are coping."

"What's that about?" I asked, as my dad picked up the remote and changed the channel. "What was she talking about?"

"No idea," my dad replied, surfing through channels as he sat in his recliner.

"That's why you had the mental health people out today," Mom accused as she stood in the entrance to the living room with a stack of dirty dishes in her hands.

"What are you talking about, Lorraine?"

"The accident. Three years ago. They brought them in, in case the anniversary of the accident brought up any old feelings."

"Well, they shouldn't have bothered because it didn't. Now can I watch the end of the news in peace?"

The two of them had another staring contest and finally my mother went into the kitchen. The water ran, plates clattered together, pots slammed, and cupboard doors closed with more force than necessary. Dad appeared to be deaf to the noise coming from the kitchen.

I went upstairs to my room. Neither the kitchen nor the living room was safe, so I found myself on my bed, music coming from my phone. I texted Chip.

*Hey.*

*Hey.*

*What are you up to?*

*Not much. Watching tv with mom. What are you doing?*

*Hiding out in my room.*

*Hiding? From what?*

*My parents had an argument—no, wait they say they never argue. They had a discussion.*

*About??*

*Mental Health workers gave a talk at my dad's work.*

*And?*

*My mom figures it's because it's the anniversary of that accident three years ago. She thinks his boss is afraid it's going to bring it all back again.*

*What accident?*

*A bad car accident. It killed a whole family. That's when my dad started drinking and having trouble sleeping.*

*That explains a lot. What does your dad think?*

*My mom's crazy??? JK He thinks it has nothing to do with that, but when mom called him out on some of his behaviours, he was not happy.*

*Oh, oh. Then what happened?*

*They agreed to disagree? I'm not sure. I haven't quite figured out those intense stares they give each other, although today it was like they were throwing daggers. Big ones.*
*What does your mom want?*

*She wants him to talk to someone. She mentioned he hasn't been eating right, and I've told you how irritable he is. I thought things were getting better, but it seems like the smallest thing triggers him. He sure didn't like the idea of talking to anyone about it, that's for sure. Maybe if he talked to someone he'd feel better, you know.*

*I have no idea how you convince someone that they need to get help, Hannah. Your dad and my mom both need to learn they don't have to go through things on their own. Sorry, I don't have any answers.*

*It's okay. Thanks for listening. I just needed to talk to someone.*

## Chapter 17

It was like walking on eggshells around my house for the next couple of days as my parents continued to give each other the silent treatment. They ate silently, got ready for work silently, and watched television silently. It was a little unnerving. Until tonight at supper when my dad came in from mowing the lawn, an empty glass in his hand. We were making supper when Dad came through the back door. I stiffened when I heard the door close.

"Lorraine did you borrow my drill?" Dad leaned against the doorframe of the back entry.

My mom turned and planted a hand on her hip. "No." Her tone was cool.

"It was in the garage on Sunday, but I noticed a loose board on the deck tonight, and when I went to get it, it wasn't there. I thought maybe you'd borrowed it." He looked at me. "How about you, Hannah? Have you seen it?"

I took plates to the table. "I haven't seen it around, and I haven't been in the garage for weeks. Sorry."

"I wonder where it could be." My dad stared at the floor, thinking. "The last time I used it was to put up that trellis along the fence a week ago, and I'm positive I put it back when I finished."

I placed the plates on the table and then a thought came to me. "You don't think someone stole it, do you?"

"What is someone going to want with my old drill? It's got to be around here somewhere." He stormed out of the house, slamming the door behind him.

My mom looked out the window over the sink. "He's going to be like a bear with a thorn in his paw until he finds that drill."

That was an understatement. My dad hated to lose or misplace things, and on the odd occasion that it happened, he became obsessed with finding it. The drill would be no different.

"Well, I guess you and I can have supper. There's no point in calling your dad. He'll be out there until dark."

---

MOM WAS RIGHT. Dad didn't come in until nine that night. I know he scoured every inch of the yard and garage to no avail. He didn't eat when he came in but went straight downstairs. We could hear him moving things around, the odd bang of something hitting the floor coming from the basement. After forty-five minutes, he finally came upstairs.

"Did you find it?" he asked my mom and me as we sat on the couch.

"Find what?" Mom replied, looking up from the program she was watching.

"My drill," he declared as if we were crazy. "The thing I've been looking for all night." He threw his hands up.

From my spot on the couch, I could see my mom's confused look.

"I wasn't looking for it," she answered. "But, I know it's not up here. Neither Hannah nor I have seen it all week. Your supper is on the counter. Have something to eat. It will probably turn up in the next day or so."

I could tell my dad wasn't convinced by the look of disbelief on his face, but he turned and went into the kitchen. Mom snuggled back down into the couch. I heard Dad open a cupboard, probably the one over the refrigerator. I couldn't concentrate on the show anymore. The missing drill kept niggling at the back of my mind. Had someone been in our yard when no one was here? And if they had, did they take anything else? You had to be pretty bold to walk into someone's yard or garage and take something. Unless they knew that no one was home. Was someone watching our house?

I looked at mom, absorbed in the show. She didn't look worried. She probably figured dad had just misplaced it. Dad was another story. There was no way he wouldn't be finding that drill even if it meant going without sleep for a week. Thank goodness I knew nothing about the whereabouts of the drill.

## Chapter 18

Jerry had his head stuck in a bush and refused to come out. I'm pretty sure he could smell a mouse or a squirrel, and no matter how much I cajoled, no dice. He was determined to find whatever was under the bush.

"Jerry," I spoke to his rear end, "Come on." I tugged on the leash, hoping to dislodge him before someone saw me and thought I was talking to the bush or worse, a person. I held Bullet's leash in the other hand, my arm stretched to the limit, just like my patience. Bending over, I grabbed Jerry by the belly and hoisted him in my arms. As we walked away, Jerry twisted and continued to bark at the bush. He finally quit barking when we caught up to Chip and the rest of the pack.

"What's wrong with him?" Chip asked, checking for traffic before we crossed the street.

"There was something in that bush back there, and he was not leaving until he found out what it was."

I didn't let Jerry down until we'd crossed the street and entered the park. The swings moved in the breeze, a mom waited for her daughter to go down the slide, and Ben was lying on the park bench, his head resting on his duffel bag.

I patted my back pocket to make sure my questions were there.

I wasn't sure if Chip had seen him yet as the dogs headed for the play structure.

Rather than follow the rest of the dogs, Bullet and Jerry headed straight for Ben.

"Bullet," I hissed, tugging as though my life depended on it and digging my heels in the grass. Neither tactic worked. What that did do was alert Ben to the onslaught coming his way. He opened his eyes the instant Bullet put his front paws on the bench and began licking his face. Ben's surprise gave way to laughter, which only encouraged Bullet to continue. Ben's arms came up to protect himself. Pushing the dog back, Ben sat upright at the same time I scooped Bullet up in my arms.

"What the heck?" Ben asked using the sleeve of his t-shirt to wipe off his face. I juggled Bullet like a hot potato as he strained toward Ben.

"All right, boy?" Ben took Bullet, tucked him under his arm like a loaf of bread, and rubbed his head. "He is a boy, right?" He glanced up at me briefly and then went back to ruffling Bullets ears and scratching his neck.

"Yeah, he is."

Noticing that Bullet was getting some attention, Jerry put his paws on Ben's leg and barked.

"You feel left out buddy?" Jerry barked enthusiastically as Ben scratched his ears. "They're quite the pair. I bet you never have a dull moment."

"No, a good day is when they decide to go the same direction and that doesn't happen very often." As if he understood my words, Bullet jumped off Ben's leg and ran for the play structure where the bigger dogs were busy investigating.

The paper in my back pocket felt like it was on fire. *Ask him, Hannah! This is your chance.* Even though my mind commanded me to say something, my mouth wouldn't cooperate. Frozen in place, I watched Jerry bask in Ben's attention. When I finally got up the nerve to say something, it was nothing to do with the questions I wanted to ask.

"Come on Jerry, we don't want to be left behind."

At the sound of his name, Jerry looked at me and then back at Ben. Ignoring me, Jerry barked at Ben when he quit scratching.

"Sorry boy, I'll see you next time."

Chip and the other dogs were lying under the bridge of the play structure. Chip leaned against the support post, having a much-needed drink of water.

"Did you ask him?" He gave me a pointed look. There were times I really hated how well Chip could read me. He'd probably watched the whole uncomfortable conversation.

"No." I looked down at Bullet and Jerry weaving between my feet.

"Give those two to me and go ask him."

I froze at his comment. "Now isn't the time." I knelt and ran a hand over Scout's coat as she lay against Chip's legs.

"Yes, it is. He's here, no one is harassing him, and you might get the answers you're looking for. The least you can do is see if he's interested in your help or in helping you with the project."

I looked over my shoulder to the park bench where Ben was sitting, his leg stretched out on the bench. He took a drink of water and then settled against the back of the bench and watched the activity around him.

"I don't know. I'd hate to bother him."

"You won't know if you don't ask, Hannah."

I looked again. "What if he tells me to get lost? Then what?" I nervously looked at Ben and a kaleidoscope of butterflies started a dance party in my stomach.

"If he says, 'Sure, I'd love to!' then you'll ask him your questions. If he says, 'No,' then you won't, and you'll find another way. Either way, you're not going to know until you ask. So, go ask." Taking Bullet's and Jerry's leashes from my hand he gestured to Ben.

"I don't have the questions with me. I forgot what I wrote down." I smiled, hopeful my lie would get me off the hook.

"I can see the paper in your back pocket, Hannah. The same place it's been for the last two weeks since you wrote them and then asked my opinion. Now, get going."

With no excuses left, I casually headed toward Ben, who was still sitting on the bench. At first, he didn't notice me, but as I got closer, and it was obvious I was coming toward him, he turned and sat with his elbows on his knees watching me approach. I considered turning around and going back. I glanced over my shoulder. Chip scowled as if he knew what I was thinking. He knew me so well. I kept walking.

I perched on the edge of the bench. "Hi, Ben."

"Hi, Hannah. What's up?"

He didn't say any more than that, just waited for me to explain why I was there.

"I was wondering—" I tugged on the hem of my t-shirt, cleared my throat, and started again, "the library is running a contest this summer. It's a multi-media presentation on social issues . . ." My voice and my courage petered out. He continued to stare at me, his hands clasped loosely in front of him, waiting. "I want to enter . . . I was thinking—" I paused again, "about doing it on people like . . . you know . . . in your situation." I finally got it out.

"And what situation is that?" His eyes never left my face.

"Well, staying in the park." I stared at my shoes.

"Do you mean homeless, Hannah?"

I cleared my throat again. "I guess. Would you help me by answering a few questions? I've noticed how people treat you, and I feel bad that people judge you without knowing you."

He looked toward the child and the mom by the slide and then back to me.

"I'd love to help you Hannah, but I don't think there's anything you can do to change the minds of the people in this town. In fact, it's not worth it. I don't plan on being here that long."

My shoulders slumped at his words. He was right. He didn't plan on being in Acadia any longer than he had to. Why would he care if people changed or not? He wouldn't be here. But that wasn't the point. I wasn't going to benefit from people changing their attitudes, either, but sometimes we need to stand up for what's right, even if it doesn't directly affect us.

"But it might help someone in the future. Someone who isn't judged for their circumstances, the way they look, or who others think they are. If they got to know you, they'd be more accepting and understanding."

"I appreciate what you're trying to do here, Hannah. I really do. I just don't think that my story is going to make a difference. Do you think that when people hear my story they're going to immediately want to get to know me? Or that they'll treat me differently?"

"Yeah, I do."

"It isn't going to happen, Hannah." He shook his head and looked at the ground between his feet. "It won't change a thing."

"How do you know if you don't try?"

"I don't want to know. I don't care. As soon as I can get things together, Acadia will be in my rear view. I'm not saying that it's not a good idea, I just don't want to be part of it."

I heard the conviction in his voice. He wasn't going to let me tell his story, but maybe he'd be willing to help me in other ways?

"How about some pictures I could put in the presentation? Would you consider that?"

He sighed.

"I'll think about it and get back to you, okay?"

"When?"

"I don't know, the next time we bump into each other."

I didn't have any choice. I was disappointed, but what could I say? I couldn't force him to do it. I thanked him and joined Chip and the pack who were lazing on the grass, except for Bullet who was walking among them as far as his leash, which Chip had firmly clutched in his hand, would allow.

"No luck, eh?"

I flopped on the ground and ran my hand over Scout's coat as she lay between us.

"Is it that obvious?"

"Like someone ran over your dog."

"Geez, Chip." I covered Scout's ears.

A confused look passed over his face. Then understanding dawned, and he rubbed Scout's head. "Sorry, girl. Slip of the tongue." Scout lifted her head and licked his face. "What did he say?"

"He said that he didn't think it would make a difference, so there was no point. That people in town weren't going to change their beliefs, so he wasn't willing to put himself out there even though he'll be leaving as soon as he can."

Chip nodded and continued to rub Scout's coat. "I can see his point of view. This town hasn't been very welcoming: the mom with the baby who avoided him, Irving harassing him outside the cafe, and the couple that got up and moved when we went for ice cream. Logan's threats were just icing on the cake. And those are the ones we know about. Who knows what else he's had to put up with."

"You're right. That's what makes me mad. The adults in this town are just as bad as Logan and the rest." The more I thought about it, the angrier I got.

Chip cleared his throat and looked pointedly at my hands. I was yanking on the grass.

"He did say he would consider letting me take some pictures of him for my project though. He's going to give me his decision the next time we see each other."

"That's something, Hannah. And you never know—he could change his mind."

Ben was still sitting on the bench when we rounded the dogs up to go home. Bullet and Jerry refused to leave without saying good-bye and skipped over to Ben as we were leaving.

He smiled and ruffled their fur. He spoke quietly in their ears. I couldn't hear what he was saying, but the dogs lapped up every word and scratch. Ben gave the dogs a wistful look when I said it was time to go. We were all disappointed when we left the park.

## Chapter 19

I was right. A week later, we still hadn't seen Ben one time. My right shoulder had permanent indentations from lugging my camera around every day, and today was no different. I placed my camera on my desk. Technically, it wasn't *my* camera, it was Mom's. I'd asked her if I could use it after the photography unit we had last year in Art. The one that had turned out so horribly for Trudy, thanks to Brady and Stephanie. I'd decided it would be a good way to practice what we'd learned rather than using my phone. The camera hadn't taken a picture all week. My sketchbook lay open beside it. I'd blocked out my project and jotted down the images to go in each square. But I had no actual pictures to put into the presentation. Today, Chip and I had gone actively looking for Ben. No luck.

While dog walking, we'd checked the park and the Milky Way. Nothing. After we'd dropped the dogs off, we expanded our search. Our first stop was the arena on the east side of town. It was home to the local hockey team in the winter and usually empty during the summer. As we walked across the parking lot toward the main entrance, everything was locked up. The place appeared deserted, so we thought we'd take a look around the back to see if there was anything or anyone behind the building. Other than some garbage piled beside the rear entrance, it didn't look like anyone had been there for months. We tried the door—locked too.

The motel on the outskirts of town was next. We walked the four blocks from the arena. The motel was a stretch of ten rooms attached to a small lobby. For as long as I could remember, it looked the same. White siding, air conditioner in the window of each unit, and flower pots with plants that struggled to look colourful. Thinking that Ben had found the money for a room, we'd asked the manager if he'd seen anyone matching Ben's description and he told us he hadn't. We called it a day, as I had to get home to make supper.

I added the can of beans to the chili simmering on the stove when my mom and dad arrived home at the same time. Mom was talking about something that happened at work and my dad had laughed in response. I stopped stirring and looked over my shoulder. Dad's laughter was a rare event, right up there with a meteor shower. I guess they weren't mad at each other anymore.

"Hannah, I'll help you finish up supper after I change," my mom called on her way upstairs.

"How was your day?" Dad tossed the mail on the kitchen counter before getting a glass out of the cupboard and pouring himself a drink.

"The usual, run after the dogs, clean up poop, save them from danger, a typical day. How about you?"

"The usual: go on a call, wash the ambulance, go on another call, have a game of cards, a typical day."

Mom breezed into the kitchen. "So, where are we at?" She asked, washing her hands.

"The chili needs to simmer. All we need to do is make the rice," I told her.

"I'll look after that while you set the table." She dug in the cupboard for a pot and measured in some water.

My dad took the mail and sat at the table while I got the dishes and utensils.

"I talked to Marty today," he told mom as he tore open a letter. Marty was a friend of Dad's that worked for the Acadia Police Department. "He was telling me that Irving had a run-in with a young man in front of Hank's cafe." Dad didn't hide his dislike of Constable

Irving. It was Constable Irving who let Brady off the hook last year when he broke his probation and threatened Trudy and me. But that wasn't what had me worried. This was the second time Ben and Irving had run into each other.

"Really?" Mom added the rice to the water and turned the burner to high.

"Yeah, Marty told me Irving thinks this young man is the one responsible for the thefts. He's been hanging around town since the fair went through."

The plate I had in my hand hit the table with a loud thump and Dad looked up from the bill he was reading.

"Careful, Hannah." He warned.

"What happened?" I asked nonchalantly, carefully setting down a plate beside him.

"According to Marty, Irving gave him a warning for loitering."

On my way to get some glasses and iced tea, I caught my mom's gaze. She gave me a pointed look that said, "We'll talk about this later."

"So where is he now?" My mom sat down at the table and started going through the mail with my dad.

"No idea. If he's smart, he's on his way out of town. People in Acadia aren't very welcoming to strangers that hang around or don't have a job."

My dad was right. Ben might be the first homeless person in Acadia, but we'd had other people move here who had trouble fitting in. It even happened at school. Chip was a perfect example. Everyone treated him like he had a contagious disease when he first moved here. If you hadn't lived here all your life, you were an outsider.

"So, you think he left?" I asked placing the glasses and iced tea on the table and sitting down.

"Nobody knows, but this happened a couple of days ago, and no one has seen him since." Dad put the bills in the rack on the counter and threw the envelopes in the recycling bin. He picked up his drink and went into the living room.

"You see, Hannah. I was right to be concerned about that man. Now the police are involved."

"The police are involved because he was standing outside a store," I answered.

A ball of tension settled in my stomach. I knew what was coming next; she was going to forbid me from using him in my project.

"We don't know his story, and that's what I want to use in my project. Everyone has a story, and his is just as important as anyone else's. Trust me on this, please. Just let me talk to him one time."

She stared at me hard for a moment and then sighed. "Okay, but you talk to him in a public place and only if Chip is with you. Understand?" She grabbed my hand from the table and gave it a squeeze. "I don't want anything to happen to you."

I nodded and squeezed her hand back.

"All right then, let's eat supper."

---

AFTER THE DISHES WERE DONE, I ran up to my room and texted Chip.

*Did you hear about Ben?*

The message delivered, and I waited for it to tell me it had been read. Why would Ben take the chance on Irving catching him in town? Minutes passed with no response. I tried Trudy. No response there either. Unable to sit still, I started pacing. Then I paced and tapped the phone against my leg, muttering to myself "Hurry up, Chip."

During what had to be my tenth pass across my room, my phone dinged.

*No.*

No? That was it? No? I plunked down on the edge of the bed and tapped out a response.

*My dad told us at supper that he almost got arrested for loitering* outside of Hank's café a couple of days ago. You didn't hear about this? The whole town is talking about it.

I started pacing, tapping, and muttering again as I waited for Chip's reply.

*No.*

It took everything I had not to scream in frustration. This time I replied as I paced.

*He may have left town. They let him off with a warning but told him they'd throw him in jail next time. We need to find him and help him!*

He replied immediately.

*We'll keep looking tomorrow. Mom's calling me. I have to go.*

I sat on the bed, took a deep breath and scrolled through our conversation. I was lucky to have Chip as a friend. He stood by me and understood why helping Ben was important. To think that when we first met, I wanted nothing to do with him. Now I didn't know what I would do without him.

## Chapter 20

We spent the next two days looking for Ben every chance we got. Usually, it was the time between walking the dogs and getting supper ready. We'd checked every place we thought he might go, but so far it was looking like Ben had left town. We sat on the bleachers at the fairgrounds, deserted now except for what looked like a bunch of ten-year-old boys playing a game of baseball at one of the diamonds.

We said nothing as we sat watching the kids go up to bat. Parents stood or sat in lawn chairs behind the backstop and cheered.

"I'm going to have to go home soon," Chip broke the silence. He'd been uncharacteristically quiet today.

"Okay," I said. "I'm kinda bushed myself."

Chip didn't respond to my comment, but instead kept his gaze focused on the ball game. A loud cheer went up when a ball was hit into right field and the runner made it to third base.

"My mom's not feeling good, again." Chip started. "Hasn't been for a couple of days now. I thought she was over the virus. She hasn't said anything, but I hear her up during the night, and she's trying hard not to let on that she's tired. She fell asleep watching television last night. Whatever made her sick before, I'm afraid it's back."

He brushed the hair off his forehead and looked right at me. A lump formed in my throat, and I was afraid to speak when I saw the fear and worry in his eyes.

My voice cracked when I asked, "Have you talked to her about it again?"

He said nothing, turning back to the ball game. Chip didn't avoid things like I did. He met them head on, and I knew he was worried. I was worried too, especially by the way he avoided my question. I was about to ask again when he started talking.

"I asked her today if she should be going to the doctor again, and she just laughed and told me she'd be fine. It was probably some bug she'd picked up at work." His voice trailed off as he added, "But I don't believe her."

As usual, I didn't know what to say. Fear wrapped its arms around me.

"What can I do to help?"

"I don't think there's anything you can do. I appreciate that you listen though. You can keep doing that."

"I have a lot of practice with that, since you do a lot of talking." I bumped him with my shoulder.

He smiled at my teasing, but it didn't quite reach his eyes.

"You just have to keep talking to your mom. You need to make her understand that while she might be protecting you, not knowing what's going on is worse. You have to let her know that it has you imagining the worst."

"I know. I can't seem to get that through to her. I want her to know I'm here to help her any way I can. But she just doesn't get it, you know?"

I knew better than anybody how difficult it was to talk to your parents. I remember how I never told mom and dad anything. They never knew about my writing until Chip invited Mom to the Writer's Café. And it took every bit of courage to tell Mom about finding Brady's water bottle with liquor in it. There were still things I couldn't talk to them about, especially my dad. But things had gotten better, one small step at a time.

"Keep trying. Don't give up, Chip. If there is something seriously wrong, your mom is going to need you to help her through it. You might want to tell her that too."

He nodded and then slapped both hands on his thighs as if he'd made up his mind. "I'll talk to her when she gets home from work tonight. You ready to go?" He picked up the backpack.

The mood was lighter as we walked home. We laughed about the antics of *our* dogs, as we'd started calling them over the last couple of days. As we came to the corner where we usually parted ways, our laughter died. We were quiet for a moment, both contemplating the conversation Chip would have with his mom.

"Let me know how it goes," I said.

"I'll give you all the highlights tomorrow. Pick you up at the usual time?"

I took a couple of steps down my street and stopped. "Of course, wouldn't want you being pulled all over town by a pack of crazy dogs by yourself."

He smiled, "Never happen."

"Yeah, right. See you in the morning."

## Chapter 21

On Monday, Chip and I were once again out walking the dogs. It was cloudy, and you could smell rain in the air. The weather seemed to have an effect on the dogs too. Bullet snapped at Jerry when he greeted him with a friendly sniff. Brute kept tangling up with Scout. And for the first time ever, Scout barked at him as if to say, "Leave me alone." Dotty seemed to be the only one unaffected. She wandered along behind the rest of the pack without a care in the world, ignoring what was going on around her. We barely talked, and when we did, it was with one-word answers, and we were impatient with the all dog's behaviour too. It seemed like we were all on edge.

"Let's go to the farm," Chip suggested after untangling Brute from a streetlight. "At least there they can roam around."

"I don't know. My mom thought we should stay away from there. We could get into trouble for trespassing." Bullet and Jerry chose that exact moment to take off in opposite directions, pulling me in two.

"There are no signs warning people, besides the dogs need to get away from each other a little. They're driving each other, and us, nuts." The dogs yanked on his arm and pulled him over to a tree where they proceeded to wrap their leashes around it in different directions.

Seeing his situation, I helped him untangle the dogs. "Fine. But if there's anything creepy going on, I'm leaving."

The dogs tried to race ahead once they realized where we were going. They didn't seem to have any misgivings about the farm, just excited to go back.

I paused at the entrance to the farm. Bullet strained on his leash and Jerry barked at me as if saying, "What's the hold up? Let's get going!" I scanned the trees. I don't know what I expected to see, but the hairs on my arms stood up as I peered into the gloom.

Chip came up beside me.

"You okay?"

I bent and peered down the path, and he followed my gaze.

"I'll go first. If you hear screaming, come running," he joked, and I swatted his arm.

"This isn't funny."

"There's nothing there, Hannah," he tried to reassure me, but it didn't work, and he knew I wasn't convinced by the look on my face. "Watch."

He started down the path to the trees and as he disappeared into the shadows, I wanted to yell for him to stop. I opened my mouth to do just that when I heard, "Come on, Hannah," from the darkness.

I stepped forward, and for the first time, the dogs didn't drag me along behind them. Instead, they hid behind my legs as if waiting for me to go first. Dotty whined and backed up until her leash was tight. Bullet's whole body shivered. A minute ago, they couldn't wait to get going and now they refused to move. Had they picked up on my fear or was there really something or someone down there?

"You're not dogs. You're chickens," I told them, straightening my shoulders and taking a tentative step. I turned to see all three of them sitting, watching me move forward. I took another step and still no movement from behind. On my third step, there was no slack in their leashes, and they were forced to follow behind me.

Inside the grove of trees, it was darker. My eyes searched the shadows between the grass and trees, where the fingers of sunlight couldn't reach. I strained my ears above the rustling of the leaves for the sound of footsteps. Tree trunks creaked as they moved, reminding me of an old man's joints as he walked. Twisting my head like an owl, I tried to be aware of everything around me. Was someone behind that tree or was it just a shadow? When the opening came into view, the dogs took off from behind me and shot toward the light.

Scout barked as we emerged before running to the house where Chip stood with Brute and Lucy. Scout bounded up the steps and joined the other two dogs who alternated between sniffing the door and barking.

"I don't know what's got into them," Chip said as Bullet and Jerry joined forces with the other dogs. It was impossible for them to all sniff at once, so they barked when they couldn't sniff the bottom of the door.

"What are they doing?" I asked as they jumped over each other in a tangle of leashes, legs, and fur.

"There must be something in there." Chip tried to push the dogs out of the way, but when he couldn't get close to the door, he looked through the living room window.

"Hannah, come here." With a sense of déjà vu, and some trepidation, I cupped my hands and looked through the window. I knew why Chip had called me over. Sitting on the floor next to the chair was a duffel bag I recognized.

I pulled back from the window in shock and then peered through the window again.

"Chip?"

"Yeah," he said, looking at me.

"Do you see what I see on the floor?"

That explained the dog's strange behaviour. They must have sensed he was here on our past visits. I let out the breath I'd been holding.

He looked again. "Oh man, that's Ben's duffel bag. Do you think he's been staying here?" He turned from the window and scanned the farmyard. "And if he has, where is he now?"

I turned to look. Nothing seemed out of place, but it was hard to tell, the tall grass hid what was underneath. The wagons, equipment, and farm tools looked the same as before.

The dogs suddenly went quiet.

"What do we do now?" I said, not sure if I wanted to hear Chip's answer.

He considered my question, and after a moment, he grasped the door handle. The dogs moved out of his way this time, but as soon as he opened the screen door, they crowded back in around his legs.

"Chip," I said as he put his hand on the doorknob, "are you sure about this?"

"He might not even be here, Hannah. Or he could be in trouble." Chip's hand rested on the doorknob waiting for my response.

The dogs barked impatiently. I was afraid Bullet and Jerry were going to be trampled.

"Okay," I said before they were crushed in the confusion.

The dogs nearly bowled Chip over as he opened the door. They streamed through the living room, sniffing the duffel bag, chair, and around the tattered couch. Bullet was the first to move into the kitchen, his nose to the floor, he circled the table in the kitchen and along the bottom of the cupboards. Scout followed him while Dotty laid down on the living room floor and Jerry tried to get onto the couch. Brute stood between the two rooms, and Lucy headed to the stairs that led to the second floor. Chip passed through the kitchen and out to the back entry. I followed.

An antique cupboard occupied the room. A dusty vase and jars sat on top.

The dogs, who had been quiet during their investigation of the house, now took up a chorus of barking. When Chip and I entered the kitchen to see what was going on, we were surprised to see Ben standing in the front door way.

We all froze, except for the dogs; Bullet greeted Ben with barks and high jumps. Jerry attempted to get off the couch, while Brute growled.

Ben caught Bullet in his arms and smiled as he got an enthusiastic face wash. "Hey, boy. How are you?" Ben ruffled Bullet's ears despite his squirming. Bullet wiggled out of Ben's arms.

"Chip. Hannah," Ben acknowledged us. "What are you guys doing here?"

"We were going to ask you the same thing," Chip said, folding his arms across his chest. His hard tone surprised me, as did Ben's reaction. His chin dropped to his chest, and he ran his hand down Scout's back before answering.

"I'm sure you've heard. The police told me if they caught me loitering around town again, they'd throw me in jail. So, I found this place. I've being lying low, only going to town when I need to or to check around for a job." He shrugged his shoulders. "Which, as you can see, hasn't been too successful."

"Are you sure this is the best place to stay?" I blurted out.

Ben sighed, "No, but I'm running out of options. I don't have enough cash to get home, and Constable Irving has been telling everyone to stay away from me."

Chip lowered his arms at Ben's confession. "We aren't like most people in town. What can we do to help?"

"Find me a job?" Ben asked hopefully.

"In case you hadn't noticed"—I gestured around me—"we walk dogs."

Ben squatted down to pet Jerry. "I'd call that a great job, but people around here wouldn't even trust me to do that." Jerry rolled over on his back, and Ben rubbed his belly.

"Do you have enough money for food?" Chip said.

"It's been a couple of weeks since the fair, and I'm surviving, but the small amount of cash I have left won't go far." At Ben's words, Dotty hefted herself off the floor, crossed over to Ben, and licked his face as if she understood the weight of his words.

"Thanks, girl." He scratched behind her ears, earning him another swipe with her big tongue. "I thought about hitchhiking, but with my bum leg, I just don't think it can handle the walking."

"We can get you food," I offered and looked to Chip for confirmation.

Chip nodded, "Yeah, but that's not going to solve your problems."

"Maybe if you helped me with my project, we could change people's minds and get you a job, so you can get back home. There's prize money too. You could use that to get home."

I crossed my fingers waiting for him to answer. I was afraid "No" would be his first response. He thought for a moment and finally stood.

"Okay, I agreed to the pictures. Why don't you tell me what else you had in mind?" He gestured to the couch. He took the lone chair as Chip and I sat down. The dogs, finally content with the amount of attention they'd received, scattered on the floor between us.

I cleared my throat. "What I'd like—if you're okay with it, of course—is to tell your story." When Ben didn't reply, I continued, "I think that people see you and your situation and assume that they know all about you." My voice trailed off at the end.

I held my breath for Ben to comment.

"You're right. People look at me, think I'm homeless, and judge me without knowing my story. They immediately assume the worst. Like they know everything about me. I guess that's the hardest part—they've discarded me right off the bat."

Pain radiated from Ben, and Dotty lifted her head off the floor, putting it in Ben's lap. He stroked her head absently, lost in thought.

"That's why we need to do the project. They would get to know the real Ben."

Ben continued to stroke Dotty's head.

"I want them to know about the guy who returns money that's dropped on the ground"—I pointed to Dotty—"protects two kids about to get beat up, and has an immediate connection to dogs."

Ben's hand froze on Dotty's head; he looked at me and chuckled before his hand started moving again.

"You're good, Hannah. Okay, what do you need from me?" He relaxed back in the chair, his hand on Dotty's head.

"It's a multi-media project, so I was thinking if we had some pictures like we talked about before and maybe some video of you telling your story or parts of it at least." All my ideas came out in a rush, and I held my breath waiting for his reaction.

"I've never been video-taped before. Are you sure about that?"

"I don't know your story, obviously, but I think if you could tell parts of it in your own words, people would connect to it better."

Ben looked out the window of the old farmhouse. I felt Chip shift nervously beside me, but my eyes never left Ben. Finally, after what seemed like hours, his eyes came back to me.

"Let's do it."

A grin split my face, and Ben smiled in reaction. Chip clapped his hands.

"Awesome! You tell Hannah your story, and we'll make sure you have something to eat."

"You don't h—"

I cut Ben off before he could answer. "It's the least we could do. Food for a story. I think that's fair."

Ben looked at me and then Chip, and seeing our determined expressions, his shoulders slumped in defeat. "All right, food for a story."

Chip and I high-fived.

"We'll be back tomorrow morning," Chip said and stood up. The dogs lifted their heads and got to their feet.

"I'm not going anywhere," Ben patted Dotty, who lifted her head, and got up.

I picked up Bullet's and Jerry's leashes before standing. The dogs in hand, we all moved to the door.

Before crossing the threshold, I turned to Ben. "Thank you."

"You're welcome. I just hope you're right about this."

I hoped so too!

*August 1, 2018*

*Yes! Yes! Yes! I am so excited!!! Ben has finally agreed to be the topic of my project. We didn't actually meet him in public, like I promised Mom, but I know once she hears his story, she won't be too angry. He's willing to work with us and that's all that matters. We made a deal to bring him food in return for his help. He said "No" at first, but I wasn't backing down this time. Whether he likes it or not, we're going to help him any way we can. It's only fair. I have to round up my sketch book and camera. I can't wait to get started tomorrow. This is going to be epic!*

## Chapter 22

Ben opened the door for us shortly after nine the next morning. Today, I had my camera and of course the dogs. They stormed into the house, checking every nook and cranny, finally settling on the floor in the living room.

Chip opened the backpack, pulled out a grocery bag, and handed it to Ben.

At first, I thought he was going to refuse, but when Chip continued to hold it out to him, he sighed and took the bag.

"I've been thinking about it and you didn't have to do this, you know. I still have some food left."

"We had a deal," I reminded him.

"But I don't want you to get in trouble with your parents. They're going to notice food missing sooner or later and you could get in trouble.

"We'll handle our parents," Chip said as he began to take things out of the backpack.

"Thanks." He put the bag on the kitchen table out of the reach of the dogs and came back to the living room and sat down.

"Well, let's get started then."

Chip handed me my writing notebook, and I opened it to my list of questions.

I cleared my throat, scared to ask the first question.

"Where is your family?" My voice was quiet.

Ben rested his elbows on his knees.

"My family is my mom. She lives in Pembrook."

I recorded his answer and read the second question.

"Can you tell me why she can't help you?"

Ben paused for a moment and looked at his feet before answering.

"My mom is dealing with some issues of her own. She doesn't have a lot of cash to spare. She worked at the local bakery in town for years and loved it, but she lost her job. That's why I left home. I had a plan; I would join the army after high school and help her out the best I could. But things didn't go as planned."

"What happened?" I asked, quickly scribbling his reply in my book.

Ben lifted Jerry off the floor at his feet and placed him in his lap. Basking in the attention, Jerry plunked his head on Ben's shoulder. I smiled at the two of them and when I heard the shutter whirr, I knew Chip was capturing the moment.

"It might help you understand if I tell you how my mom and I ended up in that position in the first place."

I nodded and poised my pencil on the paper.

"My dad was a great guy," he started. "He took pride in taking care of his family, you know. He worked hard at his job and always had time for me. He came to every one of my ball games, taught me how to fish and fix up cars." His voice cracked, "He was my hero."

I breathed in through my nose to ease the knot in my throat. Chip coughed, and I knew he was struggling to keep it together too.

"Anyway, life was good, until February 24, 2011. I'll never forget that day. I was in grade ten and sitting in history class when the principal came to the door. I didn't think anything of it. He talked quietly to my teacher and then he asked to talk to me in the hall. I couldn't figure out what he wanted. I was a good student. I didn't get into trouble; in fact, I think I'd only talked to the man once in the two years I'd been in high school." He rubbed a hand down his face. "Anyway, I knew whatever he had to say wasn't going to be good because he couldn't look me in the eye. Finally, he told me that there had been an accident at the construction site my dad worked at and that my mom was coming to pick me up."

He stopped there and looked out the window. Sorrow etched in his face. Jerry stirred and snuggled his head into the spot between Ben's neck and shoulder.

"We went to the hospital, and I had to hold my mom up when the doctor told us the news." His eyes swung back to me. "My dad was dead."

"What happened?" Chip asked.

"Aneurysm. A blood vessel in his brain exploded. He could have had it for years or months, no one knows, but it was fatal. In that moment, I knew it was my job to take care of my mom."

"I understand that feeling," Chip said. "My mom left my dad two years ago, and I knew the moment she said 'We're getting out of here' that I was the man of the house."

Ben nodded at Chip's words. "Things were never the same. My mom fell into a deep depression. She started drinking heavily and her doctor gave her some sleeping pills, which she became addicted to. That's how she lost her job at the bakery. I got a job at the local garage. The old guy who owned it taught me some general maintenance like changing oil and fixing tires. The little bit I made working after school and on weekends kept my mom and I going. But we both missed my dad. He was our rock, and without him we were lost."

He paused in thought, and I waited to ask the next question.

"So that's when you decided to join the armed forces?"

"I wanted to make my dad proud and be able to help my mom out. At least, that was the plan."

"Can you tell me what it was like in the armed forces?" A shadow fell over Ben's face.

"To begin with, it was great. I was sent down east to do my basic training, and I loved it on the base. I missed my mom, but it gave me the opportunity to send a little cash home each month. Initially, I'd wanted to be an engineer, but my drill sergeant discovered that I had extremely steady hands. In fact, he told me I should have been a surgeon, but instead of surgery they had me defusing bombs, particularly roadside bombs. My sergeant told me I had nerves of steel, as I hardly broke a sweat in simulation exercises, so I was moved to Special Forces and shipped to the coast."

Chips eyes rounded with fascination. "How long were you there?"

"I'd been there for a year before my squad was shipped out to Afghanistan. They gave us a week leave to visit our families. I went home to see my mom. It'd been nearly a year since I'd been home, and I needed to see how she was doing."

Ben went quiet after this, and I waited till his attention came back to me.

"What was it like in Afghanistan?" I said.

"It was hot, dusty, and tense," Ben replied, and Jerry's head came up as he spoke. Jerry whined and rubbed the side of his head against Ben's arm as if to soothe him. Ben stroked Jerry's back, and he settled back to sleep. "When we arrived, we were stationed in Kandahar because we were Special Forces. Most of the time we were deployed, we spent at the base."

"What did you do?"

"We did a variety of things. We played cards, looked after our equipment, and kept in shape. We had to be ready at a moment's notice."

I wrote as quickly as I could. Chip held the camera loosely in his hands, enthralled with Ben's story.

"It seemed like it was going to be a piece of cake. We had one call out to a small village close to us. A young woman discovered a bomb while she was going for water one morning. Apparently, a fierce wind the night before had uncovered it. An elder had informed one of the patrols in the area, and they called us in."

I had a bad feeling that this story wasn't going to end well. "What happened next?" Chip asked.

"We arrived in the village and an elder led us to the bomb near the village well. We diffused it without any problems. It was like all the others. My partner and I were walking back to our vehicle when he stepped on a mine buried in the sand." Ben stopped.

I waited for him to regain his composure.

He took a deep breath. "I ended up with shrapnel in my leg. But I was the lucky one." He stared out the window and then started speaking again, "At first it was a rush, you know. We'd be hanging around the base, we'd get a call, and in minutes we were on our way. It happened anywhere from a couple of times a week, to a couple of times a day. I liked living on the edge, never knowing what each day would bring. But after we lost Will"—he pet Jerry as he thought about what he was going to say next—"I started to have trouble sleeping. At first, I'd fall asleep fine, but would wake up in the middle of the night thinking we'd been sent out." He chuckled. "One night, I actually got up and got dressed before one of the guys woke me up." Ben tried to make it sound funny, but I could tell that the incident shook him up. "It progressed from that to nightmares and then to panic attacks from loud sounds."

"How long were you over there?" Ben's eyes rose to the ceiling as he calculated.

"The first tour was nine months. My team was ecstatic to have some time at home, and I spent it with my mom. It was the longest period I'd been back home for over two years, and during that time, my mom started to notice that I'd changed."

"How did you change?" I asked, tucking my fist under my chin, my questions forgotten in my notebook.

"I was jumpy. If there were fireworks on the television, I'd hit the floor. Something I'd never done before I entered the forces. My mom was concerned and told me I needed to see someone about it. When I got back to base after my visit, I went to see the doctor." Ben frowned at the memory but said nothing.

Finally, I asked, "What did he say?"

Ben huffed out a breath. "He wanted to take me off active duty. He suggested I see a counsellor for symptoms of PTSD."

"What's that stand for?" I asked.

"Post-Traumatic Stress Disorder. It's a disorder that affects people after a frightening event, like the day we lost Will. People in the military, law enforcement, and emergency services are the most likely to suffer from it."

As I scribble down what he was saying, I stopped. My dad worked in emergency services. Did he have PTSD? I pushed the thought aside.

"Then what?" I asked.

"My sergeant denied it. He said the forces weren't for wimps, and if I wanted to stay there, I'd better get over it," he laughed, not because it was funny, but to cover how much it hurt. "Anyway, as far as the forces were concerned, that was it. Get over it or get out. So, I tried to get over it."

"Were you able to?" Chip brought the camera to his face and peered through the viewfinder. Ben shifted uncomfortably at Chip's question, "Get over it, I mean?"

"As far as the army was concerned, I guess I did because I didn't go back to the doctor again. Truthfully, I just got better at covering it up, and if my teammates ever witnessed me having a panic attack or feeling anxious, I'd explain it away. At the time, I wondered why they accepted my excuses, but now I can see it was probably because they were feeling the same way."

"But you didn't know that at the time?" I asked, starting to write again.

"No, it wasn't something we talked about, which is why 'get over it or get out' worked so well."

At the lull in the conversation, Scout got up and got a drink of water out of the dish that Ben left out for the dogs. As Ben tracked Scout's path to the kitchen, Chip motioned with his head that we should go.

Scout came to stand beside Chip, and he slipped the camera into the backpack. "I think we should get going, Hannah." As he stood, the dogs got up off the floor and started to mill around the living room. Ben clipped Jerry's leash on his collar and set him on the floor.

"Are you sure you have to go?" Ben watched the dogs walk amongst us. "I think the dogs want to stay."

"We have to have them back by 10:00, so we're going to have to hustle to be on time."

I wished we could stay longer when I saw the look on Ben's face as he waved to us from the porch. The dogs seemed as reluctant to leave as I did. They were slower than normal, in fact, Bullet was behind Dotty.

"I don't think the dogs were ready to leave yet," I said to Chip as we walked in front of the pack that trailed behind us.

Once the farmhouse was out of view, Brute took his usual lead position and the rest of us fell into place.

"Did you see how Jerry reacted when Ben started talking about Afghanistan? It was like he was trying to comfort him." Chip walked next to me, both arms bouncing up like he was driving a team of horses.

"It was like he was picking up on Ben's emotions. And the way he rubbed his head against his arm? That was so cute." As if he knew we were talking about him, Jerry looked up at me and gave a sharp bark.

"Okay, this is getting freaky. The next thing you know, he'll be reading our minds."

"As long we can't read his, I can deal with that. I do not want to know what's going on inside that head of his." Jerry barked again at my comment. "You know I love you, Jerry." Now I was soothing Jerry's feelings. I shook my head.

"I can't believe that defusing bombs is an actual job in the military and the way Ben described it—never knowing from one minute to the next if you're going to have to put your life on the line. That would get to you after a while."

I agreed, "The nightmares would be the worst. I can't sleep after watching a scary movie. It must be ten times harder to sleep when you've lived those nightmares."

"I'm sure he spared us a lot of the details," Chip said.

"But he didn't tell us why he's not still in the military."

"I know."

Suddenly, I wasn't as anxious to find out the rest of Ben's story.

―――――

MOM BALANCED pizza boxes as she walked through the door.

"Dad going to be home for supper?"

"He texted that he'd be late. They were called out to an accident on the highway north of town. He thought he'd be home by 8:00."

I flipped open the first box of pizza: pepperoni and mushroom. "Ew, I hope the other one is Hawaiian," I said as I closed the box and reached for the next one. "YES! I saw that."

My mom laughed as I called her out for rolling her eyes. "It wouldn't kill you to have pepperoni every once in a while."

"Oh, yes it would." I closed my eyes as I savoured that first bite.

"Turn the television on. I want to see if there's anything on the news about the accident."

I dropped the piece of pizza I was holding onto my plate and went searching for the remote. After some digging through the couch cushions, I tuned in to the local news station. I was just about to drop the remote on the coffee table when Jacob Robinson's voice boomed through our living room. He was standing outside his construction company with microphones pointed at his face.

"I have taken my concerns over the latest rash of robberies to Mayor Aldridge and nothing has been done. Citizens of this fine town are coming to me and asking me to do something about it. Not only is property being stolen, but we now have vagrants hanging around the streets, threatening people, and begging for money. Our parks and restaurants are no longer safe for the good law-abiding folks of our town to visit. One member of the community came to me, and I told him the next time anyone is loitering around your business, you call the police. And he did. What did the police do? Nothing. They let him off with a warning." He pointed his finger at the camera. "This has to stop. That's why I'm running for mayor. I've said it before and I'll say it again: Acadia needs a mayor that's going to clean up this town. That includes thieves and vagrants." Reporters hollered questions, but he turned and entered his business.

"Hannah? You going to come and eat?" my mom called from the dining room.

I stood frozen as the reporter made some comments about what Mr. Robinson had said.

"Hannah?"

"I'm coming." I let the remote drop to the couch and sat down at the table.

"You okay?" My shocked expression said I wasn't.

"Jacob Robinson was on the news, and he said he was going to 'clean up all the thieves and vagrants.' What does that even mean?"

"Well, Ben could be considered a vagrant. It's a term used to describe homeless people who beg for money."

"You think Ben's a vagrant?" The shock evident in my voice.

"If he's living on the street, yes. And I have to agree, it's not the kind of people we want hanging around Acadia."

My hand froze over the pizza box at Mom's harsh words. *Did she see Ben the same way Jacob Robinson did?* I picked up a piece of pizza and thought about the best way to convince her that her opinion of Ben was wrong.

"I bet it was Jacob Robinson who told Hank to call the police and have Ben arrested." Then a thought hit me. "Can they do that? Can they arrest him for hanging around a business?"

"I don't know. Maybe if they have a 'no loitering' sign, but even then, I'm not sure." She frowned and rubbed her hands down her face, as if she didn't want to talk about it anymore. "We'll ask your dad when he comes home. Now eat your pizza before it gets cold."

I picked a piece of pineapple off my pizza and tried to chew it, but my appetite was gone.

My dad arrived home at 8:30. Mom and I were watching *The Big Bang Theory* and even Sheldon couldn't take my mind off what I'd seen on the news. Jacob Robinson's words kept ringing through my ears, drowning out the television.

My dad barely had his coat off, and I was off the couch.

"Dad, do you know if they can arrest someone for hanging around a business?"

"Well, hello to you too, Hannah. My day was long. Thanks for asking." He walked over to the table and sat down. He flipped open the pizza box and removed a slice.

"I'm sorry you had a hard day. Mom said there was an accident north of town. Is everyone alright?"

Dad finished chewing and wiped his mouth with a serviette.

"A few cuts and scrapes. We took the driver of one vehicle to the hospital to get checked out, but he was fine."

"That's good. So, can someone get arrested for loitering?" Dad put the slice of pizza on his plate. "Let's start with what this is all about."

I took a deep breath and told my dad about the news story.

"Yes, but only if you are posing a threat to property or others. What was this guy doing?"

"I'm not really sure, but I don't think he'd threaten anyone."

"Sounds like Robinson is trying to use him to get elected." Dad picked up his pizza and took a bite. "Using someone's situation for his own gain has Jacob Robinson written all over it. That man would stoop to any level to get what he wants. The question is: why does he want to be mayor?"

Dad looked at me. I didn't have any ideas about Jacob Robinson's ambitions.

"Who knows?"

"Well, that right there would tell you why he's using some guy down on his luck to get elected as mayor."

At least Dad didn't share the same opinion of Ben that Mom did. Dad was more likely to be suspicious of Jacob Robinson than a stranger that showed up in town.

Neither of us said a word after that. I imagine Dad was trying to find a reason, just like I was.

## Chapter 23

It was after lunch the next day, Chip and I were walking out to the farm to see Ben. I told him about the Jacob Robinson news story that he'd missed the night before, and explained why we needed to look out for Ben. Chip agreed that we needed to tell Ben what was going on. It wasn't a conversation I was looking forward to.

"How'd things go at your mom's doctor's appointment the other day?"

"Dr. Tompkins finally agreed to get her an appointment in the city with a neurologist. She's waiting to hear when that will be. He told her it could take a couple of months with the long waiting lists, which is totally stupid, but there's not much she can do."

"At least you got an appointment. That's a start." I tried to look at the bright side. I dodged a puddle as we went down into the trees at the farm. The grass was soaked from yesterday's rainfall and my feet squished in my sneakers.

Chip rapped on the door and entered the house. Ben had the chair from the living room pulled up to the kitchen table and was reading a book. He turned as we entered and greeted us with a smile.

"Hey, how are you guys today?" he said, marking his place in the book and joining us in the living room. Ben was wearing his usual jeans, and his t-shirt sported Yoda and the saying: "There is no try. Just do or do not."

"Love your shirt," Chip said. "I've got one just like it."

I rolled my eyes and slid the backpack down my arms.

"Great, another Star Wars fanatic." I pulled out a container with left over pizza in it and handed it to Ben.

"You love Star Wars, Hannah?" Ben teased.

"I do. But not to the level that some people in this room do." With my notebook and pencil in hand, I sat on the couch.

"She's right, Ben. She loves Star Wars twice as much as we do." Chip laughed at my disgusted expression and sat down beside me. "Don't you, Hannah?"

I elbowed him in the ribs and moved to the end of the couch.

"How were the dogs today?" Ben asked.

"We took them to school and ran them around the track. I think it played Chip and I out more than the dogs."

Ben smiled. He loved the dogs' craziness as much as we did.

"Before we get started though, Hannah and I have something to tell you." Chip motioned his head for me to begin.

I could not believe him. "I have to tell?"

"You heard it," he defended. "You should tell it." He leaned back on the couch.

Sometimes Chip was so frustrating. I narrowed my eyes as he ignored me and looked at Ben. *I know what you're up to. You're going to get a piece of my mind after this, buddy.*

I told Ben the story I'd told Chip and my dad. When I finished, no one said anything.

"You think he wants to use me to become mayor?" Ben looked at me with consternation.

I nodded my head. "My dad thinks so too."

"I don't know Jacob Robinson. I've never met the man before in my life. Why me?" He looked back and forth between Chip and me.

"From the little we know about Jacob Robinson, it would totally be something he would do." Chip hung his head. Ben looked at me to explain.

"Jacob Robinson is Brady Robinson's father. The little we know about him is that he uses his position as a prominent business owner in Acadia as a way to get certain privileges in the community."

"Like what?" Ben looked confused.

"Well, like being able to get his son off of assault charges, for one. Getting the police and school officials to look the other way when his son broke his probation, for another. And assaulting his own son when he got caught breaking his probation. The man is a monster." I took a deep breath to steady my pounding heart. Even after all this time, Jacob Robinson could still get me riled up.

"Wow!" Ben sat back in his chair with a stunned expression. "You don't know a little about Jacob Robinson, it sounds like you know a lot. Where is this Brady now?"

"We're not really sure. After he was charged with breaking his probation, he left town and didn't return for the rest of the school year. Rumour has it that he did some time in juvie and went to live with an aunt and uncle when he was released."

"So, this Jacob Robinson, who bullies his own son, wants to be the mayor of Acadia?" Chip and I nodded. "And people are okay with that?" His shocked expression said it all.

"Well, there are a couple of families that aren't okay with it. Hannah's and mine, and I think we could add our friend Trudy's family too."

Ben shook his head. "That's just crazy. No one in town will stand up to this guy?"

We shook our heads ruefully.

"What's he got on this town that people put up with this?" He got up and started pacing in front of Chip and me. Ben was more worked up than me about Jacob Robinson and rightfully so. Robinson was going to use Ben to get elected.

Chip looked up at Ben's statement. "His construction company is one of the biggest employers in town. People are afraid to stand up to him."

"He donates generously to the school, civic groups, and projects," I added.

"He's also involved in his local church," Chip finished.

"So, he's already got influence," Ben mused. "What does he need to be mayor for? It sounds like he holds the town in the palm of his hands."

"That's what we can't figure out," I agreed. At this point, Chip got up from the couch and paced alongside Ben.

"Men like Jacob Robinson don't get involved unless there's something in it for them," Ben declared and stopped. "We need to find out what it is because he's not using me as part of his plan."

The sound of a vehicle entering the farmyard interrupted our conversation. We watched as a beat-up truck entered the yard and parked near the barn.

A short, gray haired man dressed in jeans and a plaid shirt got out of the truck. He scanned the yard as he hitched up his pants.

"Get down," Chip whispered. We ducked over the top of the couch and watched as the man entered the barn.

"Who is it?" Ben asked.

"No idea. I've never seen the guy before."

I had. "His name is Jim Peterson. He's a local farmer."

We'd never seen him at the farm, but that didn't mean much. We'd never seen anyone here.

"He owns this place?"

I shrugged. "I guess so?"

Jim came out of the barn carrying some machinery parts and got in his truck and drove off.

We all heaved a sigh of relief as his truck disappeared through the trees.

"You better be careful," I told Ben. "You never know when he'll show up again."

## Chapter 24

The smell of cinnamon buns nearly drove the dogs and me crazy the next morning as we walked to the farm. The smell of the freshly baked buns floated around us. They were a treat from Mrs. Morris.

Chip was the pied piper this morning as all six dogs followed him with their noses in the air. The gopher hole was forgotten as they paraded behind him. Ben was sitting on the front porch when we emerged through the trees. As soon as the dogs saw him, they forgot Chip and the cinnamon buns and raced toward him. They proceeded to give his face a thorough cleaning. He never flinched, not even once; instead, he smiled ear to ear until one of the dogs swiped their tongue across his mouth. After that, he kept his mouth closed, but rubbed and petted every dog he could get his hands on. It took ten minutes for the welcome party to settle down enough for Ben to get up off the steps and invite us inside.

"I know I said you didn't have to give me any food, but if I smell what I think I smell, please hand it over," he pleaded.

Chip laughed and pulled the backpack off his shoulders. He carefully lifted out a Styrofoam container and handed it to Ben. Ben popped the top and picked up the first bun.

"Still warm. Where did you get these?" Ben asked in awe.

Chip shuffled uncomfortably. "My mom made them this morning."

Ben licked the sticky goodness from his fingers. "You be sure to thank her for me. These are the best cinnamon buns I've had, second to my mom's of course. Do you guys want one?" He held the box out to us, but we both declined. We'd both had one on the walk over.

Ben finished and snapped the lid shut and placed the box on the stove. "Now that I've had all of that sugar, we better get to your project Hannah, before I fall asleep."

Chip and I took our usual spots on the couch, and Ben sat in the chair with the dogs around him. It took them a few minutes to settle, and I noted that Jerry was again in his lap. I nervously checked the window for any sign of Jim Peterson.

"What do you want to know today, Hannah?" Ben absently stroked Scout's head as Jerry lay sleeping in his arms.

Today, we'd brought Shelley's video camera. Chip had found it in a closet at home and wanted to give it a try. I thought his phone would work fine, but he liked the idea of using the video camera. Ben eyed the camera warily. "I don't know about this Hannah. Videotaping is a whole lot different than interviewing with an odd picture." It had taken us nearly a week to convince Ben to give videotaping a try, and he finally agreed after we promised that he could decide which pieces we would use, if any, in the project. I hoped he kept his word because I was starting to get permanent writer's cramp.

"Let's see how today goes," I tried to reassure him.

Chip and I moved the couch ahead and set the camera up on a tripod behind it. I sat on the couch, and Ben sat three feet across from me. Ben and I both shifted to get comfortable.

I balanced my notebook on my leg and went over the questions I wanted to ask. So far, Ben had talked about his time in the armed forces: his job, his friends, and the places he'd traveled to. Today, I wanted to talk about why he left the military.

Ben sat with his back straight and both hands on his knees.

"You both ready to go?" Chip asked from behind me.

Ben nodded, and I replied, "Yes."

"Action!" *Really?* I rolled my eyes. Ben's eyes never left me.

"Ben—" I began, only to be jolted by "Louder" from behind me. I swiveled around and glared at Chip. "Please?"

Turning back, I gave Ben a smile and started again. "Ben. You've told us about the struggles you had while in the armed forces." I paused clearing my throat before I asked my question, "Can you tell us why you left?"

His knuckles turned white as he gripped his knees. "First of all, I didn't leave."

At his reply, I flipped through my notebook looking for where I'd written that he'd left. Before I could find it, he continued. "You assumed I left, and I never told you otherwise," he shrugged. "It didn't seem like that big of deal at the time. I didn't think I'd ever have reason to tell you what really happened because I've never told anyone."

He drew in a breath and held it as if he was waiting for me to say, "Forget it." I waited patiently for him to begin. He huffed out a heavy breath as he ran his fingers through his hair.

"You have to understand, by this point, I was hardly sleeping. Most nights, I'd lay on my bunk staring at the ceiling, and if I did fall asleep, I'd wake up sweating, wrapped in my blankets from the nightmares." He crossed his arms over his chest protectively. "Being sleep deprived meant I was not the most pleasant person to be around during the day. I'd lose my temper over the littlest things."

He looked past me out the window, lost in thought. I started to tell him we could quit if he wanted when he started to speak.

"If I was trying to pinpoint the exact moment I noticed that I was changing, it would be one specific day during lunch. We were in line and the guys were horsing around and one of them bumped my tray. The next thing I knew, I had the guy against the wall with hands around his throat. It was dead quiet. I let him go and apologized, but after that everyone avoided me." He stared at his hands clasped in his lap.

"It didn't happen again for months. I kept it under control. If I felt like I was going to lose it, I talked myself down, but it got harder and harder each time. The lack of sleep and the tight grip I tried to keep on my temper started to affect my job. I was jittery and jumpy all the time. We'd do a simulation, and where before I had nerves of steel, my hands shook so bad that I couldn't cut the wires on the dummy bombs they gave us. If I'd been deployed, I could have killed someone, or myself." His hands fisted, and I could see them shaking.

"My commander took me off active duty. He told me to get some rest and when I felt better to come back." He unclenched his fists. "I lost it." He looked into the camera. "I threw a chair through his office door window, and when he tried to prevent me from doing further damage, I took a swing at him. Before I could swing again, the military police were there, and I was arrested." He dropped his chin to his chest and then looked up. "I loved the military. I wanted it to be my career, but I was in no shape to do my job, and now I was charged with assaulting an officer."

Chip broke in before Ben could continue, "They didn't help you? The reason you lost it was that you hadn't slept in what . . . a year? And you couldn't sleep because of your job. It wasn't your fault you were in this mess."

Ben grinned as Chip defended him. "I needed you for a lawyer," he said. "They didn't see it that way. They saw a guy with a short fuse who could go off at any minute. They put me in jail and a week later, I was court-martialed. They gave me a dishonorable discharge and showed me the door."

"Where did you go?" I said, no longer bothering to take notes, listening to his story instead.

"I had a little money. I sent most of my money home to my mom, but I thought since I hadn't had a holiday in over year, I would take my time going home. That was a mistake."

"Why?" Chip came and sat down beside me. He leaned closer, knowing this would be the hardest part of Ben's story.

"Remember I told you about my dad and how he always came to my baseball games? It was more than that. He coached my Little League team for years. He loved baseball and taught me everything he knew. One of my best memories is when we won the league championship when I was ten. My dad was so proud. His love of baseball brought us together, and we'd always talked about going to Toronto to see a Blue Jays game, but he died before we could make that dream happen. Even though dad was gone, it was something I wanted to do in his memory."

"The Blue Jays? I'd love to see one of their games." Chip's face lit up.

Ben chuckled, "I was pretty excited and sad at the same time. It wasn't something I thought I'd do alone, you know? But I was so close that I couldn't pass up the chance." He rubbed the back of his neck. "The game was great. I got a seat on the first base line, right where my dad said we'd sit. The seat next to me was empty, and I imagined that my dad was sitting right there with me, watching the game."

"Did the Jays win?"

"Of course, they did. I even caught a foul ball in the fifth inning. It was perfect. After all I'd been through, I felt like my old self."

"But you said it was a mistake," I reminded him.

"It was about 10:00 at night when I left the stadium and headed back to the hostel."

"A what?"

Ben blinked and gave Chip a confused look. "You've never heard of a hostel?" Chip shook his head.

"It's like a hotel, but cheaper. Students usually stay there."

"Huh," Chip tilted his head, "a lot cheaper?"

"Yeah. I think it cost me a hundred bucks."

Afraid we were getting off track, I interrupted. "So, you were going back to the hostel—"

"Right," Ben picked up the story. "It wasn't located in the best part of the city, but having been in the military and given that there were crowds of people, I felt confident I could make the two-kilometer walk. Things were going great, until I turned onto Church Street. I felt alone on the deserted street as I walked from one pool of light to the next. But you'd think with a name like that it would be safe, right? I was just about to the hostel when four guys came around the corner toward me. They seemed to ignore me as they passed, and I thought nothing of it until pain exploded in my head. I bent over from the blow and they pulled the backpack from my shoulders and took off. Everything of any value was in that backpack. I stumbled to the hostel, and the manager called the police. It all happened so fast that I couldn't give the police much to go on."

"What did you do then?"

"I still had some cash, but not enough to get me home."

"What about your mom or your friends?"

"Mom didn't have any money and my army buddies wouldn't take any of my calls. I can't blame them. I thought for sure I could get my identification replaced and find a job in the city. That was my second mistake."

I could see that Ben was upset, so when he stopped, I asked, "Can we take a break?"

Relief swept over Ben's face, and I realized that his story hadn't been hard to hear, it had been hard to tell.

Chip dug around in the backpack and pulled out a container of cookies. "Mrs. Morris gave us these, too. They're her famous chocolate chip cookies. You'll never taste anything like them." He popped the top off and handed them to Ben.

"I don't know, my mom was a baker, remember? My expectations are pretty high. Besides, I've already had cinnamon buns. I could end up in a sugar coma at this rate."

I didn't hesitate when Ben handed the container to me, there was nothing on earth like Mrs. Morris' cookies and I wasn't going to pass them up.

Chip took a couple and put the lid back on before handing the container to Ben. "You can save the rest for later."

"Thanks," Ben said and bit into his cookie. "My mom would never forgive me if she heard me say this, but these are delicious."

We chewed in silence, savouring the flavour.

While we ate, I noticed that Ben looked tired. Telling us had exhausted him, so before Chip could start the camera up again, I said, "How about we leave the next part of the story for tomorrow?"

Ben looked relieved at my words, and I knew I was right. We chatted for a while longer then got our stuff together. Ben held the door open for us as we juggled our equipment.

"I'd give you a hand, but . . ." his voice trailed off, and we knew why. It wasn't safe for Ben to be in Acadia.

"Hannah and I can manage." Chip stood at the bottom of the stairs.

"See you tomorrow, Ben."

"See ya," He answered.

As we came to the path's entrance, I glanced back and saw Ben standing in the open door. The pain from our discussion was etched on his face. I waved, and he gave a half-hearted wave in return before closing the door. With a heavy heart, I followed Chip and the dogs into the trees.

## Chapter 25

The days started to take on a familiar pattern: pick up the dogs, walk out to Ben's, and learn more about his life. Each time we visited, Ben and the dogs became more attached to each other. There wasn't enough time to interview Ben when the dogs were there, so if it was nice out, we'd take them outside and let them run around the farm yard, except for Bullet because we were scared he'd run away and Dotty because she'd just rather lay in the sun.

Today, we'd brought some tennis balls for the dogs to play fetch with. It kept all three of us busy tossing balls, and it wasn't long before we were all panting. We collapsed on the front porch amid tails, noses, and paws. Ben brought some water for the dogs from the old pump he'd discovered by the barn, and Chip dug some water bottles out of the backpack for us. I took a sip of water and took in the scene around me. Brute had Chip on the ground, and as they wrestled around, Chip's laughter rang out over the yard. Ben had his back to the front of the house; Jerry sat in his lap with his tongue lolling out. Ben's eyes crinkled as he took in the sight of Chip and Brute while he gently stroked Jerry's back.

The rest of the dogs were scattered around the porch doing their best to avoid the arms and legs of Chip and Brute rolling on the ground. Dotty rested her head on my lap, and it was at that moment I realized how happy I was. Part of that was seeing Ben happy. I understood now what it was about the dogs that seemed to transform Ben into a different person. Yesterday, he'd told us about the dog he had as a boy. Murphy was a gift from his dad on his eighth birthday. They'd done everything together. Next to losing his dad, the loss of Murphy was one of the hardest things he had to live through.

"Enough, Brute. I give up. You win," came from the pile of dog and boy. Brute stood with his front legs on either side of Chip's head, gave a bark in victory, and then swiped his big tongue up and down Chip's face before prancing over to Ben and lying down.

"Ew, Brute. That's just rubbing it in," Chip scowled at the dog as he wiped slobber off his face with the sleeve of his shirt.

"You play dirty," Ben said as he rubbed Brute's back, to which the dog replied by rolling over and barking for a belly rub. "And you're bossy too." Ben laughed and gave Brute what he demanded.

"Well, the dogs should be good and tired when we take them home today," I said, "except for you Miss Dotty." I ruffled her fur. "You didn't join in at all."

Dotty looked up at me with her eyebrows raised as if to say "I'm fine with that" and then closed them again.

"I'm afraid the party's over." Chip got up and brushed off his jeans. "Time to get you guys home."

As if they knew what he was saying, they got to their feet and stood patiently waiting for their leashes. With their leashes on and a last drink of water, we herded the dogs down the steps to the yard.

"Are you coming back after lunch?" Ben asked from the porch.

"Yeah, we'll try to be back by 1:00," I called over my shoulder as the dogs ambled to the opening in the trees.

Tired dogs meant a slow trip back to town.

"That was fun," I said to Chip.

"More fun than the roller coaster?" he teased.

"About a hundred times. Not once did I fear for my life."

"Ben enjoyed it too. I've never heard him laugh like that before." Chip slowed for the gopher hole, but the dogs were too tired.

I hoped he was still happy when we went back later.

LATER THAT NIGHT, as I helped mom do the dishes, dad hollered from the living room.

"Lorraine!"

She dried her hands on the dishtowel, throwing it over her shoulder as she went to the table to collect the rest of the dishes. "What?"

"Jacob Robinson, Acadia's very own Montgomery Burns. The paper interviewed him about his campaign to clean up Acadia." Dishes forgotten, my mom and I sat on the couch. "Listen to this: he claims that the homeless guy, the one that was 'loitering'—he made air quotes around the word—is the prime suspect for the robberies occurring over the last few weeks." When did my dad start using air quotes? My dad snorted. "How does he know who the prime suspect is? The guys were telling me no one's seen the homeless guy around town for a couple weeks. He probably isn't even around. I still say Robinson has cooked up this idea just to get himself elected." He snapped the paper and folded it in half. "I'd still like to know why he wants to be mayor," he mumbled to himself as he moved on to the next story.

---

THE NEXT DAY, as we set up the camera in the living room at the farm, I told Chip about the article.

"He won't get put in as mayor, Hannah." He adjusted the legs of the tripod. "The people of Acadia are smarter than that."

I wasn't so sure. Principal Struthers was a smart guy, and Jacob Robinson had pushed him around without too many problems. There was no way my parents would vote for him, but not everyone in town was as lucky as we were to have made his acquaintance.

The door flew open as we finished setting up. A tide of fur rolled into the living room. Tails wagging, the dogs were energetic as they circled around Chip and me.

"Brute, get out of here before you knock the camera over," Chip scolded, getting behind the dog and pushing him out from behind the couch with his legs. Brute turned and stuck his head between Chip's legs, a bad move because now Chip had him in a head lock, and he had no choice but to back out of the space.

Ben was the last to come in. He had a wide grin and Jerry in his arms.

"You're spoiling that dog." I took a reluctant Jerry from his arms and set him on the floor. "He'll only walk halfway home and then whines until we pick him up. Chip actually suggested a dog stroller or wagon the other day."

Ben bent over and stroked Jerry's back. "He's my pal. If he needs a lift, I'm there to help out." Jerry appeared to understand, as he barked and then licked Ben's face.

"Think of the other dogs. They could get jealous." Ben froze at my joke .

"Do you think so?"

"Nah, they don't care who pets them as long as they get their fair share." I patted Lucy on the back, and she ignored me and went to lie down.

"Your lunch is over there." I pointed to the grocery bag on the table.

"Thanks, Hannah. You know you don't—"

My hand came up. "Don't say it."

"It's just that—"

"Nope." I lowered my hand, grabbed my notebook, and sat down. "A deal's a deal."

Ben sighed and sat down. "Are there cookies in there?" He smiled hopefully.

"There might be. Or was it cake. I can't remember," I said to Chip who was still setting up behind the couch, "Or did we eat them on the way here?" Finger to my lip, I pretended to think about it.

"Ha ha, you two," Ben considered us, not laughing at all. "You know better than to get between and man and his cookies."

Chip appeared from behind the couch. "I think we're ready to go."

Ben sat up straight and stared at the camera—quite a change from the first day when he stared at the floor most of the time. I hoped he was up to this today. Yesterday, he told us about how he lost all his money and identification. Today, I wanted to ask him about how he ended up in Acadia.

"When we left off yesterday, you'd just arrived in the city. What happened next?"

The happy expression disappeared from his face like the tide from a shore, slowly and completely.

"Between the bus fare and getting robbed, I was pretty much broke." He studied his hands, then clasped them together and looked at the camera. "There weren't a whole lot of options.

I got up early that first morning, and by noon I had a job."

"Doing what?"

"Working at the fair. I stopped for a coffee at a local café and overheard a family talking about how excited they were to go to the fair. Four buses and one admission ticket to the fair and I was in."

"How did you go about getting a job? You should have applied for the fortune teller position. You could have done a way better job." Chip chuckled to himself.

"Thanks, I think. They had signs up, so I asked around and got a job."

"So, you traveled with the fair until you got here," I asked jotting down some notes.

"My plan was to save enough money till I got close enough to get home. But, what I didn't count on was what a jerk my boss would turn out to be." He stopped, and I looked up from my notebook.

"You didn't get along?"

"That's an understatement." He ran a hand through his hair. "He watched me like a hawk. I couldn't turn around without bumping into him. I didn't get along with the other workers either. Let's just say they were into things I wasn't, so they didn't trust me. I think that's why my boss watched my every move and implied that ever since I was hired they were short money every day. This was the second time that week that he accused me of stealing, and I lost my temper. I put my fist through the trailer wall and left. We arrived in Acadia the next day, and he told me if anything else happened, he'd fire me. The run in I had with a bunch of punks was the last straw. I was stuck here after that."

I didn't know what to say. I couldn't imagine Ben doing something like that. Chip got up and shut off the camera.

Finally, Ben said, "I just want to get home, but it doesn't look like that's going to happen anytime soon." He dropped his head in his hands.

"We are going to get you home, Ben," I said with conviction. "We're going to win the prize and get you home."

"I don't know, Hannah. I think you're naïve if you think that telling my story is going to change people."

"We won't know unless we try." Chip put the camera back in the backpack and sat down again. "Even if we can convince the right person, someone that would give you a job so you can get back home, it will be worth it."

Ben studied Chip. "You're right. It's not like I have anything to lose."

"Yay!" I jumped from my seat, and we all high fived.

"I appreciate your enthusiasm, Hannah. I'm not convinced it's going to work."

I was ready to burst with excitement. Despite Ben's reluctance, I was certain this would work. Chip's ear-splitting grin mirrored mine.

"The only thing I have left to capture is you with the dogs," I said, "We'll come around tomorrow during our walking time and film them."

"Sounds good," he agreed.

Chip slid on the backpack and we said our goodbyes.

"What do you think?"

A truck passed us on the road going slower than usual. I tried to get a glimpse of who it was, but it picked up speed and drove into town.

"I think it's going to be great." Chip walked backward in front of me. His hands in his pockets and that wide grin he had at the farm still on his face.

*August 5, 2018*

*We finished our interview with Ben today. He's still not convinced that my plan is going to work, but at this point, he's got nothing to lose. Chip, however, is confident it will. No surprise there! Mr. Optimistic is always sure things will work out. Despite what I told Ben, I'm still not sure that my plan is going to work. It's a long shot, but it's all I could think to do. There's no way I could talk to people and try to convince them that Ben needed our help. Writing is how I share my feelings and the project is the perfect way to get my feelings across. I know what it felt like to be Ben. For people to look right through you like you aren't even there. My classmates at school judged me, just like the people of Acadia judged Ben. I protected myself, didn't let anyone close because they might hurt me, just like Ben did when we first met. But I'm convinced once they hear his story they'd view him differently. If I don't win, I'm going to have to think of another way to help Ben. I just didn't know what it would be.*

## Chapter 26

We arrived at the farm with the dogs just after 9:00 to take pictures and videos with Ben. We'd brought along treats to bribe the dogs to sit still long enough for us to get organized and snap some photos and a quick video, but we soon realized we needed way more treats to keep this unruly group together. I'd fished Jerry out of the trees at least three times and every time I thought we were ready for a picture, he'd run off again. Ben held Bullet so he wouldn't take off, which meant every other picture had Bullet licking Ben's face. The only two that seemed to realize what we were trying to do were Scout and Dotty. They never moved, not once. Out of treats and out of patience, we had one photo and no video. The dogs thought it was a game and every time we got three or four of them settled down the rest would take off for a romp through the grass. This wasn't my best idea!

"This is impossible," Chip threw his hands up in frustration. The camera sat on the tripod and he caught it before it toppled to the ground as Brute bumped it on his way by. "We're running out of time."

"Well," I added, "the dogs are getting some exercise at least."

Ben sat on the steps of the porch as the dogs ran around. He and the dogs were the only ones enjoying our photo session if the happy barks and the grin on his face were any indication.

As if they heard our frustration, the dogs circled around Ben and sat looking at us.

Chip and I looked at each other in shock.

"Take a picture and then turn on the video," I waved at the camera. Chip jolted in surprise and snapped some pictures.

It was a good thing I'd prodded him because the dogs sat still for all of one minute. And then, in unison, they started to lick Ben's face, having a contest, or so it seemed, about who could get the most of his attention.

It quickly dissolved into a mass of dog and man with Ben in the middle. I could hear his laughter amidst the barks and yips.

"Okay, okay." Ben made a futile attempt to get the dogs away. "Enough already." The dogs ignored him and continued their affectionate attack.

In a change of tactics, Ben went limp and lay on the stairs. Confused, the dogs stopped and when he didn't move, they started to whine and nudge him with their noses.

"I think I've got enough," Chip said and shut off the camera. Ben slowly got to his feet. It was amazing that through all their wrestling, the dogs always avoided Ben's injured leg. Before the dogs pounced again, I had their leashes ready and started to round them up. They weren't too happy about it and dragged their paws in the dirt when we went to leave.

"See you tomorrow," I called as we entered the path through the trees.

"I'll be here," Ben replied.

———

"HOW LONG DO you think it's going to be before Jim or someone else discovers Ben's staying in the farmhouse?"

This was something that had been weighing on my mind for awhile.

"We've been going out here for nearly a year Hannah and the only time we've seen someone was the other day when that Peterson guy showed up. I think if our plan works, he'll be gone before anyone knows he was here."

"If he's caught, it would be trespassing. I'm just afraid Ben could get in more trouble. And the way Jacob Robinson is trying to use him, this could end badly before we finish the project."

"We just have to get everything put together and entered, then wait and hope that you win."

"It's not the money that's the issue; I want the people in this town to be more accepting and respectful of others."

"There are people who have thought this way for a long time Hannah. Your project is going to have to be powerful if it's going to change minds."

I'd written powerful pieces before, but this would be a real test of my abilities. I wanted to change long-held beliefs, but I was sure that if people just got to know Ben and his story that they would be compassionate to his situation. The fact that it would foil Jacob Robinson's election plans was just a bonus.

"We'd better get to work then," I said to Chip as we walked the well-beaten path to town.

## Chapter 27

"This image next," I pointed to the pictures on the computer screen. Chip and I were sitting at his kitchen table, the computer in front of us along with the storyboard I'd sketched out for my project.

We were working at his place today because his mom wasn't feeling good, and he wanted to stay close in case she needed him. We'd walked the dogs quickly, if that's possible, and skipped our usual visit to Ben. The submission date for the contest was a week away, and we'd only just started to put it together.

"Let's get the pictures and videos in order and then we can do the voice-over for what you want to say." Chip brought up the pictures and videos we'd downloaded. I scanned the screen to find the ones I wanted.

An hour later, we were just putting the finishing touches on the pictures and videos when Shelley came out of her room. She had a blanket draped around her shoulders.

"Hi, Hannah. How's the project going?" She plugged in the teakettle, took a cup from the cupboard, and added a tea bag.

"It's going great, thanks to Chip. I don't know what I'd do without his computer genius." I ruffled his hair as he focused on the computer. He ignored me.

"Finally, all that time playing computer games has paid off," his mom teased leaning against the counter.

Chip's face turned red. "Enough, Mom. And enough from you too." He gave me a disapproving glare.

"Are you blushing, Chip?" I'd never seen Chip blush in all the time I'd known him.

"No, now stop it and let me work." Shelley and I both laughed at his discomfort. She made her tea and slowly lowered herself into a chair at the table. She picked up her mug to drink, and I noticed it took both hands to get it to her lips—her hands were shaking so bad. Noticing my stare, she gently placed the cup on the table and put her hands in her lap.

"How are you enjoying being an assistant dog walker, Hannah?"

"It's great! I really love the dogs now that I've gotten to know them. And they're pretty well behaved now. It took a while for them to get used to being with other dogs, but they get along for the most part."

Chip ignored our conversation, focusing on the work he was doing.

"Who's your favourite?"

I smiled. "It's hard to have a favourite. Dotty is the most even-tempered, she just goes with the flow, but the others get frustrated when she walks too slow. Brute, he's the leader of the group, he's always out in front, barreling along. Scout is the most loving. I think she has a crush on Chip." I eyed him as I said this, and the red flared up on his face again.

"Hannah—"

"Well, she does. She walks right beside Chip everywhere we go." Chip glared at me and then started clicking the mouse with more force than necessary.

"Bullet is exactly as his name implies. He goes from zero to sixty in a second, and that's why he's hardly ever off his leash. Jerry is older and not in much of a hurry. The rest of the dogs give him grief just like they do Dotty. He's got a crush on Ben." I stopped and thought for a moment. "No, I wouldn't call it a crush. It's more like a deep connection. Jerry seems very attuned to Ben's moods."

"I've heard about that," Shelley nodded, her voice quiet. "Dogs that seem to pick up on their owner's moods. I've heard that they train dogs for people that suffer from seizures and PTSD. It's quite fascinating."

"Then there's Lucy, the collie. She just likes to get out in the fresh air. And that's the whole crew."

"Well, it sounds like fun." She picked up her tea and went to the kitchen. "Would you like to stay for supper Hannah? It's Taco Tuesday."

I glanced to see Chip's reaction to her invitation and asked, "Do you think we'll be finished today?"

Engrossed in what he was doing, he didn't answer at first, "Yeah, I think so."

"I'd love to stay," I said to Shelley. "I just have to let my mom know."

I quickly typed a text to my mom: staying at Chip's for supper. She didn't reply for a full ten minutes and then I only got a quick "Okay." She must be busy at work.

Chip didn't need my help at the moment, so I went to the kitchen. "What can I do to help?" I asked Shelley.

"Would you cut up some tomatoes and lettuce while I get the ground beef frying?"

Shelley handed me a knife and a cutting board. We worked in silence except for the sizzling beef. I watched Shelley at the stove. I couldn't tell if it was the steam from the pan or if she had a fever, but she kept wiping her forehead and her face appeared flushed.

My stomach growled as the smell of taco seasonings filled the air.

"It will be ten more minutes, Hannah. Do you think you can wait that long?" Shelley joked.

"Sorry. Lunch was a long time ago, and it smells so delicious."

Ten minutes later we were sitting at the table loading up our taco shells. Chip's was piled so high with toppings that I didn't know how he was going to hold it together, let alone get it in his mouth, but he did it.

Chip and I did the dishes while Shelley relaxed on the couch. She'd eaten as much as I had, but not as much as Chip. No surprise there—he had the appetite of a starved wolf. And now she was watching one of her crime dramas. I wanted to ask Chip about the shaking and sweating, but there was no way Shelley wouldn't hear us talking. Chip and I joined her when we were done.

My phone buzzed in my pocket, and I saw I had a text from my mom.

*Time to come home, Hannah.*

I looked at the text and thought it was strange. My curfew was usually 10:00 during the summer, and she knew I was at Chip's.

I tapped out: *Why?*

To which she replied: *Just come home, please.*

*That's strange. Why won't she tell me why I have to come home? Did something happen with Dad? Was I in trouble?* I shoved my phone in the pocket of my shorts and stood.

"Where are you going?" Chip said. "The show's not over yet."

"My mom texted. I have to go home." I walked to the door. "Thanks for supper, Shelley. It was delicious."

"You're welcome anytime, Hannah," she said from the couch where she was wrapped in her blanket with a cup of tea. "Say 'Hi' to your mom and dad for me."

"I will. See you tomorrow?" I asked Chip, who had come to the door to see me out.

"For sure. Is everything all right?" His voice was laced with concern at my quick departure. He knew it was strange for my mom not to let me stay later.

"I have no idea. I guess I'll find out when I get home." I opened the door. "We'll finish up the presentation tomorrow?"

"Only your voice-over left and then it's done. So, make sure you know exactly what you want to say."

"I've got it all written out. I'll practice tonight so I'm ready for tomorrow." I stepped through the door.

"Night, Hannah."

"Night, Chip."

---

I BENT over and clutched my knees. I'd run the four blocks from Chip's and now I stood on the front step trying to catch my breath. My dread built with each step. In my mind, I'd imagined all types of catastrophes. Dad had been hurt at work. Mom lost her job. Something happened to my grandparents. Afraid to open the door for fear of what Mom might have to tell me, I tried to calm the panic racing through my body with a deep breath.

I walked through the front door to see my parents sitting at the kitchen table. The remnants of their meal were gone, and they each had a cup of coffee sitting in front of them. I tried to read their faces to determine what was going on. My mom kept throwing worried glances at me and my dad. My dad's face, however, was a thundercloud. I tentatively pulled out a chair and sat down.

My dad gave me a long look, and I realized that I was the cause of the dark look on his face. I knew in that moment that this wasn't going to be good.

My dad took a deep breath, as if to get control of his temper, and my stomach dropped. Prickles of fear ran up my spine, and I looked at my mom. The worried look was still there, but she said nothing.

"I had an interesting conversation today at work," he started. "One of the guys was on his way to visit his parents and took the road south of town." At the mention of the road, my stomach dropped. I felt the color drain from my face, but said nothing. My dad turned his stare toward me. "Imagine my surprise when he told me that he saw you and Chip coming out of the trees at the farm south of town."

I swallowed a huge gulp and opened my mouth to speak, but my dad wasn't finished.

"Your mom was equally surprised when I told her." I shifted my gaze to see my mom staring at me as well. "She also mentioned that she'd told you not to go out there. Do you mind telling us what you were doing there, when you were forbidden to go?" He clasped his hands on the table and looked at me expectantly.

The prickles down my spine had changed to full-grown stabs of fear. Dad's gaze didn't waver, neither did Mom's, and I shifted uncomfortably.

"I know mom told me not to go out there, but—" I trailed off under their scrutiny. "I . . . we . . . Chip and I discovered that's where Ben was staying when he disappeared." The last of my confession coming out in a rush.

"Ben?" Confusion replaced anger on my dad's face. "Who is Ben?"

"The guy that was warned about loitering? I asked you about it. Chip and I took the dogs out to the farm"—I peered at my mom when I let that little tidbit slip and she frowned—"a few days after he disappeared. He had nowhere to go and barely anything to eat. So . . . so Chip and I took turns bringing him food, and then he started to bond with the dogs and one thing led to another and we were going out there every day." I ended on a whisper.

My parents looked at each other, and I could tell they were not happy with my confession, so I rushed to continue, "Ben agreed to help me with my project. He told us the story about why he's been hanging around town and how he was trying to get home to his mom." My parents still hadn't said anything, so I barreled ahead. "Chip and I interviewed him and took some pictures and videos. I'm going to enter it for the multi-media project at the library. We just put everything together tonight. I think it's going to make a difference." My parent's lack of response had me.

"Hannah—" My mom placed her hands flat on the table. "I appreciate that you want to help Ben, and I think it's terrific that you are going to raise awareness for his situation with your project, but that doesn't change the fact that I specifically asked you not to go back to the farm."

She was right. I'd blatantly gone against what she'd asked. I lowered my head.

"I'm sorry." And I truly was. "But I can't just let him starve. No one wants to help him. Thanks to Jacob Robinson, the whole town is against him! They have him convicted just because he doesn't have a job or place to live. That's not right!" My pleas had no effect on my parents. The determined set of Dad's clenched jaw told me my explanation had fallen on deaf ears. Frustration leaked out of me like air from a balloon. Why couldn't they understand?

"So," my dad started, "for disobeying your mother you're grounded for the next week."

My head whipped up. "A week! I can't be grounded this week!" Frustration forgotten, anger rushed to take its place.

"I'm sorry, Hannah. But that's what it's going to be." My dad put his hands on the table, pushed himself out of his chair, and went to the living room.

"Mom?" I made one more attempt to change her mind.

"It's a week, Hannah. And next time, I hope you'll listen to me when I ask you not to do something."

She got up and joined my dad in the living room.

Not wanting this to be the end of the argument, I followed them.

"Can't you see how important this is to me? I want to help Ben. No, I need to help Ben because he has no one who has his back, and I know what that's like. He's a nice guy who needs some help. Please let me help him."

Dad didn't take his eyes from the television. "It's our job as your parents to make sure you're safe, Hannah, and the only way we can do that is to make sure you're at home."

I stared at them watching their stupid show. I used every reason I could think of to appeal to their sense of justice, but when they ignored me I gave up and went to my room.

*August 10, 2018*

*I hate my parents! Someone saw Chip and I near the farm and tattled to my dad about it. So, I'm grounded for a week! A week! Because Mom told me not to go out there. They are so unfair! A day, maybe two, but seven days? I have people who count on me and now my parents have made it impossible for me to help them. I'm never speaking to them again.*

I threw my journal on the bed. Writing about it wasn't helping. That ball of anxiety that was in my stomach while I sat at the kitchen table was back and it was bigger than ever. What am I going to do? What could I do? I started pacing, my journal forgotten. It was useless anyhow. The only thing that was going to make me feel better was if Dad changed his mind. Fat chance that would happen. I knew from the look on his face when he got up from the table, he'd made his mind up.

I continued to pace. My parents didn't understand the consequences of me being grounded for the next week. Chip needed me to walk the dogs. It was a two-person job. Without me, they'd drag him all over town, literally. And the deadline for the library project was a week away, and I still had to add my voice to the presentation and then polish it up. Finally, what about Ben? It would all fall on Chip's shoulders to make sure he had enough to eat. What a mess!

The first thing I needed to do was to tell Chip. He wasn't going to be happy. I texted him: *Hey* and settled in for a nice long wait, most of which I'd spent pacing. I was shocked and then concerned when my phone buzzed back immediately.

*I was just about to text you.*

I frowned at my phone. Chip was going to text me? Chip never texted me first, and he always took forever to reply. Something was up with him. I hoped it wasn't something to do with his mom. Adding that concern to my parent problem made my anxiety skyrocket.

*What?*

I could see he was writing a reply.

*Your mom called my mom.*

Uh, Oh. This wasn't going to be good!

*What did she say?*

I cringed because it could be something bad or it could be something good. It was bad.

*She told my mom about us being out at the farm and helping Ben.*

*And?*

*And she's worried we'll get into trouble. She did agree to let me go out tomorrow and take Ben some food. But we're not to go out there without permission again.*

*So, you're not grounded.*

*No. Are you?*

*Yeah, a week stuck inside these four walls.*

*Say "Hi" to the dogs for me. And Ben too.*

*I will. I'll text you tomorrow, and we'll decide how to get your presentation finished.*

*Okay…*

*Keep your chin up, it's just a week. What could happen in a week?*

## Chapter 28

My mom knocked on my door the next morning.

"What?" I moaned and pulled my pillow over my head.

"Don't take that tone with me," she said from the vicinity of the door. "I left you a list on the kitchen counter. There's a few things I'd like you to do today."

I pulled the pillow off my head and propped my head up on my hand, "What do you mean 'a few things?'"

"A few things that you can do since you'll be home all day." She pulled her head back and started to shut the door.

"Like what?" I replied sulkily.

The door opened again, and she stuck her head back in. "Like vacuum the bedrooms and clean the upstairs bathroom."

I opened my mouth to disagree.

"Don't say a word, Hannah. You're getting off pretty easy if you ask me. Those jobs will take you all of an hour. That leaves you the rest of the day to do what you want until it's time to get supper ready, which reminds me, the instructions are on the counter."

"Fine," I huffed, flopping on my back and pulling the pillow back over my face. My mom didn't reply, she shut the door and left me alone.

An hour later, I was putting the vacuum back in the storage closet and grabbing the cleaning supplies when the doorbell rang. Chip stood on the other side with a sad smile and puppy dog eyes.

"Stop it." I grabbed a fistful of his Yoda t-shirt and pulled him into the house.

"Your parents didn't happen to change their minds, did they?" he asked hopefully.

I shook my head and waved at the kitchen table.

"So, it's me and the dogs on our own today?"

"I'm afraid so. Do you think you can handle it?"

"No problem. Besides, I called Alex just in case you couldn't make it, and he said he'd help me out," he shrugged sheepishly.

"It didn't take you long to replace me." I did my best to look hurt. Chip's sad smile and puppy dog eyes were back.

"Sorry. I'm just not sure I can handle them all on my own. Although, I'm not sure how Alex will work out either. I told him he couldn't bring his phone or any games, so we'll see how it goes. Anyway, I thought I'd check just in case your parents had changed their minds."

"Nope, I'm here every day for the next seven days. But they didn't say anything about visitors." We both perked up as the thought came to me.

"Okay, I'll be back this afternoon after I walk the dogs and check on Ben." He stood in the doorway and gave me a wave.

"Later," he called and shut the door.

---

I THOUGHT KEEPING busy would be the best way to keep my mind off Chip and the dogs. I'd vacuumed, cleaned the bathroom, cut all the vegetables for supper, and cleaned my room. To say I was going crazy was an understatement. Out of chores to do, I played games on my phone to pass the time.

When the doorbell rang, I ran to the door and yanked it open and instantly burst out laughing.

Chip and Alex stood on my front step, and they both looked like they'd been put through the ringer. My first impulse was to hug Alex because I hadn't seen him in awhile and for helping Chip, but after a closer look, I wasn't sure he'd let me. He had a scrape on his forehead, his shirt was ripped around the collar, and he was missing one shoe. Chip didn't look any better. He had a cut on his chin, his favourite Yoda t-shirt had the sleeve hanging off, and both of his knees were skinned.

"What happened?" I asked as I motioned for them to come in. "I worried about you all morning and it looks like I had reason to." I pointed to the kitchen table and got down some glasses. I poured us all a glass of iced tea and when I got back to the table, both of them had their heads on their arms. "Tell me what happened."

"What didn't happen," Alex mumbled into the table.

Chip lifted his head. "Where would you like us to start?" It seemed he could barely keep his head up.

"I guess with how you got so messed up." I looked between them curiously. Alex raised his head and took a long drink of iced tea while Chip talked.

"It started about five minutes in. I went and picked up Scout, Bullet, and Dotty before I picked up Alex."

"So, things started off okay?" I looked back and forth for confirmation.

Alex shook his head no.

"I thought," Chip said, looking at Alex who had his head down again, "that I'd give Bullet to Alex right off the start. Let him get used to the dogs. My mistake was to hand the leash over at the same time I was telling him to really hang on because Bullet likes to run."

"That bit of information came a little late." Alex lifted his head and dropped it again.

"So, before we even had all the dogs picked up, Alex and I were running through the park after Bullet, who decided that if he was going to have a taste of freedom, he was going to make the most of it."

Alex's head came up again. "And making the most of it included running through the park and through five different yards. It wasn't until we'd cornered him by a shed, that we grabbed hold of his leash."

His head dropped back onto his arms.

"Where did the cuts and scrapes come from? Did you fall while you were chasing him?"

"No," from Chip.

"Yes," mumbled Alex.

My head went back and forth, as they answered at once.

Chip explained, "Alex got pulled through Mrs. Temple's hedges." Mrs. Temple was Chip's next-door neighbour whose hedge—with its razor-straight sides and top—was the talk of the neighbourhood. "He didn't think to let go of the leash until it was too late and he was in the bushes."

"That's where I got this." He pointed to his forehead. "Everyone's going to think I'm a Harry Potter wannabe."

I could see why Alex was concerned. He prided himself on not following the crowd.

"But that doesn't explain what happened to you." I pointed to the dried blood on Chips chin.

Alex sat up at this point and started to laugh.

"Now, that was funny. You should have seen it, Hannah."

"You suddenly seem a whole lot better," Chip said raising his eyebrows in anticipation of Alex's response.

"So—" I prodded.

"So," Chip started and stopped and then looked at Alex who was ready to tell the story if Chip didn't, "Jerry—"

"What happened to Jerry?" I turned to Chip.

"Nothing happened to him. He may have, well, he had a run-in with a cow." Alex drew circles on the table avoiding my gaze.

"Where on earth would Jerry come in contact with a cow?" I got out of my chair and started pacing. If I kept getting this much exercise, I was going out for the track team.

"Alex thought it might be a good idea to take the dogs out in the country. When I said we couldn't go south of town, he suggested we head out to the west side of town. Not a great suggestion."

Alex agreed, "Yeah, we should have gone east. But how was I to know it wasn't a good place to walk dogs. I don't have a dog." He threw his hands up. "I didn't know the fields of wheat and canola come right up to the town limits." Then he looked at me. "Did you know there was a dairy farm out that way?"

I shook my head. Clearly, he hadn't been enjoying the view back on our Ferris wheel ride.

"But, we went west, and like Alex said, there's a dairy farm right next to the road. They must milk the cows early because they were all out in the pasture . They had their heads stuck through the barbed-wire fence and were eating the tall grass along the side. They didn't seem too concerned about a pack of dogs coming up the road, but Jerry sure took offense to them being on his road." Chip took a drink of iced tea and carried on. "Jerry ran right up to one cow that had her head out of the fence and proceeded to bark his displeasure. Well, the cow didn't take too kindly to Jerry either and took a swipe at him with her head."

I put my head in my hands. I could see clearly how this was going to end, and it wouldn't be good for whoever had a hold of Jerry at the time.

"And the fight was on. Unfortunately, Jerry went under the fence and I had his leash, so I went too."

"That explains the torn shirt then." I pointed to his sleeve.

"Yeah, and if I smell a little rich it's because Jerry dragged me through the pasture for a while."

"What did the cow do?"

"After Jerry quit barking, she went back to eating. They ignored us, and we were able to crawl back through the fence."

"Well, you had a pretty eventful hour." I poked Alex with my finger. "So, Alex, is dog walking a job you'd like to do for the rest of your life?"

He glared at me. "I don't want to do it for the rest of the week." He was so funny when he was grouchy. "I have to go." Alex got up from the table. "Thanks for the iced tea, Hannah. And I guess I'll see you tomorrow, Chip."

"Don't be late," Chip said as Alex shuffled to the door.

"Yeah, yeah," he waved and let himself out.

As soon as the door closed, I said, "Did you go see Ben today?"

"Not yet. I'm going to go home and shower and change my clothes. If I can't stand the smell of myself, I doubt that Ben will."

"Wait, I think we have some leftovers from supper last night that you can take." I rummaged around in the fridge and put what I could find along with some fruit in a bag. "Tell him I'll be out to see him as soon as I can."

"Okay, and I'll talk to you tomorrow about finishing up the project. I can come over tomorrow night if that's okay with your parents."

"I'll ask. Talk to you later."

It was only noon, and I wondered how I was going to spend the rest of my day. Thinking I'd put the time to good use, I got my writing notebook and went over my script for the project. What would people think? Would all this work make a difference? I wasn't sure, but I had to try.

After an hour of practicing, my voice resembled a frog's, but I felt ready to do the voice-over for the project. That done, I grabbed a book off the shelf in my bedroom and read.

## Chapter 29

It wasn't mom who woke me up the next morning, it was Chip. Or more specifically it was a text from Chip. My stomach fell. Two mornings in a row I had woken up to a text from Chip. This couldn't be good.

Rubbing the sleep from my eyes, I tried to focus on his message.

*My mom's in the hospital.*

*Oh, no! What happened?*

*We were watching television last night and she got up to go to bed and fainted.*

*Do they know what's wrong?*

*We're still at the hospital, and they are going to run more tests this morning.*

My heart sank for Chip. I knew that this was probably his worst fears realized.

*What about the dogs?*

*Alex has it covered—at least I hope he does.*

This was the worst time to be grounded. I wished Trudy wasn't at camp. She loved dogs, and we could've used her help.

*What about Ben?*

*I took out the food you gave me yesterday, I'm sure there is enough there for two days.*
*I'll try to get out there this afternoon.*

*You'd better tell him about Alex. He might have to help us out there too. I hope your mom is okay.*

*Me too.*

The day stretched out in front of me. I finished the chores mom had left me and tried to read my book. I couldn't motivate myself to go over the script again for the project. By 2:00, I was sitting on the couch, worrying about Shelley. My fingers itched to text Chip, but I knew that he would tell me what was going on as soon as he knew. I texted Trudy to let her know about Chip's mom.

I was in the kitchen getting supper ready when my mom walked through the door. Her shoulders drooped, and it looked like it took all her energy to hang up her jacket. She bent down to pick up her lunch from where she'd dropped it and groaned as she straightened.

I stopped peeling potatoes as she slowly made her way to the sink and put her dirty lunch dishes in it.

"Rough day?" I stated the obvious.

"You could say that." She leaned against the counter. "Did you talk to Chip today?"

I rinsed the peeled potato and dropped it in the pot before answering.

"He called me this morning. Did you see Shelley today?"

Mom nodded and tucked her hair behind her ear. "Yeah, she came in last night and spent most of today having tests run.

"And what did they find out?" I stopped peeling to look at her. She avoided my gaze, instead focusing on the refrigerator across from her. "Mom?"

"They didn't have any results back when I left work, and I couldn't tell you what they were anyway. It's better that you hear it from Chip." She pushed off from the counter. "I'm going to take a quick shower before supper and try to wake up."

It was not a good sign that my mom refused to tell me what was going on with Shelley. If things were great or it was something minor, she would have told me. My phone lay on the counter and each time I passed it, I checked to see if Chip had texted. Nothing. Dad arrived home as I put supper on the table.

"How was your day, Hannah?" he said as he followed his after work routine. He had his drink, but instead of heading to his recliner, he leaned against the counter.

"Good."

"What did you do today?"

"Nothing."

He studied me as I took the pitcher of iced tea from the fridge. "How's Chip making out with the dog walking?"

"Fine."

Apparently tired of my one-word answers, he took his drink and sat down at the kitchen table. Mom joined us as we dished up our plates. Mom and Dad discussed how their days had gone, I ate silently, and their conversation flowed around me. I was about to put my dishes in the sink when my dad said something that had me returning to my chair.

"There was another break-in last night," he mentioned after a long silence, "Proctor's Garage."

"You're kidding? What did they take?" Mom asked.

"According to the guys at work, they took some tools from the garage. They're getting bolder, Charlie has surveillance cameras." He got up from the table and put his dishes in the sink. "The police are checking them to see if they can identify who it was." Grabbing his drink, he sat in his recliner to watch television. "Let's see if Jacob Robinson has anything to say about this." He scrolled through the channels to the local news station.

It took everything I had not to join my dad, but mom already had the sink full of water when she asked, "Give me a hand with these, Hannah?"

I took one more glance at the screen before grabbing a dishtowel. When we finished, I went to my room and Mom joined Dad. My patience was at an end. I texted Chip.

*You home yet?*

It was only 7:00, and I knew visiting hours went till 8:00, so the chances of him being home were slim. The text was marked delivered, but not read. Grabbing my project script, I read it over a few times. Reading the script made me think of Ben, which made me think of the break-ins, which made me think of Jacob Robinson, which made me sick to my stomach. I got a glass of water and picked up my book with the idea that it would take my mind off everything going on, but then I started thinking about Chip and whether Shelley was okay, and the loop started all over again. On my third attempt to read the same sentence, I gave up. Maybe being busy would take my mind off things. I started with the clothes strewn on the floor. Some were definitely dirty, and others were questionable, so I scooped them all up in my arms and went down to the laundry room. I didn't acknowledge my parents as I passed the living room. Clothes in the wash, I grabbed a banana.

"You hear from Chip?" my mom asked as I started up the stairs.

"Not yet." I kept going, and once I reached the safety of my room, I checked my phone. The time said 8:15. I thought Chip and his grandparents might be home by now. There was no answer to my text and even though it killed me, I left my phone on the bed, while I tidied up my desk. My room had never been this clean.

It was nearly 10:30 before Chip replied. I was just getting into bed and had put my phone on the nightstand when I heard it ding.

*Hannah? You still awake?*

*Just. How's your mom doing?*

*Tired from all the tests, but I think she feels better. It was a long day.*

*Do they know what's wrong?*

*We didn't get any results back yet. It takes a couple of days.*

*How did Alex make out with the dogs? I'm sorry I couldn't help.* ☹

*I haven't talked to him yet. I'm afraid to ask.*

*Are you going to the hospital tomorrow?*

*Yeah, going with grams and gramps in the morning.*

*I wish I could help you out, but if I snuck out now and my dad found out, I'd be grounded for eternity!!*

*Things will be fine. I just hope Ben is okay.*

*Me too. Talk to you later.*

*Night, Hannah.*

I lay in the dark and tried to sleep. I counted sheep, did deep breathing, and even turned on music. Nothing worked. My mind kept circling back to everything that was going on in my life. First, I thought about Shelley and imagined the worst things that could be wrong with her. I hoped it wasn't something life-threatening like cancer. Then, I thought about Ben. How was he making out at the farm without food and visits from the dogs? Did he think we'd abandoned him? What would he do if no one showed up for another day? What if he decided to go into town on his own? Who was responsible for the break-ins? It wasn't just stealing something that was lying around, it was deliberate breaking and entering. And what were they doing with it? Selling it? Storing it somewhere? But where? I flipped from one side to the other. I fluffed my pillow. I flipped it over. My mind would not quit coming up with scenarios of the people that I cared about being in danger. Finally, I thought about the dogs and how happy they were and that's what it took for me to drift off into a troubled sleep.

## Chapter 30

After I tossed and turned all night, every part of my body hurt the next day. My head felt like it weighed a hundred pounds and every muscle was sore. My parents were gone to work when I hobbled downstairs and saw today's to-do list on the counter. Too tired to make myself breakfast, I poured a glass of orange juice and collapsed on the couch. I must have fallen asleep, because the doorbell woke me up. Pushing my hair out of my face, I opened the door to find Alex and he wasn't alone. Bullet jumped three feet in the air before digging his claws into my legs.

"What are you doing here?" I picked Bullet up and did my best to avoid his enthusiastic face wash by turning my head back and forth, which wasn't easy with how it felt. I gave up.

"Bullet's been acting really strange and I thought that maybe he missed you. I asked Suzy, his owner, and she said it was okay to bring him over to see you. This is the most energy he's had all day."

Cradling Bullet to my chest, we went into the house. On the couch, Bullet immediately curled up in my lap and closed his eyes.

"How did you make out today?" Alex stood uncomfortably in the middle of the living room. He couldn't seem to decide if he should sit down or not. Finally, he lowered himself into Dad's recliner.

"It's taken me a while to figure which dogs to hold in which hand, but it's getting better. I just hope Shelley gets out of the hospital soon, I don't know how long I can keep this up."

"Tell me about it. I give you credit for being able to walk them by yourself, Chip lasted all of one day on his own."

"Well, I do have a secret weapon," he said with a sly smile.

"Really? Well, don't hold out on me—what is it?" Alex reached into his pocket and I could hear the rustling of plastic. Bullet's head suddenly came up and looked to Alex.

"Bacon. All dogs love bacon." As he held up the bag, Bullet barked, shot out of my lap and was in Alex's in seconds. "See. They'll do anything for this stuff." Alex broke off a piece and held it out for Bullet, who snatched it from Alex's fingers and then came back and arranged himself back in my lap.

"And you didn't think to share this before?"

Alex shrugged and smiled. "I can't give away all my secrets. My grandpa feeds it to his dog all the time, behind my grandma's back, of course. I figured if it worked for him, it'd work for me too."

I scratched behind Bullet's ears and realized that I'd missed him too. Who would have thought? Thinking about the dogs got me thinking about Ben.

"I'm worried about Ben." I didn't look at Alex when I admitted this, keeping my eyes on Bullet.

"I'm sure he's okay, Hannah. If worse comes to worse and Chip can't make it out there, I'll take him some food."

My hand stopped moving, and Bullet batted my hand with his head. I kept scratching.

"You don't have to provide the food, Alex. Stop here first, and I'll give you some food to take to him." I could tell he was going to argue with me. "No." I put my hand up to stop him from talking. "Chip and I took this on. We'll get you the food."

With a resigned sigh, Alex stood up. "Okay, let me know if you want me to make a delivery tomorrow." He picked up the end of Bullet's leash. "Come on, Bullet. It's time to get you home."

Bullet whined and looked at me to intervene. "Sorry, you've got to go buddy." I told him with one last scratch under the chin. He hopped down and headed for the door, not caring if Alex followed or not.

"Thanks again for bringing him over. I missed him too. I miss them all really."

"Later," Alex said as he hurried out the door behind Bullet.

After Alex left, I texted Chip. He should've been at the hospital by now and hopefully had some news about his mom.

*How's your mom today?*

No answer, which wasn't a surprise. They were probably keeping Shelley company while they waited for the test results. I looked at my to-do list and got started on my chores to pass the time. I still didn't have an answer by noon, so I texted Alex.

*Did you hear from Chip?*

Alex replied immediately.

*No*

Alex was the same in text as he was in person, the fewer the words, the better.

*They must still be at the hospital. I'll make something up for Ben if you'll drop it off. I'll have it ready in half an hour.*

*K*

I rolled my eyes. I looked through the fridge for something to make sandwiches.

I put the food in a bag along with some bottled waters and set it by the door.

I was cleaning up the kitchen when the doorbell rang. Alex was playing a game on his phone when I opened the door. "Hello, Alex."

"Hey." He walked in without looking up from his game.

I picked up the bag and held it out to him. "Alex."

"Just a sec." He continued to play as I stood holding the bag. "Okay," he said finally and shoved his phone in his pocket.

"You know where you're going, right?"

"Yep, take the road south of town and until you get to the clump of trees and take the path that goes into it." He turned to go.

"Ben doesn't know you, so he may not come out right away. Just tell him we sent you and it will be all right. If he doesn't come out, just leave the bag by the front door." At least, that's how I hoped it would happen. I wasn't convinced that Ben would come out if it was someone he didn't know, even if he did say he knew us. "Text me after you drop it off."

Alex flicked his hand good-bye.

---

I CHECKED my phone again and settled in for another exciting day. There was still no answer from Chip. I went to my room, got my book, and settled in to read for an hour or two.

Less than an hour had passed, and the doorbell rang again. Thinking it might be Chip I ran down the stairs and pulled open the front door and frowned.

Alex stood with the bag of food in his hand.

"Why didn't you drop the food off?" I asked gesturing at the bag.

He handed the bag to me. "He wasn't there."

"I told you to leave it by the front door." I didn't take the food, hoping Alex was going to turn around and deliver it like he said he would. "Did you forget what I told you?" Barring the door, I crossed my arms in case he tried to leave the bag and looked down at him from the threshold.

"I just didn't think there would be much point," he shrugged.

"What do you mean no point? He could be hungry Alex, that's the point!" Alex's calm, indifferent attitude didn't match my frustrated, urgent one.

"I'm pretty sure he'll get meals at the jail." He lifted the bag to me again.

I froze. "Jail? What are you talking about Alex?"

"I met three police cars coming back toward town on my way to the farm. I couldn't tell for sure, but I thought there was someone in the back of the second cruiser. When I got to the farmhouse, the place had been ransacked, not that there was a lot of stuff to go through, but I looked around the house. They'd checked every room. Even the barn and sheds. I don't know what they arrested him for, but I'm almost positive it was Ben."

I slumped against the doorframe. This is exactly what I was afraid would happen. That he'd get arrested for trespassing. And after the warning he had received, they'd throw him in jail for who knows how long.

"Sorry, Hannah." Alex put the bag on the step and turned to go.

"Wait!" He stopped and turned to look at me. "Sorry. It wasn't your fault. I'm just glad you were there. Otherwise, we'd never know what happened."

"No problem." He started down the walk.

"Alex, would you come with me to the police station?"

He stopped to look back at me. "The police station? Why would you go there?"

"Because I want make sure Ben's okay."

"Why not? I've got nothing better to do—other than win another level in Fortnite, but that can wait." He waited on the sidewalk as I threw the bag of food into the house and locked the door. I skipped down the steps and grabbed his arm. We took off running toward the police station.

When we arrived, I knew immediately that things were not normal at the Acadia PD. Jacob Robinson stood on the steps of the two-storey building surrounded by reporters and camera people. His two goons stood on each side of him. Jacob's lips were moving, and he was pointing at the police station behind him. We were about ten feet away before I could hear what he was saying, ". . . have lived up to my promise to clean up our town. That means that the residents of Acadia can sleep easy tonight knowing that the thief who has been helping himself to your hard-earned possessions is now behind bars. And it might help you to know that this thief is the same vagrant that has made himself a nuisance and an unwanted presence in our town." He stopped to give that time to sink in and then began again. "I am so committed to the safety of this town that I have started to protect its citizens before I'm even elected." He stopped and smiled into the camera. "That's dedication."

*Dedication. Ha! More like making himself look good to the voters of Acadia.* The reporters held their microphones in his face and began shouting questions.

"Were you the one who discovered him?"

"How did you know where to go?"

"Who is he?"

His hands came up and he motioned for the reporters to be quiet. "The name of the man is not being released at this time, but as soon as it's made public, I'll let you know."

*Yeah, right! He's now the spokesperson for the police?* Alex and I stood at the back of the crowd doing our best to blend in.

"He makes it sound like he was the one who arrested Ben," Alex said out the side of his mouth.

I didn't answer because I wanted to hear the answers Robinson was giving to the reporter's questions. He said a local farmer had noticed some activity around there recently. Today, he'd noticed a young man fitting the description of the vagrant that had been in town a couple of weeks ago. He felt it was his civic duty to report the matter to the police. *Yeah, right!* Robinson added he was almost positive the man had a criminal record. That was enough! I wasn't going to stand around and listen to his lies any longer. I grabbed Alex's arm and we moved around the group in front of the building, making our way to the entrance of the police station. I looked over my shoulder once before opening the door and sliding in with Alex right behind me.

I hadn't been inside the police station since our grade three class trip. It didn't look the same as I remembered it. There was a small waiting area with a receptionist on the other side of the plexiglass. I stood on tiptoe and spoke through the hole in the glass.

"Excuse me. Can I speak to Ben please?" I asked.

Looking up from her computer, she asked, "Ben?"

"The guy arrested at the farm south of town. Can I talk to him?" I pleaded.

She came to the glass. "I'm sorry, but unless you're his legal representation, which I'm guessing you're not, you can't see the prisoner."

"Can you tell me what he was arrested for?"

"No, I'm sorry, I can't." She went back to her seat at the computer.

Dismissed, I turned to Alex.

"I have to go home. If my parents find out that I left, I'm going to be in big trouble." Alex didn't reply. "Can you go to the hospital and tell Chip what happened? Get him to text me. We need to decide what we're going to do. Ben needs our help. I don't know what's going on, but we need to figure out how the robberies are connected to Ben and Jacob Robinson. Can you do that?"

"Yeah, I'll go right now."

"Thank you." We stopped at the corner. I started toward my house, and Alex continued on to the hospital.

The house was empty when I got home. I picked up my phone and waited for Chip to text me. I opened my browser and typed "Robberies in Acadia" into the search bar. A long list of links appeared. As I looked through the first one, there was an article about the robbery at Proctor's garage. The article quoted Jacob Robinson, "We need to get a handle on these robberies. Acadia has always prided itself on being a safe place to raise your children. If the local police don't start getting some results, no one will feel safe." There was no quote from the mayor. It seemed that Jacob Robinson had a number of friends in the media.

The next story was about Jacob Robinson speaking at the local Chamber of Commerce. He talked about how important it was to keep Acadia safe, again, and his vision for the town as a leader in the region. The next detail caught my attention. He went on to explain how he had a possible business venture that could bring more revenue to the town. He didn't give any details about the venture, only that it could result in a spike in the local economy. Whatever that meant. Was it something to do with the mill?

The rest of the links had Jacob Robinson appearing at numerous events where he promised to clean up the town, find the thieves and bring economic prosperity. The mayor was rarely mentioned, even the pop-up ads were for Robinson's campaign.

My phone dinged with a text.

*Ben got arrested??!!*

*Yeah, but I don't know what the charges are.*

*See what you can find out.*

*Looking right now.*

*Keep me posted.*

*Okay.*

I went to start supper.

———

THE NEWS WAS on as we ate supper. My dad had mentioned the arrest when he got home from work. People were saying that Ben had been charged with the robberies that had happened.

We all turned our attention to the television when the announcer said, "In local news, an arrest has been made in the rash of robberies plaguing Acadia over the last month. Ben Carter was arrested and charged with four counts of robbery and one count of breaking and entering. The police received a tip that Carter was hiding out at an abandoned farm south of Acadia. He will appear in court on Monday."

I dropped my fork to my plate. "They make it sound like he did it." I spoke to my plate. "I know he didn't do it." I pleaded for my parents to believe me and not the announcer on the television. "We have to do something."

"What can we do Hannah?" Mom said, dropping her fork on her

plate. "We only know what he's told you. Who's to say that it's true? It could all be a story he's created."

"Your mom's right. The system will assume Ben is innocent until proven guilty. We have to be confident that's what will happen."

I knew my parents were trying to protect me and there was the possibility that everything that Ben had told us was a lie, but my gut was telling me that he'd told us the truth. There had to be something we could do. With Chip's Mom still in the hospital and me grounded for five more days, whatever we could do was going to have to wait.

I practiced my script for the project and went through the pictures of Ben. Each photo was more proof to me that Ben was not guilty of the charges, but how were we going to prove it?

## Chapter 31

Chip spent the next two days at the hospital with his mom before she was released to come home. The test results were inconclusive so far and the doctors had ordered another round to determine what was making her so sick. They weren't trying to find the problem but rather ruling out others. It didn't make sense to me, but they'd given her new medication they thought might help with her symptoms. At least she was well enough to leave the hospital. I put the finishing touches on my multi-media project, while Chip stuck close to home just in case his mom needed him, which left Alex on dog duty and texting as our only contact.

*We need to find out what evidence they have on Ben.*

*You're not grounded tomorrow, are you?*

*No. I think he is going to have to enter a plea tomorrow. Should we go and try to find out what we can?*

*Good idea! I'll see if Alex will walk the dogs for one more day.*

Ten minutes later, Chip texted back.

*He said he'd do it. Court starts at 10:00, according to the website. I'll pick you up at 9:45.*

*See you tomorrow.*

I sat on the front step the next morning, waiting for Chip. He was right on time. We arrived at the courthouse with ten minutes to spare. Reporters surrounded Jacob Robinson, who stood on the steps. He was dressed in a suit and tie as he addressed the crowd.

"Is it true, Mr. Robinson, that you provided some of the evidence that will be presented at the preliminary hearing for Ben Carter."

His chest puffed out like a rooster. The only thing missing was the comb and tail feathers. Or not, as the wind lifted his hair straight up to fan around his head. "I'm not at liberty to say." But his smile said it all. "I'm just doing what any good citizen would do. Now, if you'll excuse me, I must get inside."

Chip and I sneaked around the group of reporters and made our way up the stairs and inside. Jacob Robinson was nowhere in sight. A security guard sat at a table to our right, and I immediately recognized him as the bailiff during Brady's trial.

"Excuse me," I asked, and he looked up from what he was doing. "Can you tell me which courtroom the Ben Carter arraignment is in?"

He obviously didn't recognize us as he checked his computer.

"It's in courtroom four. Last one on the right at the end of the hall." He pointed to the far end of the hallway and we started toward it. "Right next to the one you were in last year," he added. Both Chip and I stopped and looked at him, but he was staring at his computer.

The door to the courtroom was open with a few people scattered throughout. Jacob Robinson sat in the front row, behind the defendant's table. The last time he'd been there he was supporting Brady. This time he was there for an entirely different reason. He considered us as we took our seats in the second row but said nothing. We both returned his levelled gaze before looking to the bench.

"Things haven't changed much since we were here last," Chip said, loud enough for Robinson to hear.

"Yeah, things seem really familiar," I responded innocently. "Really familiar."

Chip shrugged, "Some things never change."

"You got that right."

Robinson said nothing, his red face the only indication he heard us.

The courtroom continued to fill with reporters and several people from town. There was Charlie, from Proctor's garage, and a couple of the people mentioned in the newspapers as missing property in the last month.

At 10:00, Judge King entered the courtroom with a stack of files in his arms. He dropped them with a thump on the bench and took his seat. He raised his arms to loosen his robe and opened the first file.

A new bailiff, a woman, read the case number.

Ben shuffled slowly into the courtroom, his limp worse than I'd ever seen it. An officer led him to the chair beside the defence attorney and removed his handcuffs.

Judge King read from the file. "Benjamin Carter, you are accused of four counts of robbery under $500 and one count of breaking and entering. How do you plead?"

Ben and the defence lawyer stood. "Not guilty, your honour," Ben answered, and they both sat back down.

The prosecutor stood. "Your honour, I ask the court to deny bail at this time as the defendant is a flight risk due to his transient lifestyle."

"Your honour," Ben's lawyer stood. "That is totally unreasonable. I ask the court to consider his service in the military defending our country. Every day for over a year he risked his life to protect civilians and military personnel in Afghanistan. Is that any way to treat our veterans? Lock them in jail? My client is the victim of circumstance. He was in the wrong place at the wrong time."

The judge considered the request.

"I understand your concern. However, for the safety of the community, bail is set at $5,000."

Ben stared at his hands resting on the table. The judge might as well have denied him bail because we all knew Ben didn't have $5,000. He couldn't even get enough money together to get home; there was no way he was getting out of jail.

The bailiff came over and helped Ben to his feet. He turned to us as she led him out of the courtroom. It was then that I noticed how his appearance had changed. There were dark circles under his eyes, his cheeks were sunken, and it looked like he had lost weight in the week I'd been grounded.

"He looks terrible," I stated the obvious.

"And there's no way he's going to get out on bail with the bail set that high," Chip added.

As the judge moved on to the next case, Jacob Robinson hustled out of the courtroom. Chip and I were close behind and not at all surprised when he stopped to answer a reporter's question.

"Mr. Robinson, were you called as a witness?" Robinson stopped, and when he turned around, a smile took up most of his face.

"No, I wasn't. But I was happy to see that Judge King did all that he could to protect the fine people of Acadia." The reporters yelled over each other with more questions. And, shocker, Robinson didn't listen to anyone. "I'm sorry, but I have a pressing personal issue to attend to. Thanks for the questions and for taking time to cover the real story."

The reporters shouted more questions as Robinson whirled around and left the building. Chip and I were close behind as he crawled into his car and drove out of the courthouse parking lot.

Chip and I watched as his car disappeared around the corner. "That's strange," Chip noted as we walked down the courthouse steps.

"What?" I asked.

"Robinson. I've never seen him cut short an opportunity to talk to the press. Not on television, not in the newspaper, or in person for that matter. It's awfully strange that he would cut things short today."

"So, why was he in such a hurry today?" I said.

Chip looked thoughtful, "I'd say he's up to something."

## Chapter 32

The next day, things were back to normal. Not quite normal, but as normal as they got for Chip and me. This was the first day back with the dogs, and I can honestly say, I think they missed us. Each time we picked one up there were welcome barks, numerous licks to the face, and a spring to everyone's step. Alex joined us. He said it was just in case we ran into trouble with the dogs, but I really think they'd started to grow on him. It seemed like a good idea to have him along, as the dogs were pretty hyper.

Chip suggested that we take them to the farm. I wasn't excited about the idea.

"I want to check things out, Hannah. I want to see where he had all this 'stolen property' hidden," Alex nodded as I looked between the two of them.

"Are we really going to find anything?"

"We won't know if we don't look," Chip replied, setting off in the direction of the farm.

Bullet and Jerry tugged on the leash to follow, and I sighed, trailing behind.

The first thing we noticed when we entered the yard was that the front door was open. The dogs were up the stairs and into the living room as if they'd been shot from a gun. The house looked like it usually did, except for the turned over chair and the kitchen table pushed against the wall. The dogs' noses never left the floor, and if the number of trails was any indication, there had been more than six people in the house.

It was Alex who looked out the window over the sink and noticed the tire tracks in the grass. "Chip. Hannah. Come and check this out." He motioned us over. We left the dogs to continue their search and joined him at the window. "I've never seen tire tracks over here, have you?"

The tracks came right to the back door. Chip must have had the same thought because he went to the back entry. Everything looked exactly the same, except the jars on the washstand were knocked over. Chip went to open the door. Without turning the handle, the door popped open. Chip looked at me. When we'd been here a couple of weeks ago, the door had been shut.

"Ben could have been out here and left it open," I said in answer to his unspoken question. "Or maybe it was Jim?"

"It's possible, but there are two sets of tracks." He pointed to the footprints on the linoleum.

Opening the door wider, I could see the muddy footprints ended on the top step.

"How did they get in the house? There's only muddy tracks on the top step," I said to Chip.

Chip studied the area in front of the stairs. The two parallel lines of flattened grass signified a vehicle. "They backed up to the steps and lowered the end gate."

"They were loading something into the truck? The house looks exactly the same, just messed up."

Alex joined us at the doorway. "Unless . . . they weren't picking something up but rather dropping something off instead."

We all moved at the same time, searching for footprints, but they didn't go into the kitchen. They stopped at the other doorway. Fear skittered down my spine, and I stepped back as Alex wrapped his hand around the doorknob. Chip nodded his head. The door creaked as Alex opened it. Alerted by the sound, the dogs crammed into the back entry. I picked Bullet up to keep him from shooting into the darkness. Scout stood beside me whining, and I stuck my knee out in front of her to prevent her from going down too.

"Wait here," Chip said. I wasn't sure if he was talking to Alex, me, or the dogs, but I was fine staying right where I was.

Chip flicked on the flashlight of his phone and shone the beam down the stairs. From my vantage point behind them, I couldn't see anything. Chip's foot landed tentatively on the first step, and soon, he was swallowed up by the darkness. Alex followed behind, and I stayed to control the dogs, which was not an easy feat as they poked their noses around to see what was happening.

Chip yelled from the basement, "Send Scout down, Hannah. I don't think there's anything that she can get into."

Hearing her name, Scout pushed past me.

"What's down there?" I asked from the top of the stairs. I couldn't see anything but the top five steps and the occasional beam of light from Chip's phone.

"Nothing," Alex's voice travelled up the stairs, "but a furnace. But there was something here not that long ago. The dust is disturbed over here in the corner."

I could hear the two of them talking but couldn't make out what they were saying. Bullet wiggled in my arms, and I held him tighter to my chest. Suddenly, Scout barked. I heard Alex say, "What is it girl?"

Scout barked again.

Chip said, "Way to go, Scout."

"What did you find?" I yelled down the stairs.

"We'll be up in a minute and I'll show you," Chip answered. I tapped my foot as I listened to them talk to each other. "Hurry up."

"Hold your horses," Alex replied from the bottom of the stairs. Scout shot out from behind them, and I moved as she reached the landing to avoid being barreled over. Alex pushed the dogs back from the door and Chip came into the back entry, closing the basement door behind him.

"Look what Scout found," Chip said as he opened his fist. I was shocked at what it held. Jacob Robinson's bodyguard had worn the same pin at the fair. The one that had blinded me.

"What do you think it means? How did it get here?"

Alex took the button from Chip's hand. "It means that someone who supports Jacob Robinson was in the basement."

"Thanks, Captain Obvious," Chip said and took the button back. "Whoever was in the basement dropped this. What we need to find out is who it was and what they were doing here."

"How are we going to do that?" *Great question, Alex.* We looked at Chip waiting to hear his answer.

Chip thought for a moment. "First, we need to find out what evidence they have on Ben."

"And how do you suggest we go about doing that?" Alex voiced the same skepticism I had.

"I don't know," Chip replied. "We need to talk to someone with connections to the police."

"They're not going to tell a bunch of kids about what they've got on Ben," Alex scoffed. "We tried to get in there once already. There's no way that receptionist is going to let us talk to anyone."

"No, but they might tell someone like . . . Hannah's dad." Chip's eyes lit up at the idea.

"My dad? Why do you think they'd tell my dad?" Was he nuts? "My dad isn't so sure that Ben isn't the one doing the robberies. I'm not sure I'll be able to convince him to help."

"What about Marty? He's a friend of your dad's and a police officer. Your dad could just casually mention Ben. If he can find out what evidence they have, we might be able to figure out a way to prove Ben's innocence."

"I don't know, Chip. I just finished being grounded for a week and now we're back here. If my dad finds out—I'll be stuck at home for the rest of my life." A week was bad enough. Dad would go through the roof if he knew I was back here.

"Don't mention that part. Just say that we don't think Ben is guilty and see if he'll ask around."

A sick feeling settled in my stomach as I thought about bringing this up to my dad. I wasn't sure I could convince him without letting on to what we'd discovered.

"I'll think about it."

"Don't think too long. We need to find some proof that Ben's innocent before he goes to trial."

I nodded.

"Okay." Chip looked around. "Let's get the dogs rounded up and head back to town."

---

I STRUGGLED to rip a piece of paper towel off the roll by the sink while blood dripped from my finger. I'd cut it while attempting to chop some peppers. I wrapped my finger and got an awkward grip on the pepper. So far, I'd managed to cut my finger, open a can of tomato paste instead of tomato sauce, and almost put sugar in the chili instead of salt. Supper was a disaster, and it was all because I couldn't stop thinking about the best way to approach my dad about the evidence against Ben.

I glanced at the clock. He'd be home in less than an hour, and I still didn't know what I was going to say. Hey, Dad, can you ask one of your friends at the police station what evidence they have on Ben? *No, too direct.* Hey, Dad. Did you hear they arrested Ben for those robberies? I wonder how they knew it was him? *Subtle, but he wouldn't ask around if he didn't know.* Hey, Dad. We think that Ben's innocent. How can we prove that? *Might work. But then again, he may just say stay out of it.* The possibilities swirled around in my head. I wished I had time to sort this out in my journal, but I had a meal to ruin. Then it came to me: act casual, find out what he knows so far, and go from there. That I could do. Feeling confident I had a plan, I finished the chili and left it to simmer.

When Dad walked through the door, I was on my phone, scrolling through videos. Rather than jumping up and peppering him with questions, I forced myself to play it cool.

"How was your day?" He asked on his way through to the kitchen.

"Good," I replied. "Yours?"

"Good." He sat in his recliner, drink in hand.

I pretended to be engrossed in a video while Dad studied something on his phone. The minutes ticked by. It was now or never.

"Anything interesting happen at work today?" I tried to be casual.

"Hmm?" Dad looked up from his phone.

"What's new in Acadia?"

"I'm just reading about that guy's arrest. What did you say his name was? Ben?"

"What does it say?" I asked, knowing what it said.

"That he was the one responsible for the robberies." He continued to read.

"No, he isn't." At the forcefulness of my tone, Dad raised his head and studied me.

"I agree. It seems a little too neat and tidy." He turned his attention back to his phone. "It says here that Jacob Robinson was part of the arrest. Now, the whole situation stinks to high heaven if he's involved."

"Does it say what they have for evidence?" I asked innocently.

"No." He continued reading. "The article doesn't say, but they must have something or they wouldn't have arrested him." Then almost to himself he said, "It just seems too perfect."

"Don't you know someone down at the police station? They'd know about the evidence," I said, hoping Dad would take my suggestion and run with it.

He kept reading. "I'll check with Marty next time I see him."

I figured that was as close as I was going to get to dad doing anything, if I pressed for more, Dad might become suspicious. It was a start. I turned my attention back to my phone. Picking my iced tea up off the coffee table, the glass cooled my hands. What I really I wanted to do was put it to my face to cool down the heat. I breathed a sigh of relief. Now we just had to wait to see if dad could find anything out.

## Chapter 33

"Did you talk to your dad?"

"Good morning to you too." I took Bullet's and Jerry's leashes from Chip, closed the door, and started down our walk to the street.

"Sorry. Good morning." Chip sheepishly followed us down the street.

"Yes. He was going to talk to Marty and see if he knew anything, but don't hold your breath. I'm not sure when he'll see him again."

"Well, it's something at least."

The sky was full of clouds this morning. A relief after the hot, sunny days we'd been having. The dogs pranced along. No, that's not true, Bullet and Brute pranced, the others loped, and Jerry trotted to keep up.

"I was thinking—" Chip said.

"Uh-oh."

"Funny. Seriously, I think we need to go and check out Jacob Robinson. That button we found is connected to him somehow."

"What are you thinking?"

"That we go by his construction company. Maybe we can find something that will help Ben."

"What are we looking for?"

"Anything that might give us a clue that he's involved. It's really strange that we have a rash of burglaries right around election time, don't you think? And it's pretty convenient that Ben is the target for those burglaries."

"Dad says Jacob Robinson doesn't do anything that doesn't benefit him. We need to find out why he wants to be mayor. That's the ticket to seeing if there's any connection between him and Ben's arrest."

"I don't think we're going to see anything at his business, but we need to start somewhere." I wasn't convinced that this was the best way to find anything out, but I guess he was right, we had to start somewhere.

Robinson Construction was in the industrial area of town. Located on the service road past a farm equipment dealership and a trailer company—a box-shaped building in the center of a large compound protected by a chain link fence. Equipment and building materials were scattered throughout. Six trucks loaded with wood and tools sat parked in front of the building.

Trying to look as inconspicuous as possible, we walked past the business.

"We got trucks," Chip said, gesturing with his head, "full of tools."

"There have to be at least fifty trucks in town, that isn't proof that he's involved."

"True. I just wish we could get a closer look without raising suspicion."

We were nearly past the building when Scout started sniffing the ground. She broke off from the pack and headed towards the fence. This was not the way to avoid suspicion, and even though Chip tried to get her to come back, she was determined to follow the scent she'd picked up.

When she reached the fence, she started whining and scratching at the grass. The rest of the dogs, seeing Scout had found something interesting, ran to follow her.

"Come on girl," Chip said to her, trying to get her back on the road.

She continued to sniff along the fence until she reached the end and then went back again.

"I don't know what's wrong with her. The last time she acted like this was when we were in the basement at the farm." Chip handed me the leashes for the other dogs and knelt down beside Scout.

"What do you smell, girl?" he asked, scanning the compound to determine what she was focused on.

At that moment, two men came out of the building. The same ones from the speech at the fair and the news conferences. I ducked down beside Chip, hoping they wouldn't notice us. I had no interest in finding out if those muscles were for real.

"We need to go over to the old mill," the bigger one said as he rounded the front of one of the trucks. "Robinson wants the office emptied out. The dozer is scheduled to arrive at—" I missed the rest as he opened the door and got in the truck. The engine roared to life, backed up and left the lot.

"Did you hear that?" I turned to Chip in disbelief.

"What are they talking about? A dozer out at the old mill? What would they need a dozer for?" Chip stood and pulled Scout from her continued investigation of the fence.

"I thought he said he was going to get it up and running again. Not tear it down." I thought out loud. "We better get going before someone else comes out."

Chip nodded and started back the way we came.

"After we drop the dogs off, we should go check it out."

I knew this was coming. Chip never backed down from getting to the truth, no matter how dangerous it was.

"The place gives me the creeps. I'm not sure it's a good idea." I recognized the firm line of Chip's mouth and I sighed in resignation. "You're not going to change your mind, are you?" His look never changed, and my shoulders slumped.

"Nope."

I worried this wasn't going to turn out well.

IT TOOK us half an hour to reach the old sawmill. An eight-foot chain link fence surrounded the area. A huge chain ran through the main gate, fastened by a padlock. Chip pulled on the lock, but it didn't budge. Neither Chip nor I were skinny enough to slip through the gate.

Chip looked to his left and then to his right. "Let's check around the outside, maybe there's a hole in the fence we can sneak through."

We headed right and started walking along the fence. Weeds grew about three feet high and made it hard to walk. Chip went first, and I followed closely behind.

"Do you think there's anything living in the grass?" I asked as I tiptoed through the forest of weeds.

"Like what?" Chip replied.

"I don't know—snakes, small rodents, huge bugs," I answered as my eyes scanned in front of me.

"Nah, I don't think we'll come across anything like that."

"I hope you're right," I replied, unconvinced.

By the time we made it to the corner of the fence we hadn't come across any holes big enough for us to squeeze through. Chip turned the corner and started to head along the north edge of the fence.

"Come on Hannah, I think I see a hole up ahead."

Chip took off running. When I finally caught up to him, he was standing beside a small hole close to the ground. I grabbed on to the fence and gulped huge mouthfuls of air. My heart felt like it was about to beat out of my chest.

"You think we can fit through there?" I managed to get out. The hole didn't look big enough for us to get through and it would mean crawling through the weeds, which I was still not convinced didn't house all sorts of creepy creatures.

"It's going to be tight, but I think it will work," he said. "You go first."

"Me? Why do I have to go first?" I snapped.

"I'll hold the fence and make sure you don't get stuck. Then I'll go through and you can do the same for me."

Chip pulled the weeds away from the fence and started tramping them down with his feet. I crouched down in front of the hole and looked through.

"What about the weeds on the other side?" I asked.

Chip stuck his leg through the hole and did his best to flatten the weeds for me.

"How's that?" he asked.

I eyed the hole skeptically and did a thorough scan of the area for anything that moved. When nothing appeared, I put my arms through the hole and crawled through. Chip was right. It was a tight fit, but I made it without getting hung up on the fence. I brushed my clothes off and turned to help Chip. He was half way through when the back of his shirt caught on one of the fence wires.

"Hold on, you're caught," I said and untangled his shirt from the wire.

Chip stood up and looked toward the three buildings that made up the old mill. A large one that had once been painted white had since lost its paint and only gray, rotting wood remained. A smaller one, which I assumed was an office, and, finally, a shed constructed of poles with a covered roof for storage.

"Where do we start?" I wondered.

"Well, let's check out the office building first. It looks like the only building that isn't about to fall down," he reasoned.

The ground surrounding the mill had once been covered in gravel, but now the weeds had taken over, and we picked our way toward the office. Wooden steps led up to the door and Chip gingerly put his foot on the first one. Testing each step to be sure it would take his weight, he reached the landing and motioned for me to follow. When I got to the top, Chip was using his hand to clean the dirt off the window of the door.

"Can you see anything?" I asked.

"Not really," he replied as he cupped his hands to his eyes and looked again. "Maybe a desk and a couple of chairs."

I noticed the rusty padlock hung on the door and asked, "Is it open?"

Chip grabbed the doorknob and turned it. The door didn't open and appeared to be stuck. He put his shoulder against it and pushed. It opened a couple of inches, and I looked over Chip's shoulder to see what was inside. I couldn't make anything out. Blinds covering the windows made it impossible to see anything.

"Is anyone in there?" I whispered.

"It's too dark to tell," he replied and went to give the door another push.

"Wait," I grabbed his arm. I knew Chip was excited about playing detective and all, but I was petrified. There was no telling what we'd find inside, and if we were right—Jacob Robinson trying to get Ben to take the blame for the robberies—we could be in danger.

"Why?" he questioned.

"What if someone is in there and they're just waiting for us to come in so they can bash us on the head?" I argued. My mind went to the worst possible scenario. Isn't that what always happened in horror movies? You know the person shouldn't enter the house, but they do anyway, and guess who ends up dead? I didn't want to end up dead. I peered into the room again and tried to make out if there was anyone inside. I couldn't hear anything, but that didn't mean there was no one here. If we got caught and my parents found out—they would kill me! If I wasn't dead already.

"There are no vehicles around. It's the perfect time," Chip replied. "I'll go in, you wait here. I'll tell you if the coast is clear."

Before I could convince him of why this was a terrifically bad idea, he gave the door another shove. He now had a wide enough space to enter the office. As he took two steps forward, I moved to his spot in the open doorway. I lost track of him as he entered the office. My eyes strained to make him out in the gloom. It seemed like an hour but was probably only a few minutes before Chip called, "It's all clear, Hannah."

I entered the office and let my eyes adjust to the darkness. As they did, I took in what I could see: a desk littered with take-out food containers and pop cans, two old office chairs with worn leather seats and arms, filing cabinets, and what looked like an ancient photocopier. I scanned the room to find Chip and saw his silhouette on the far side of the room. He was squatting down beside something on the floor.

"Hannah, crack the blinds a bit," Chip said.

"What is it?" I asked.

"I can't see Hannah. Open the blinds."

I walked to the window nearest Chip and turned the handle. Slowly, light seeped into the room, and as I turned around, I saw what Chip was already looking at—a tower of objects haphazardly thrown together stacked in the corner. Items ranged from lawn chairs to bicycles, garden ornaments to kids toys, lawn mowers to power tools. Power tools! I moved closer to the pile as I caught sight of what looked like a drill.

"Holy cow! Where do you think all this came from?" Chip gestured at the pile.

The minute I saw the drill, I knew where all this stuff had come from.

"Careful, Hannah." Chip got to his feet beside me.

"I think that's my dad's drill," I said moving a rake out of the way.

"Let me get it. One wrong move and this mess could come crashing down." Chip pushed aside the cushion from some lawn furniture and stuck his arm through the legs of a chair. With the tips of his fingers, he grasped the drill around the barrel and carefully pulled it out of the pile. Chip handed it to me, and I turned it over, knowing exactly where the initials would be if it belonged to my dad.

"Is it his?"

"Here are his initials: MW in white paint. Dad marks all his tools the same way."

Chip studied the pile. "I think we can safely assume all of this is stolen property." He smiled, pleased with himself.

"We also know that Jacob Robinson sent his henchmen out here earlier today."

"Do you think they were doing it without his knowledge?"

"I doubt it. Robinson has eyes and ears everywhere. I'm sure they aren't acting on their own. I don't think they were hired for their smarts."

"The question is, what do we do now? Do we take your Dad's drill to the police? It doesn't really prove who put it here."

"You're right, it doesn't. But if we can find out who's been out here, then we can prove that Ben isn't guilty."

"Take your Dad's drill, and I'm going to put everything back the way it was before we got here."

While Chip closed the blinds, I stuck my head out the door of the office to check to see if the coast was clear. The lot was still empty.

Thankfully, we didn't see any vehicles on our way back to town. A girl carrying a drill down the street wasn't something you saw every day in Acadia.

"Do I tell dad that we found it at the old mill or do I just put it in the garage and let him find it?"

If I told him where we found it, there was a good chance that he would lose his mind over me trespassing again. If I say nothing and he just happens to find it, he won't feel compelled to help Ben at all. He'll just think he misplaced it, and the real thief will get away with one less charge.

"Why don't you wait and see if your dad talked to his friend. If he did, that might make him a little more open to hearing about his drill and where we found it."

"Good idea. I'll play it by ear."

We arrived at my house. Trying to appear casual, we sneaked into the garage.

"We need to hide this for now," I said, scanning the workbench and shelves that lined the walls. Not surprisingly, Dad's garage was immaculate. Each tool had its own outline on the pegboard above the workbench and his power tools were lined up neatly on top. The empty spot where his drill sat was like a beacon. "But where? He knows if things are moved an inch."

Chip moved over to a box on the floor along the wall. "How about in here?"

He tucked the drill into the bottom of the box and covered it with some rags Dad used to do whatever it was he did in here. "I've gotta run. I told Mom I'd be home to make supper for her."

"How's she doing?"

"Better, but she gets tired easily."

"I noticed her sweating the other day when I was over. And she was shaking so bad she could barely drink her tea."

"Yeah, that just started happening. Hopefully, the doctor can figure out what it is. I'm hoping that if I do some of the more taxing chores, she won't be so exhausted."

"What's on the menu tonight?"

"I'm thinking my world-famous dogs and beans."

I shuddered at the name. "Please tell me that's not what I think it is."

"Depends. Did you think it was hot dogs and beans?"

"Of course, but it's a terrible name. What would Scout and the others think?"

"I guess you're right. I'll come up with something better."

I hoped so. Chip left, and I set to work to make supper myself.

―――――

I DIDN'T HAVE a chance to quiz my dad before supper, since he didn't get home from work until after mom and I had finished eating.

Mom sat at the table and talked to Dad while I started the dishes. Moving the dishes quietly around in the sink, I hoped to pick up on their conversation. They discussed their day and then I heard Dad mention Marty. My ears strained to hear what he was saying.

". . . saw him at Hank's café today. Hank was quizzing him about Ben."

As soon as dad mentioned Ben, I dropped the dishcloth with a spray of bubbles and sat down at the table. He knew what I was going to say without me having to say it.

"Hannah, before you ask, you have to understand, he's not supposed to be talking about a case. He did say that they had some evidence that Ben was the thief. Hank said that people were contacted to come in and identify their property. It doesn't sound good for Ben."

I stared at my hands. If what dad said was true, we were going to have to find out where the stolen items at the mill had come from. I couldn't take the chance of telling them what we'd discovered just yet. I had just finished being grounded for a week. I couldn't take the chance on getting grounded again.

"Is there anything we can do, Mike?" Mom asked.

"It sounds pretty cut-and-dried from what Marty was saying."

"We have to do something, Dad."

"Hannah—" Mom cautioned.

"Ben didn't do it. I know it. We can't let him go to jail for something he didn't do."

"We have to let the police do their job, Hannah. Interfering in a police investigation could land you in a whole lot of trouble."

"Your dad's right. We have to stay out of it, Hannah."

*August 15, 2018*

*Chip and I struck gold at the old mill today. Not real gold. More like my dad's drill. But it's the proof we need to prove Ben's innocence. I haven't told them we found it yet. I'm waiting to see what the police do. The downside to all of this is my parents have forbidden me to do anything that might help Ben. I tried to convince them that we needed to do something, but they don't think we should get involved. I'm surprised at their trust in our legal system, it's not like it worked for us before. If Trudy and I hadn't stood up for Chip, Brady and his friends would've gotten away with beating Chip. I know he's innocent and with the whole town against him and Jacob Robinson using him to get elected, Ben needs someone on his side. Chip and I are going back to the old mill tomorrow to see if we can find anything that will connect Jacob Robinson to the robberies. My parents might be willing to stand by and see what happens, but I'm not. And I know Chip isn't either.*

## Chapter 34

Today we were crouched in the weeds at the old mill. The weeds and grass still creeped me out, but if we were going to help Ben, we needed to see if there was any action around there. I focused on the mill to keep my mind off what might be lurking in the grass.

Chip thought that whoever had stashed the stolen goods in the office would be back for them at some point and we wanted to be there when they did. Chip had wiggled through the fence when we got here to make sure the stolen property was still in the office.

"It's still there," he panted as he slid down on his belly beside me.

I handed him a bottle of water from the backpack. We'd come prepared with snacks and water in case we had to spend the whole afternoon watching the mill. We walked the dogs and then packed up and found our spot along the fence.

"Do you think anyone will show up, Chip? That stuff could stay there and we'd never know who did it. I mean, whoever planted the stolen property at the farmhouse did their job. Ben's in jail."

"I just don't think someone is going to leave the rest here. My gut is telling me that we don't know the whole story."

. . .

## Watch Me

THE SUN BEAT down on our backs. The taller weeds gave a little shade, but it was still hot. I slapped a mosquito that landed on my arm. The heat and bugs were starting to make me irritable. Nothing had happened in the hour we'd been here, and I realized that I was not going to be able to last much longer.

Pigeons cooed as they flew in and out of the shed, and magpies dived among the trees. The birds and bugs were the only sounds we heard.

I laid my head on my arms and that's when I heard a low rumbling. I lifted my head to tell Chip when his hand landed on my arm. He held his finger to his lips and then pointed to the gates of the mill. A truck with a Robinson Construction logo on the side sat parked at the gate. The door opened and someone got out, unlocked the padlock and pushed the gates open. The truck drove to the office and backed up to the stairs.

My heart nearly stopped when two familiar men got out.

"Those are the guys—"

Chip's hand covered my mouth. I pushed his hand out of the way and watched silently. It was Jacob Robinson's bodyguards. Was it my imagination or did they look even more menacing than they had yesterday? The thud of their boots on the stairs to the office matched my heartbeat. I imagined myself melting into the ground in the hope they wouldn't see me.

I peeked through the weeds as the bigger man came out of the office with some garden tools and threw them in the back of the truck. He went back in and the other man came out with a lawn chair. They went back and forth until everything that had been stacked in the corner of the office was now in the truck. The smaller man closed the end gate and they drove out of the compound.

"Come on." Chip stood up and threw the backpack on his shoulders.

I scrambled to get off the ground as Chip ran through the weeds lifting his legs high to clear the taller ones.

"Hold on." I dodged a rock and nearly ended up on my face.

"I want to see where they're going. Hurry." He stood on the road waiting, bouncing from one foot to the other.

When I got close, he started walking down the road, and I jogged to catch up.

The truck entered the town limits and turned right.

"I think they're going back to the construction company. Let's hurry."

We ran full out—for six blocks.

The truck was parked in front of the building. We stopped at the corner of the fence.

"What do we do now, Chip?"

"We go get a picture of all that stuff in the back of the truck and we take it to the police."

"Okay, how do we do that without getting caught?"

Chip scanned the area.

"We wait until there's no one around and then act like we're walking by and take a picture."

The service road was busy. Trucks and machinery drove back and forth. This wasn't going to be easy. Between all the businesses, there was a constant stream of activity. Finally, there was a break in all the traffic.

"It's all clear my way. How does yours look?" Chip asked, his eyes glued to the road on the right.

"After this truck, it's clear." As soon as the truck was even with us, I shouted "Now," and we started toward the trucks.

Chip pulled his phone out of his pocket, opened his camera app, and then held it next to his leg. We got closer to the truck and casually stopped behind it. Chip checked the area once more before lifting his hand and taking a picture.

"Get one with the Robinson sign in the background."

"Good idea. Then that ties it to Robinson." He stepped back and took another picture.

"And maybe take one from the side to show the truck logo."

Chip stepped around the truck and snapped another shot.

The door of the building opened, and we ducked down behind the truck. It was the smaller bodyguard, and I could see him coming around the front as I peered over the box. Chip and I sneaked behind the other trucks and hid. The engine started and pulled away from the building.

When we were certain he was gone, we stood up and ran along the fence to the corner. We slowed to a walk and continued to my house.

It wasn't until we were sitting in my living room that we looked at the photos.

"Do you think it's enough?" I asked, looking over Chip's shoulder.

"This one shows the stolen property." He flipped to the next picture. "This one shows the truck in front of Robinson's building and you can even see some of the stuff in the back." He looked up at me. "I think we've got enough to prove Ben's innocence."

"Do we go to the police now? We could ask for Marty. Tell him what we found."

Chip thought for a moment and then gave a firm nod.

"Let's do it."

———

AFTER A COMPETITIVE GAME OF ROCK, paper, scissors on the steps of the police station, it was Chip who stood in front of the hole in the plexiglass. The door had buzzed when we entered, and Chip waited patiently at the window for the receptionist. When she didn't acknowledge him, he gave me a questioning look. I shrugged my shoulders. It was amusing to watch Chip's first experience with the indifferent secretary.

Chip sighed loudly, and the secretary finally graced him with her attention.

"What can I do for you today?" she asked, coming to the window.

"We'd like to speak to Marty, please." Respect and politeness laced Chip's request.

"Marty? You mean Constable Duffield?" she corrected.

Chip looked over his shoulder for me to confirm, and when I nodded my head, he told her that was correct.

"I'll see if he's free."

The clicking of her heels receded as she walked down the hallway on the left.

"Well, she seems to be having an awesome day," Chip commented when she was out of ear shot.

"If by awesome you mean she could tear your head off just for looking at her the wrong way, then yeah, she's having an awesome day."

At the returning click of footsteps, Chip turned back to the window.

The receptionist waved to the chairs where I was sitting.

"Have a seat. He's just finishing up a call and then he'll talk to you." The phone rang, and she sat down at her desk to answer it.

We sat and waited.

"Do you know what you're going to say?"

"I think I've got it worked out. This guy is a close friend of your dad's, right?"

"Yeah, they've known each other for years. Marty's been to our house a few times. He'll take it seriously."

The door to the inner office clicked, and Marty opened the door. He frowned when he saw us sitting there.

"Hannah? What can I do for you today?"

Chip stood and held out his hand. "I'm Chip Cavanagh. We were wondering if we could talk to you about the case against Ben Carter."

"Really?" He looked at both of us. "Okay, step into my office." He held the door open for us to pass through. "Take a left. It's the second office on the right." He trailed behind us. We entered his office and sat in front of his desk.

Marty sat down. "All right, so the Ben Carter case. What can I do for you?" He looked back and forth between us.

I looked at Chip.

"We . . . what if—" He cleared his throat and took a deep breath. "We were wondering . . . "

Marty raised his eyebrows looking intently at Chip. "Go on, Chip. Just spit it out."

"What would happen if we had proof that Ben didn't rob those people—that someone else did?"

Marty leaned forward—his elbows on the desk—and studied

Chip. "Are you saying you have evidence that would exonerate Ben Carter?"

Chip glanced at me before addressing Marty. "We think we may have evidence that Jacob Robinson or someone who works for him may be involved in the burglaries that Ben Carter was arrested for."

Marty leaned back in his chair, his hands flat on the desk, looking back and forth between us.

"Let's start with where you got this evidence, shall we?"

"Hannah and I discovered some of the missing property at the old mill."

"The old mill? What were you doing out there?"

"We overheard two Robinson employees mention something about the old mill one day when we were walking dogs past the business."

Marty frowned and tilted his head to the side. "Why on earth would you be walking the dogs out on the service road?" He raised one eyebrow and looked at me.

"We suspected that Jacob Robinson had something to do with Ben getting arrested." Both of Marty's eyebrows shot up, and I finished with a whisper. "We thought that Jacob Robinson was using Ben to get elected."

He absorbed my words for a moment and then blew a breath out and pursed his lips.

"You do realize what you're accusing him of, don't you?" He gave each of us a pointed look and he continued after we both nodded. "Jacob Robinson is a powerful businessman in this town. You can't go sneaking around looking for evidence that he's trying to frame someone to get elected."

He stopped speaking and considered us both. Realizing that he was finished, Chip said, "That's why we took pictures of what we saw."

"Pictures? You kids went and took pictures?"

"Yes, sir. Hannah and I thought it would be the only way to prove that he was involved." I nodded to back up Chip's point.

"Let me have a look." Chip punched in his password and opened the picture app before handing it to Marty.

"There're three pictures. We tried to take some with the buildings so you would know that we didn't just take a random picture somewhere."

Chip and I waited while Marty swiped through the next two photos. I squeezed my hands together in my lap, secretly hoping that he'd believe us.

"I'm going to send these pictures to my email," Marty finally said.

"Okay. Does that mean you're going to use them to arrest Jacob Robinson and let Ben go?"

Marty put his hand up. "Let's not put the cart before the horse. First, I'm going to print the pictures you took, see if I can match them to the stolen property we have listed, and then I'll need to ask some questions." He grabbed the mouse sitting next to his computer and gave it a shake. He started to type.

"There's one other thing." Chip reached into his pocket and pulled out the pin we'd found at the farm and placed it on Marty's desk.

"Where did you get this?" Marty pinned Chip with a hard look.

"At the farm south of town where Ben was arrested. We found it in the basement," he paused before adding, "well, it was Scout who found it."

"Scout? Who's Scout? Wait—I don't want to know. Obviously we can't run it for fingerprints," Marty said, earning Chip another hard stare.

"His bodyguards were wearing these when he gave the speech at the fair." I hoped this would help Marty make the connection between the two.

"Unfortunately, a large number of the people in Acadia are wearing these, but I'll check into it." He put the pin in a clear plastic bag. "Is there anything else you want to tell me?" He looked back and forth at the two of us.

Chip shook his head.

"Ben didn't do this." My words rebounded around the quiet room, followed by silence and the squeaking of Marty's chair as he faced me.

"I said I'd look into this, Hannah. Let me do my job. I don't want Ben convicted of something he didn't do anymore than you do."

I searched his face to see if he believed me. Satisfied that Marty would get to the bottom of it, we stood and thanked him for his time.

"Thank you. If what you say is true, Ben will owe you his freedom."

Chip and I let ourselves out of the office and proceeded to the front entrance. The receptionist gave us a curious look but said nothing as we exited the building.

"Do you think he believed us?"

"I think he was skeptical to start with but having those pictures on your phone was the proof we needed to get him asking some questions."

"We did what we could."

"I wonder what Ben's lawyer is doing to help him? It's so frustrating not being able to talk to him."

"Do you think your mom could go visit him? She's known about him from the start. She could at least find out what the lawyer is doing?"

"I can ask her, but I'm not sure she can get in to see him, either. My dad would be the obvious choice, since Marty is his friend, but I'm not sure he'd do it either."

We walked in silence, Ben's fate hanging between us.

## Chapter 35

It took an hour of pleading and begging to convince Mom to go see Ben. In the end, I think she did it just to get me to be quiet. I'd started the moment she'd walked through the door after work. She refused initially, and then demanded to know what Chip and I had discovered that required her to go. To say she wasn't happy would be an understatement. When I told her that Chip and I had been to the old mill and we'd taken pictures of the evidence in the back of the truck, she went from unhappy to angry.

"I can't believe you purposefully went out there, when your dad and I forbid you to go."

"I'm sorry, but—" she cut me off before I could say more.

I'll go and see Ben, but Hannah you have to promise me that you will not get involved in this anymore. The next thing you know, I'll be going to visit *you* at the police station."

"I'll do whatever you say. Just please, see if they will let you in to see Ben." At this point, I would have agreed to eating kale for the next month if it meant that my mom could visit him.

She studied me. "You promise to stay out of it?"

"I promise." I laid my hand over my heart.

She studied me for a moment.

"Fine. I'll stop by the police station after work. Now, how's supper coming along?" she asked, taking the empty containers from her lunch and putting them in the sink.

"It'll be ready at six." I set the table while mom repacked her lunch for tomorrow.

Dad arrived just as we were dishing up supper. I placed his plate in front of him and set my own down.

"I saw Marty today at the gas station as I was filling up on my way home from work." Dad filled his fork with stew. "He told me you and Chip had been to the police station today."

I gulped. I was so focused on getting Ben free that I never considered Marty would talk to Dad.

"He said you and Chip had brought in some evidence that might prove Ben was innocent."

I glanced at my mom. She calmly chewed her supper. No help there.

"We just happened to come across some information we felt the police should know." I scooped up some stew and chewed while my dad considered what I'd said.

My dad put down his fork and steepled his hands in front of his mouth.

"The thing is, Hannah, you don't know these people. You don't know what they're capable of. I'm worried about your safety."

"It was just a couple of pictures taken from the road." I gave him the basic details, skipping over others. Hoping that was the end of it, I took another bite of stew.

I thought I was home free until my dad asked one more question.

"So, let me get this straight. You just happened to be walking by Jacob Robinson's business and you noticed stolen property in the back of one of the trucks? How did you know that the trucks were going to be there?"

I gave my dad a blank look. My face felt like it was on fire. "We followed the truck back from the old mill." My dad's face was the same colour as mine, but if I had to guess, it was about twenty degrees hotter.

"You were at the old mill?" The clang of his fork hitting his plate jarred me from my panic. "Please tell me you didn't go into the compound."

"We didn't go in today." His eyes narrowed at my words. *Shoot! Too much information!*

My dad nodded. "Did you go in another day?"

"Maybe?"

"Maybe? Maybe? You just got finished being grounded for a week for going to the farm and now you're snooping around the mill?"

"Well, you didn't say anything about the mill. You said not to go to the farm."

"Let me be perfectly clear then. I don't want you going on any property whether it is posted with 'No Trespassing' signs or not. Got it?"

"Got it."

He picked up his fork and stabbed a piece of meat before jamming it into his mouth. I quickly finished the rest of my supper.

I lay on my bed after finishing the dishes and texted Chip.

*Good news or bad news?*

*Good news, of course!*

*Mom is going to go to the police station tomorrow to check on Ben.*

*Excellent!*

*Bad news . . .*

*Uh, oh.*

*I may have let it slip to my dad that we'd been out to the old mill. :0*

*I don't like where this is going . . . What did he say?*

*I'm not allowed to go on any property—trespassing sign or not.*

*Good news . . .*

*Okay.*

*He didn't ground me, again.*

*That is good news!*

*Your turn.*

*????*

*How's your mom feeling?*

*Pretty good today. The doctor put her on new medication that seems to be working.*

*Good news!!!!*

☺

*Pick me up in the morning with the dogs.*

*Of course.*

*Night, Chip.*

*Night, Hannah.*

## Chapter 36

Chip and I were sitting on the front step the next day when my mom pulled in the driveway. We both stood as she got out of the vehicle and opened the passenger door.

"Do you need a hand, Lorraine?" Chip asked her, jumping off the step and meeting her at the door of her SUV.

"Thanks, Chip." She handed him two bags and held two herself.

"What's this? Takeout?" I opened the front door for them to go through.

"I thought we needed a treat. Besides, it's Friday." Mom dropped her bags on the counter. "Chip, you might as well join us. Is your mom feeling up to coming over? Has she received her test results yet?"

"She was feeling pretty good when I left to come here about an hour ago. She's supposed to get the results at her next appointment."

"Great! I'll give her a call and see if she wants to come over." My mom put her bags on the counter, pulled her phone from her purse, and dialed Shelley. As she was talking, she motioned to the cupboard and mouthed, "Set the table," as she listened.

With the table set, we waited for her to get off the phone and tell us about her visit with Ben.

Mom ended the call at the same time as Dad came through the front door.

Seeing the take-out bags on the counter he asked, "Hey, what's the occasion?"

"I thought we deserved a treat. Hannah's been doing most of the cooking all summer, and it's Friday. We're all tired and could use a break."

My dad didn't reply, just got a drink and went in the living room.

Finally, I asked the question I'd been dying to ask since she walked in the door. "Did you get a chance to go and see Ben?"

Mom took containers out of the bags and set them on the table. "I did. Marty let me in to see him for about five minutes."

"What did he say?"

"I had to introduce myself, first. When I told him who I was, I think he was relieved. He had a very pronounced limp when he sat down to talk to me. He mentioned it was an old injury, and I left it at that."

My gaze met Chip's knowing the real cause of Ben's limp. Not noticing our exchange, Mom went on.

"When I asked about what happened, he told me that he was at the farm and suddenly the police were there. He mentioned there was an older man with them, but he didn't know who he was."

I bet it was Jim Peterson.

"They told him he was trespassing and that he was under arrest. When they searched the house, they found stolen property in the basement and added that to the charge as well. He said he didn't know how it got there, but he'd gone into town the day before to get some food and someone must have planted it then. He's got a court-appointed lawyer that he thinks is okay. He also said he hasn't been sleeping well, which is probably why he looks so terrible. I talked to Marty on the way out, and he confirmed that Ben has been having nightmares nearly every night."

The doorbell rang, and Mom let Shelley in. She joined us at the kitchen table.

"I was just telling Chip and Hannah about my visit to see Ben. He's doing well. We have to do something for this boy. Even with the pictures that Hannah and Chip took, I'm not sure it's enough to get the charges against him dismissed."

"I agree," Shelley said. "Everyone I talk to seems to think he's guilty. Your pictures show that the robbery charges are false. It would have to be the owners that were pressing charges, right? If we can find out who owns the farm, maybe they'd consider dropping them."

"Come eat, Mike." Mom dropped spoons into each of the cartons.

As we dished up, the conversation continued.

"Hannah, maybe your project can help rally some support for Ben," Chip suggested as he bit into his spring roll.

My mom stopped spooning fried rice onto her plate. "That's a great idea! You've got it ready to go, don't you?"

I nodded and finished chewing before answering. "Yeah, we finished the voice-over, and I submitted it two days ago. I'm just waiting to hear back from the library. The winners will be chosen next week, and the three finalists will be presented at the library on Friday. They will also make an appearance on the local news and have their projects shown on television."

Shelley clapped her hands. "Perfect. That way the whole town will get to see your project and hopefully raise some awareness for Ben's plight."

"When do we get to see your project, Hannah?" my dad asked, having been silent throughout our conversation.

"You want to see it?" I couldn't keep the shock from my voice. I guess I still wasn't used to sharing things with my parents that I felt deeply about. I always thought they weren't interested, and I was too frightened to share with them.

"Of course, we do." Mom replied in an enthusiastic voice.

I looked at Chip, who nodded his head. "Okay. How about after supper?"

Everyone agreed. After supper, I went to my room and got my computer.

My fingers shook as I logged on and clicked the file containing my project. I placed the computer at the end of the table, so we could all see.

The presentation opened with pictures of Ben as my voice narrated his story. In the middle, a video where Ben shares his experiences and the symptoms of his PTSD had my dad sitting up in his chair. At his movement, my mom tore her eyes away from the screen and studied him. My voice came back on, sharing Ben's current situation and how he desperately wanted to get back home but didn't have the money to get there.

The slide show ended, and I looked around the table. No one spoke. My dad sat staring at the computer looking like he'd been hit by a ton of bricks. Concern was written all over Mom's face as she noticed his reaction to the video. Finally, Dad seemed to snap out of the trance he was in.

"We need to help him. You've got an excellent presentation there Hannah, but we can't rely on you winning the contest to get the word out. I'll go down to the police station on Monday and have a chat with Marty to see how we can move this along."

The table was silent after my dad spoke. I'd never heard him talk so forcefully about anything other than when I got in trouble.

"That would be great. Thanks, Dad." Then he got up from the table and went to the living room.

"What was that all about?" I whispered to my mom.

"Something about Ben's story obviously hit home for your dad." She looked into the living room where he sat in his recliner staring out the window.

"I guess now we wait and see if the project gets chosen."

Chip nudged me. "I have no doubt that you are going to win. But in the meantime, what if we put up posters around town? It worked for getting my dog walking business going. Maybe it would work to put up some posters looking for support for Ben?"

I pulled the computer in front of me and the four of us got to work designing a poster asking for information and looking for donations to help Ben out. I printed fifty. Chip and I made a plan to hang them up the next day as he and his mom got ready to leave.

Later that night, as I lay in my bed, hundreds of doubts started to creep in. What if the evidence we found wouldn't be enough to get the charges dismissed? What if the owners of the farm were determined to press charges? What if people ignored the posters or ripped them down? What if my project didn't win and Ben's story would remained unknown? What if Ben is wrongly convicted?

*August 19, 2018*

*Everything is happening at once. We are going to do our best to get Ben out of jail. Tomorrow, Chip and I are going to put up posters looking for information and help. Dad is going to talk to Marty. And if I win the library contest, we'll have some money to give to Ben. I hope this all works out!*

## Chapter 37

The next day, loaded with posters, tape, and tacks, Chip and I set out to paper the town. We started on Main Street, tacking one up on every light pole and bulletin board we could find on the west side of the street, then crossing to the east side we did the same. Chip even wallpapered the pole outside of Hank's café, even though we were sure they would be removed right after we finished.

We were taping a poster to a pole outside of the Milky Way when a Robinson Construction truck cruised alongside us. Inside the cab were "the bodyguards" as I now referred to them. I felt their stares as they went by. Once past us, they sped up and continued down the street toward the industrial section of town.

"What was that about?" Chip asked, watching them drive away.

"No clue." A sense of foreboding tickled up my spine. In about five minutes, Jacob Robinson was going to find out who was helping Ben.

"Maybe we should take a break and have an ice cream?" Chip suggested. I glanced once more down the road before following him into the Milky Way. As we walked through the door, I noticed posters advertising various events in town taped to the window.

"We should ask George if we can put up a poster here," I commented to Chip as we sat at the counter.

"What can I get for you today?" Erma placed both hands on the counter. She held up a finger. "Let me rephrase that. Chip what would you like today? Since I know Hannah's getting a double scoop of Tiger Tiger."

I was shocked for a moment and then burst out laughing as she smiled. I could never tell if Erma was joking or serious.

"I'll have a double vanilla, Erma."

"Coming right up." She moved to the ice cream cooler to get our order. When she returned and handed us our cones, Chip asked, "Erma, do you think it would be okay to hang one of our posters in the window?"

"That depends. What's it for?"

"It's for Ben Carter. You remember—the guy who sat beside us having ice cream a few of weeks back?"

"I do. I hear he got himself in a bit of trouble. Got arrested for those robberies that have been happening around town."

"Well," Chip started, "we have evidence that proves he didn't do it. But, he's also being charged with trespassing by the owner. We're trying to rally some support for him to be released and maybe some cash to get home."

"The owners are pressing charges you say?"

Erma gave Chip an intense look.

"Yes."

She turned her head and yelled to the back of the store. "George!"

George came out of the door that led to the back. "What are you yelling about woman?"

"Hannah and Chip were just telling me that the owners of the farm south of town are pressing charges for trespassing against Ben along with the robbery charges."

A dark look washed over George's face.

"Da— I mean darn Jim." He turned on his heel and went into the back.

"What's going on?" His confusion matched mine.

"Jim Peterson isn't the owner of the farm, we are."

Chip and I shared shocked looks. "You are?" we asked in unison.

"We've rented it out for the last twenty or so years. No money in farming, so we bought the Milky Way. Jim farms the land. Maybe that's who the police got a hold of when they arrested Ben. Jim's not the friendliest guy. Doesn't take to outsiders much. Still he should have told us about it."

"Do you think you could go to the police station and tell them?" Chip asked hopefully.

"Sure. We told Ben that if we could help him out we would. Nobody's using the old farmhouse anyway."

Chip and I high fived.

"I'll tell you what else we'll do," Erma spoke up, "you can put on your poster that anyone wanting to donate to Ben's cause can leave donations here. And to kick it off we'll donate two hundred dollars."

"This is awesome!" I grabbed one of the posters off the pile. "Do you have a marker?"

"Sure do." Erma pulled one out of her apron and handed it to me.

I added to the poster that the Milky Way would accept donations to the rest of the posters in the pile, while Chip held my cone and continued to eat his.

"You don't know what this means!"

Erma just smiled at my excitement.

"I think we do, dear. I think we do," Erma replied. "Now, you get those hung up around town. Keep the marker and fix the ones you've already put up. And on Monday, George and I will head over to the police station and get this all straightened out."

Chip took the posters and marker and handed me my quickly melting ice cream cone.

"Thanks, again," I said over my shoulder as we left the store. Once we were on the sidewalk, I started jumping up and down. The splat of my ice cream hitting the sidewalk wasn't even enough to get me to stop.

"We're going to get Ben out, Chip! Can you believe that George and Erma owned the farm all this time? And they donated two hundred dollars! We need to go fix the rest of our posters and then go home and tell our parents."

"You're right. It's amazing. You know what else is amazing? That you just dropped your ice cream on the ground and you're not even upset." He pointed to my ice cream melting on the sidewalk. "That has to be a first," he said, amused.

I scraped the ice cream back into my cone and threw it into the garbage can beside the light pole. I wasn't going to let Robinson intimidate me. We were going to free Ben.

"Nothing can upset me now. We're going to do this!"

---

AN HOUR LATER, we burst through the front door unable to contain our excitement and were greeted by the smell of chocolate chip cookies baking.

"You two look happy. How did it go?" Mom placed a tray of chocolate chip cookies on the counter.

"You will not believe this!" I told her, reaching for a cookie and then waving my fingers in the air when I burned them.

"Give them time to cool. What won't I believe?"

I took two glasses from the cupboard and got the pitcher of iced tea from the fridge.

"George and Erma own the farm south of town." I poured a glass for Chip and me. "They're going to the police station on Monday to talk to Marty. And here's the best part—they donated two hundred dollars to get Ben back home."

My mom stopped dropping spoonsful of dough onto the cookie sheet and turned to stare at me.

"They own the farm and they donated money! Can you believe it?"

"Believe what?" Dad walked in the back door with his drill in his hand. Chip saw it too and nudged me. I guess we hadn't hidden it that well after all.

"Hannah and Chip stopped at the Milky Way today and found out that George and Erma own the farm, and they donated two hundred dollars to Ben."

"Hey, that's great! If we all go down on Monday, maybe we can get them to drop the charges right away! I'll give George a call and see if they want to go together."

"Can we go too?" I asked, wanting to be there if Ben got out.

"It might take a while and you and Chip have dogs to walk in the morning." My shoulders drooped because he was right. "But I'll tell you what—if Ben gets out, I'll text you."

It wasn't what I'd hoped he'd say, but it was the second-best thing. I wanted to be there when Ben got the news that the charges were dropped. The fact that they wouldn't be didn't enter my head. I knew we could make this right for Ben. *Whoa! Where did that come from? I'm going to blame this optimism on Chip.* The pictures we'd taken of the stolen property in the back of the Robinson construction truck and George and Erma being the owners of the farm should be all that was needed to free Ben. I couldn't wait to get that text from dad the next morning.

## Chapter 38

I'd nearly dropped my phone trying to check it and walk Bullet and Jerry at the same time. The dogs seemed to sense that something big was going to happen today, which explained why Dotty was slower than usual. Bullet acted like he'd drank ten gallons of coffee instead of water this morning. It was taking every one of my dog-wrangling skills to keep them in line. *I should have brought bacon.* I'd checked my phone at least four times and there was still no text from dad saying to come to the police station. I was ready to jump out of my skin. I slid my phone into my back pocket as Jerry sniffed out a tree to see if he liked it enough to pee on it. Deciding "no" and tugging on his leash, he set off for the next one.

"How long do you think it will take?" I asked Chip who stood waiting for Brute to do his business on the tree that Jerry had just rejected.

Knowing I was talking about Ben, because I'd asked him this question three times already, Chip said, "I don't know, Hannah. I'm sure there's paperwork and lawyers involved, so it could take a while."

We were on our way to the park. We'd decided not to take the dogs too far today in case Dad texted while we were out walking the dogs. The park was only three blocks from the police station and we could be there in five minutes.

Dad phoned George last night after supper, and they had agreed to meet at the police station at 8:30 this morning. It was now 9:30, and I had expected to hear from them by now.

I sat on the bench and lifted Jerry up onto my lap. He laid down, content to let me stroke his ears. If I was going to come back in another life, I'd want to be a dog. The only things you had to do were eat, sleep, and walk. And if you were lucky, someone would scratch your ears for you. That had to be the life.

It was early enough in the morning that we had the park to ourselves. Bullet sniffed around the bench and finally found a ray of sunshine peeking between the trees and settled himself on the grass and went to sleep. Chip handed me Dotty's leash and she found a spot in the shade and closed her eyes. Scout, Lucy, and Brute were not going to waste one minute of their time in the park. Chip took three tennis balls out of the backpack and let the dogs off their leashes to play fetch.

My mind wandered. I didn't have to worry about Ben or the project. My body relaxed against the bench and I smiled at the dogs' antics as they played. I realized how lucky I was to have Chip as my friend. He was the funniest, most loving, most responsible person that I knew. He never worried about what others might think. He did what he wanted, whether it was wrestling with three dogs like he was doing now or standing up when he saw something was wrong. His courage gave me courage. If it wasn't for him, I certainly wouldn't be walking dogs, and I for sure wouldn't be standing up to Jacob Robinson and the whole town to help Ben. I didn't know where or who I'd be if I hadn't met him.

My phone vibrated, and Jerry lifted his head off my lap as I reached to pull it out of my pocket. It was a text from my dad.

*He's out.*

I jumped off the bench.
"Chip! He's out. Let's go!"

Chip turned from playing with the dogs, a huge grin splitting his face. With his attention on me and not on the dogs, they all jumped at the same time and knocked him to the ground. It seemed that they knew this was something to celebrate and licked his face.

"Enough! Come on you guys, we have to get going." As he flailed away to avoid the love the dogs were giving him, I picked up the leashes and ran down the hill to rescue him. Once I had the dogs under control, as under control as you can have six dogs, Chip stood and brushed the grass off his clothes and used the sleeve of his t-shirt to wipe his face.

"I think they know that something's up," I said as I handed him the leashes for the four big dogs.

"We better hustle. I don't know how long they'll be at the police station."

We headed to the park entrance and my excitement vanished when Logan and Mason walked through the opening in the fence, coming toward us.

An evil smirk spread over both their faces when they spotted us.

I froze. Bullet and Jerry looked back in confusion, wondering why we had been in such a hurry and now we had stopped. Dotty, as always, stood at my side. Chip had stopped and eyed the boys warily.

"Well, look who we have here," Logan sauntered closer and I instinctively stepped back. "What's up losers? Look at these poor dogs, Mason—stuck on leashes when they could be running free. I think they should be able to roam around, don't you?"

Neither of us responded. I just wanted to get away from them and get to the police station to find out about Ben.

"I think you're right, Logan." I watched as Mason moved beside me. As he got closer, Dotty gave a low growl. "Aw, look. She's trying to protect you." I kept my eyes glued to Mason as he ignored Dotty's growl, coming closer. "It's okay, girl. I'm not going to hurt you. I just want to help you."

At his words, Dotty sprung forward, her teeth bared and barking. Mason jumped back in surprise. His face white.

The rest of the dogs took up Dotty's lead and soon they were lunging and barking at the two boys. Not wanting to get bit they backed off, giving us a wide berth.

"Okay, okay. We'll leave you alone," Logan said to Scout, who was straining at her leash. Once around us, they took off running.

I patted Dotty's head. "Thanks, girl."

It took us a few minutes to get the dogs calmed down. Scout refused to move until Logan and Mason disappeared.

"We better hurry or we're going to miss everything!" I led the dogs to the entrance again.

We ran the three blocks. When we turned the corner to the police station, we were surprised to see a group of people standing out front.

*What the heck?* As we got closer, I could make out George, Marty, and my dad standing around Ben. In front of them was a group of reporters. One from the local newspaper and another one I recognized from the television station. They had microphones out, and Marty was talking to them. It wasn't until we reached the group that I could hear what he was saying.

". . . Thanks to the work of a couple of local kids, we were able to determine that Ben Carter was not responsible for the thefts in Acadia. By bringing forward evidence that proved his innocence we are dropping the breaking and entering charges." He stopped and waved to us. "In fact, they're here right now. Hannah. Chip. Come up here."

The reporters turned to where we were standing at the back of the crowd and microphones were shoved in our faces.

"Where did you find the evidence?"

"What led you to believe that Mr. Carter was innocent?"

"How well do you know Ben?"

It felt like a game of dodgeball as questions were lobbed at us. I wanted to duck and run, but then I saw Ben and the smile on his face was bright enough to light Acadia for a year.

"We know Ben very well." My voice cracked, and I cleared my throat. "We met him well over a month ago, right after the fair was in town. The Ben we know would never do the things he was accused of, so we set out to prove that."

"It wasn't too hard to figure out he'd been framed," Chip joined in. "We just followed the clues."

Their questions answered, the reporters turned back to Marty.

One of the reporters piped up, "What about the trespassing charges? If he's standing here, those have obviously been dropped as well."

Marty moved to the side and let George step up to the group.

"As the owners of the farm where Ben was staying, we've also dropped the trespassing charges. We didn't know that he was staying out there, but we understand that sometimes people are in dire situations and rather than make things worse, we would like to make them better."

"So, you don't care that he was staying at your farm without your permission?"

George frowned at the reporter. "Isn't that what I just said? This young man, due to circumstances beyond his control, has found himself in a bad way. Rather than kick the boy when he's down, we should be giving him a hand up. That's why Erma and I have agreed to collect any donations that the good folks of Acadia wish to make in order for that to happen. He was trying to get home to his mother when he landed in our town. And rather than helping him out, we put him in a worse position than he was already in." George let his words sink in for a minute before finishing. "I'm referring to certain members of this community using Ben as a means to get elected."

At those words, the reporters threw out more questions. Marty nudged George out of the way.

"Thanks, George. I think we'll leave it at that." George just smiled.

"With the new evidence you've received, have you made any arrests for the burglaries?"

Glad for the change of topic, Marty replied, "As we speak, two men are in custody for the thefts. Charges to a third accomplice are pending investigation. Now, that's it for questions. As you can imagine, I've got work to do."

The reporters shouted out more questions, but the group turned and headed toward the sidewalk where Dad parked the truck.

I handed Bullet's and Jerry's leashes to Chip and ran toward him.

"Dad!" My arms went around him, and I squeezed.

"Thank you!" Then I turned to George and hugged him as well.

He didn't really know what to make of it and gave me an awkward pat on the back. Ben stood next to my dad.

"I'm so glad you got out," I told him, suddenly shy and not sure what to say.

"I am too," he said quietly. "I don't know how I'll ever thank you and Chip for all you did." His voice was husky, and I could see tears forming in his eyes.

Chip, who'd been standing behind George and my dad, moved closer. And Ben's face lit up when he saw the dogs. They must have picked up his scent at the same time because when Ben squatted down they engulfed him. They barked their greeting and proceeded to give their trademark face wash. I was afraid that Bullet and Jerry would be trampled, but Ben picked them both up and set one on each leg.

"I think they missed you," I said when they finally calmed down enough to just circle him and take the odd swipe at his face.

He laughed, and it had a ring of joy to it. "I missed them too." He ruffled the fur of whichever dog stood still long enough for him to get a hand on. I looked over to Chip and saw he had his phone out and was shooting a video of the reunion.

"So, son, what's your plan now?" George asked when Ben stood with Bullet and Jerry in his arms. Jerry's head rested on his shoulder, and as usual, Bullet was squirming to be let down. I took him from Ben as he considered George's question.

"I still need to find a way to get home. I've talked to my mom a couple of times and she's not doing so great."

"Let me look after that." George clamped a hand on Ben's shoulder. "We'll find a way to get you home."

Gratitude suffused Ben's face, and he nodded.

"Until then, you can come and stay with Erma and me. We got an extra room."

"But I can't pay you," Ben confessed looking down at the ground.

"I'm well aware of that. If you feel you need to compensate us in some way, I'll put you to work at the store."

Ben's face cleared, and he nodded. "That I can do."

Dad walked around to the side of his truck. "I've got to get back to work. Can I drop you guys off somewhere?"

At that moment, a police cruiser pulled into the driveway and everyone turned as two officers got out and opened the backdoor. A pair of shiny, black loafers appeared first, followed by a dishevelled Jacob Robinson. His hair askew and his jacket wrinkled, he pulled his arm out of the grip of the officer trying to help him. Parked behind the cruiser was a black sedan. A man in a suit got out, carrying his briefcase.

"Get your hands off me," Robinson growled at the officer, who ignored him and started to lead him to the entrance of the police station. The reporters who were about to disperse crowded around the trio.

It was then that Robinson noticed us standing beside Dad's truck and lunged for us.

"You haven't heard the last of me Williams. You either, George. My lawyer's going to get me out of here in no time and then I'll be coming for you and those two snot-nosed kids."

The officer pulled Robinson back.

"Would you like to add issuing a threat to your lengthy list of charges?" Marty asked calmly.

Robinson's lawyer spoke quietly in his ear, and he let the officers lead him away, but not before throwing a threatening look over his shoulder before entering the police station.

"Good riddance to bad rubbish." George opened the passenger door and motioned for Ben to get in the back seat. "Take us to the store. We're going to celebrate. You kids come down after you've dropped the dogs off. Ice cream is on me."

Chip and I looked at each other and then nodded at George.

"We'll be there as soon as we're done."

Ben pulled open the back door and moved to get in, then stopped and turned to us. "I really don't know how to thank you," he said, and I could see in his eyes that he meant every word.

"You don't have to thank us," I said. "We just did what was right."

"Hannah's right. We couldn't let you go to jail to get some jerk elected."

Ben smiled and got into the truck. The dogs whined and barked as the truck pulled away and we started down the street. It was time to drop them off at their homes. Sensing that's what was happening, they seemed reluctant to get there.

"I think I'm still in shock," I said to Chip as we left Dotty's house. I couldn't wrap my brain around the fact that at this moment Ben was sitting at the Milky Way having ice cream with George and Erma.

"I know. Honestly, I wasn't sure they were going to let him go."

"What do you think is going to happen now?" I asked as I turned on to Main Street and started toward the Milky Way.

"I hope that the two guys working for Robinson get charged with the robberies. And we find a way to get Ben home."

I hoped that too. The way things had turned out couldn't have been better. I tilted my face to the sun and smiled.

## Chapter 39

"Take these out and put them on the table with the rest of the food, Hannah." Mom passed me a tray of veggies and dip. I walked out onto the deck and looked at the balloons and decorations attached to the deck railing. The table was covered with food and people milled around with plates and drinks. I made room for the veggies on the table and filled a glass with iced tea, which I nearly spilled when Scout jumped up on my leg.

"Hey, girl. Careful." I stroked her fur, and she hopped down, taking off to play with the rest of the dogs.

Ben was talking to my dad and George. My dad had a glass of iced tea in his hand and Ben was drinking a pop. They were both laughing at something that George had said.

Small groups of people clustered around our backyard. Besides my mom and dad, George and Erma were here, along with Chip and his mom. Trudy was home from camp and Alex was introducing her to the dogs. The dogs hadn't come alone, Christy and Mr. and Mrs. Morris were there along with assorted people from town. The town had really come around to Ben, and we'd raised enough money in two short weeks that he was going to be able to fly home.

Chip sidled up beside me. "What's Dr. Tompkins doing here?"

"Ben must have invited him. Dad told me George took Ben to see him about his leg."

Chip nodded. "I'm going to be sorry to see him go."

"Me too. The dogs are going to miss him." In the last two weeks, Ben had helped us walk the dogs every day. We went out to the farm most days. They ran, played fetch, or laid in the sun, like Dotty. Ben looked better every day. He'd gained some weight, thanks to Erma's cooking, and he had a permanent smile on his face. Despite all of this, he wanted to get home to see his mom and make sure that she was looked after.

The summer was coming to an end, and Chip and I were going to be starting high school in a week. Mom and I had gone to the city yesterday to get school supplies. The big day was getting closer.

George banged his bottle with a spoon and waited for the conversations to quiet down.

"First, I want to thank Mike and Lorraine for hosting this great get-together as we wish Ben safe travels home." There was a round of applause and whistles.

"Second, I want to thank all of you who showed up today to send Ben off and for your generosity." More clapping and hollering.

"Third, I want to present Ben with a little something to see him home." George pulled an envelope from the pocket of his shirt and handed it to Ben.

Ben stood staring at George, shock written on his face. Finally, George took his hand and placed the envelope in it.

"I can't—" Ben started.

"Look son, there was some cash left over from your plane ticket and you might need a few dollars to get on your feet again. Take it. We wish you only the best in the future."

Ben looked down at the envelope in his hand and then scanned the crowd in the backyard.

"I don't know what to say." He stopped and looked at the envelope again. "Thank you doesn't even come close to how grateful I am for all your help. Hannah and Chip, if you hadn't believed in me from the start, I'd probably be staring at the walls of a jail cell right now. It's because of you that I get to go home."

The crowd of well-wishers clapped again. The real thieves had been arrested on the day Ben was set free and had been in jail ever since. When they realized that the evidence against them was air tight, they'd implicated Jacob Robinson, who was also facing charges, but because he had a high paid lawyer, he was out on bail. The scandal also meant he had to withdraw from the mayoral election, something he was not too pleased about because it also meant that his plans for the old mill were also going up in smoke. Apparently, he bought the old mill at a reduced price and planned to sell it back to the town for the new sports complex. Once Robinson's illegal dealings hit the news, the town had rallied around Ben, except for Irving, of course, whose view of Ben hadn't changed.

My multi-media project won third place. I'd like to think that some of the support for Ben happened because of it. It appeared on the news and there was a write up in the paper. I was proud that the $50 prize I received was tucked in the envelope Ben was holding.

"And thanks to all of you who have been so generous. To George and Erma"—he raised his glass to them—"Mike and Lorraine, and everyone who made it possible for me to go home. I'll miss you all." At that, Jerry jumped on his leg looking for attention. "Yes, I'll miss you too, Jerry." And scooped Jerry up in his arms.

We cheered and clapped, and the dogs barked.

The rest of the afternoon was spent visiting and laughing. The crowd thinned out and there were only a few of us left. Dad and Ben sat in lawn chairs in the shade talking. They'd done a lot of that over the last couple of weeks. When I asked mom about it, she just said, "They have some experiences in common," which was really vague. What those shared experiences were, I could only guess had something to do with Ben being in the military and dad driving the ambulance. I was sure they'd both seen things that were hard to forget. I just know my dad had been drinking less and that an appointment card to see a counsellor next month was pinned to the fridge. Curled on Dad's lap was the newest addition to our family, Belle, a golden retriever puppy.

Chip and I sat on the bench swing. We hadn't had a chance to talk much today. And as the celebration wound down, my mom and Erma were cleaning up the table with Shelley's help.

"Your mom is looking better," I said, breaking the silence between us.

"The specialist discovered that she has Parkinson's," Chip replied as he watched her. "The medication they put her on seems to be making a difference. Other than the medication, there's not much they can do for her. Grandpa and Grandma want us to move in with them. Mom refused, for now. If she gets to the point where she needs more help, then we'll move."

"But she's going to be okay?"

"Yeah, she's okay for now."

I smiled and dug my toe in the ground to keep the swing moving.

"I was thinking this morning," Chip said, "I guess that stuff Madame Astraea said might not have been completely wrong."

"Yeah, I had no idea at the beginning of summer that this was how it was all going to turn out.

You ready for school to start?" I asked.

"Not really. I'm going to miss walking the dogs every day. Although, Mr. and Mrs. Morris asked if I'd walk Brute after school. You? Are you ready?"

"I think I am," I replied, taking a sip of iced tea. "Two years ago, I would have been petrified, but lately I feel confident that it's going to be okay. I know there are going to be challenges, but now I know I can meet them, you know?"

Chip turned and smiled. "I have no doubt you will."

END OF BOOK Three

BREAKING the Rules Series

**Please leave a review on Amazon!**

To get the upcoming news about my next series, a time-travel adventure, visit

www.hrhobbsbooks.com

and get on my mailing list!

## Acknowledgments

It's always difficult to write the acknowledgement page as there are so many people to thank when it comes to getting a book out into the world. Here is my humble attempt.

To you, the reader, a HUGE Thank You for taking the time to read my story. This is no greater compliment to a writer, than having someone read their book and if you left a review, well, you ROCK!

To my editor, Rachel McCracken, for coming in mid-edit and providing invaluable feedback and polishing my manuscript to a shine.

To my beta readers: Karen H., Carla H., Shirley P. and Karen K. Thank you for your feedback, your keen attention to detail and patience reading a really messy copy of *Watch Me*.

To my friends, near and far, who have supported this crazy dream of mine. Some of you I've known many years and others I know virtually, but you always amaze and humble me with your enthusiasm and support. This wouldn't be possible without you!

To my children and their families, who, by this time, are not surprised by any new adventure of mine. I hope to model that you're never too old to follow your dreams.

Finally, to my husband, Terry, who keeps the house running,

washes dishes and makes meals, while I write. Your support means the world to me!

I admit that I'm sorry to be saying "good-bye" to Hannah and Chip, as they have been a large part of my life over the past two years. They have carried my message of empathy and compassion for others in both heartbreaking and hilarious ways and I will miss them dearly.

## About the Author

H. R. Hobbs has loved books for as long as she can remember, and it's the reason she became a teacher, and, most recently, a writer. An educator for nearly thirty years, H. R. Hobbs writes realistic fiction that connects to teens and young adults. A mother to three grown sons and grandmothers to three little darlings, she resides with her husband in the small prairie town where she was born and raised. *Watch Me* is the third book in her Breaking the Rules Series.

facebook.com/hrhobbsbooks

twitter.com/hrhobbsbooks

instagram.com/hrhobbsbooks

Made in the USA
Las Vegas, NV
29 December 2020